BOMBSHELL

BOMBSHELL

ALISON HAMMOND

WITH LISA BENT

bantam

TRANSWORLD PUBLISHERS
Penguin Random House, One Embassy Gardens,
8 Viaduct Gardens, London SW11 7BW
www.penguin.co.uk

Transworld is part of the Penguin Random House group of companies
whose addresses can be found at global.penguinrandomhouse.com

Penguin
Random House
UK

First published in Great Britain in 2024 by Bantam
an imprint of Transworld Publishers

A CIP catalogue record for this book
is available from the British Library.

ISBN 9781787635258

Typeset in 11.25/16.25 pt Sabon by Falcon Oast Graphic Art Ltd
Printed and bound in Great Britain by Clays Ltd, Elcograf S.p.A.

The authorized representative in the EEA is Penguin Random House Ireland,
Morrison Chambers, 32 Nassau Street, Dublin D02 YH68.

MIX
Paper | Supporting
responsible forestry
FSC® C018179

For you, Mum  Maria

1

Glancing round the rink, Madison decided there must be something wrong with her skates. The white surface of the ice glowed prettily under the golden fairy lights all strung up by the beautiful Victorian bandstand in London's Hyde Park. You couldn't have wished for a more Christmassy scene, thought Madison, as she looked at the skaters bundled up in their winter clothes, smiles on their faces, breath misting in the cold air as festive tunes blared out. Beyond the rink, there were food stalls, fairground rides, and a selection of stands selling Christmas gifts that they'd promised the kids they'd return to later. It was perfect. Exactly the fun she'd wanted to kick off the month of December.

However, there was one problem. Her skates.

There *had* to be something wrong with them. Yes, they had been hired from exactly the same not-very-helpful assistant who had fitted out her husband, Rich, and the kids, Chloë and Jordan. But while the three of them had taken to the ice with a few initial wobbles until they found their feet, Madison had been on her bum more times than she cared to count.

Rich glided up to her and came to a sharp stop, his skates making a scraping sound on the ice.

'You know you're meant to let go of the wall, babe?' he said, and before she had time to get annoyed, he flashed her the million-dollar smile that still made her heart melt – and saw him adored by fans of the TV show he presented, *House Mates*.

'I quite like the wall, thank you very much,' Madison said primly, tightening her grip with both hands and attempting to edge along just an inch or two. Oh, God. She could feel the skates moving with a life of their own. She tensed and then, somehow, they were whizzing out from underneath her and, yes, she was down again, landing in the meltwater that was pooling by the side of the rink. That wasn't *normal*. Maybe one of the blades was adrift.

'For f— *Father Christmas's sake*!' She caught herself as Chloë, aged six, came into view, looking like Bambi on ice but somehow staying on her feet.

'Mum!' called Chloë. 'Come and skate with me!'

'In a minute, darling,' said Madison, beaming at her daughter and trying to get up in a dignified fashion. 'Mum's still getting the hang of this.'

'But we've only got half the time left,' said Chloë, with a little frown.

Madison was caught between relief and disappointment – she'd had a vision of the four of them swooshing effortlessly round the rink holding hands, discovering that – at forty years old – she was unbelievably talented at ice skating, having never tried it before. She shut her eyes briefly and tried to channel the vision of herself she'd had on the way here, skating backwards on the ice, throwing in the occasional pirouette or casual jump for good measure. But water from her latest fall had seeped into the seat of her jeans. A soggy bottom was *not* part of the vision. It was time for action.

'There's something wrong with Mummy's skates,' Madison said decisively. 'I'm going to try to change them. Can you skate with your brother for a bit?'

'He's going really fast,' said Chloë. They looked out and saw Jordan weaving in and out of the crowds, moving to the beat of the music. Madison felt a burst of love for her two kids. She was so proud of them.

'Well, you can go really fast too, I'm sure,' Madison said encouragingly. 'If you want. Girls can do anything boys can, right?'

Madison wondered if she saw the flicker of a smile on her daughter's face. She wished she could provide a more direct example of that at this precise moment, especially as Rich had taken up his effortless swooshing around the rink again and looked like a film star. She clocked one or two women giving him an admiring glance as he passed them. She guessed she'd have to get used to that, especially if his career took off as they were hoping. He'd been talking about having his own show for years, and now it might finally be a possibility. Chloë waved at him, and as he caught sight of his daughter, his face lit up. He skated over and held out his hands to them both. Madison appreciated the offer but shook her head.

'Come and skate with your dad?' he said to Chloë, who beamed.

Madison watched them moving together on the ice, blending in with the other skaters. 'Right, then,' she muttered, beginning to make her way back to the entrance. She could have sworn it was further away. Had she really shuffled only ten metres from the start?

Madison leaned over the wall and called to the assistant, who was wearing flashing green-and-red antlers. She was deep in conversation with another girl, who was rolling a cigarette whilst dressed as an elf, wearing a badge saying 'Santa's Little Helper'. 'Hello! Hi – could you help me a second?'

The girl rolled her eyes and tutted, irritated at being interrupted. 'What is it?' she called.

Never been disrespected by a girl in flashing antlers, and not going to start with that now, Madison thought, taken aback by the complete lack of customer service. She tried to draw herself up to her full height. 'Could you come over here, please?' she called.

Sighing heavily, Antlers came over and raised an eyebrow. 'Yeah?'

'There's something wrong with my skates,' said Madison.

'Wrong size?'

'I don't think so. They're just very . . . slippery.'

The antlers began flashing in a faster rhythm. Madison wondered if they indicated the girl's growing impatience with her.

'They're ice skates. They're meant to be slippery.'

The elf came over, and asked if Antlers had a light. The girl dug around in her pocket and passed her one. Meanwhile, Madison was trying to reduce her building irritation.

'This woman's saying her skates are slippy,' said Antlers, and Santa's Little Helper sniggered.

'Look, I know how it sounds,' said Madison, 'but they *are* too slippery. I cannot stay upright. There's got to be something wrong with them. Like' – she cast about – 'the suspension.'

'Suspension? It's skates, not a four-by-four,' said Santa's Little Helper, puffing out cigarette smoke. Madison's Winter Wonderland vibes were disappearing rapidly. The elf turned to Antlers. 'Look, when you knocking off? Some of the lads from

4

the Penguin Dodgems are heading to the pub, and Aaron's promised me a hot dog.'

'The fit one?' said Antlers, excitedly.

'Yeah!'

'Excuse me, but we still haven't solved the issue of my skates,' said Madison. She wasn't normally one to push things, but she was a paying customer and, as a reasonably good dancer, surely it shouldn't be that hard to translate her moves to ice.

Antlers looked at her. 'Look, Miss, I don't mean to be rude, but the skates aren't the problem. *You* are. You've been clinging to that wall since you got here. Most first-timers do the same thing, so don't worry about it. What you need to do is just . . . *let go*. Trust yourself.'

Madison felt the heat of anger and embarrassment rise to her cheeks, which stung against the cold air. She had applied herself to being good at everything since her school days. As an adult she wanted everything she did to be perfect – and when the kids arrived, well, she had to be the best mum: outings, birthdays and Christmas had to be exciting, amazing and memorable. Her visions were big, but a pro skater first time? Maybe not. She opened her mouth to speak again but Santa's Little Helper squeaked in excitement and pointed at the rink. 'Look! Isn't that Rich Sykers?'

'Who he?' said Antlers.

'That one off the telly. The home-makeover show? He's quite fit for an old bloke.'

Madison suppressed a smirk. She'd wind Rich up about it later.

'My mum *loves* him,' Santa's Little Helper was saying as Antlers nodded in recognition. 'I wonder if there's any way we can get a photo of him, a video or something . . .'

'You want a video of my husband?' Madison said, as Rich skated over to her.

The girls' jaws dropped.

'Everything OK?' Rich said, looking between Madison and the two staff members.

'Fine,' said Antlers, eyes wide and voice shaking. 'Your wife's skates are just very, very, very faulty. We're going to refund the whole session and invite you back for a freebie. With complimentary drinks and food after.'

'Great,' said Rich. He glanced at his watch and turned to Madison. 'I guess we should round up the kids. Nearly time to be off. I've got a bit of a headache as well.' He grimaced.

Madison tried not to let herself feel a beat of disappointment. She'd thought they'd stay for longer – check out the food, buy a few decorations for the tree, even go on a couple of rides.

'Really?' she said, voice low as she turned away from the prying ears of the two girls. 'I think the kids were hoping we'd stay longer.'

'Sorry, babe,' Rich said. 'I'm just knackered.'

He did look tired, she thought. Yes, he was still movie-star handsome, even more so than when she'd met him – an Idris Elba lookalike, his beard now flecked a little with grey, but that suited him. Then she noticed his eyes seemed a little hollow, his skin a little dull. She felt a flash of guilt. Rich worked so hard – he was often away filming, or doing long hours on-set.

'Of course,' she said, her voice soft. 'We can head straight home after this. Run you a bath, make you dinner or phone for a takeaway?'

Rich smiled, but somehow it didn't reach his eyes.

Madison waved the kids over and they came obediently.

'Can we come again, Mum?' Jordan said, unlacing his skates.

'Definitely,' said Madison. 'We've got free tickets, actually.'

Jordan punched the air with his fist and Madison laughed – what did it matter that she wasn't the world's best skater when the kids had enjoyed it so much? Next time, she'd just wrap up warm and watch them all from the side. *Or maybe I could try not to pressure myself so much.* 'Can we get hot chocolate?' Chloë was saying. 'And go on the rides? I saw this massive slide and—'

Truthfully, Madison shared in her disappointment. She wanted to stay on and do all those things but she needed to manage her daughter's expectations, make sure this outing still felt like a treat. 'We're going to have hot chocolate at home,' she said.

Chloë pushed out her bottom lip and looked at her with doe eyes. 'But I thought . . .'

'I know,' said Madison. 'But at home we can put marsh-mallows in it.' She hoped there were some left in the cupboard. If not, she'd have to pop out. 'And you can do all the frothy milk by yourself.'

Somewhat placated, Chloë nodded, but Jordan thrust his hands into his pockets, downcast.

'We'll come back soon,' Madison promised. 'And it'll be even more fun.'

'With Auntie Jess and Sienna?' said Chloë.

Madison always smiled at the mention of 'Auntie Jess'. Jess was her best and oldest friend from school, and for years, whenever Madison heard her name, the first mental image that came to mind was of Jess as a fifteen-year-old, pouting in the cloakroom mirror as they tried to get away with wearing makeup they hoped was undetectable to the teachers, but noticeable to the boys. She could never quite believe that she and Jess were now proper grown-ups, that their families were so close and they were raising their children side by side in the neighbourhood where they'd grown up.

She helped the kids pull off their skates; the cold air made their fingers stiff. Madison rubbed their hands in hers to warm them – she smiled as she remembered her own dear mum doing the same. Then she bundled a pink bobble hat on to Chloë's head and wound the matching scarf round her neck, leaving only her eyes visible, and tried to persuade Jordan that he *would* feel cold soon, once he'd cooled down after skating, so maybe it was a good idea to put his jacket on. Somehow that turned into a negotiation about Xbox time, and then—

'Babe, you're OK to film this, yeah?' Rich said, holding out an iPhone with a sparkly cover on it. Madison glanced around. Antlers and Santa's Little Helper were flanking Rich, and looking at her expectantly. 'Sasha' – Santa's Little Helper – 'was just saying her mum's a big fan of the show and could I do a little cameo?'

'Oh, sure,' said Madison. She grumbled inwardly, then ticked herself off. It wouldn't take long. In any case, it was part of the job and what made Rich so popular – he had a reputation for being super-friendly to his fans. It was only going to get more intense, she reminded herself, so she'd better get used to it now.

Rich worked as a handyman on *House Mates*, in which pairs of friends gave each other's homes a makeover. It was fronted by the eternally youthful Scandinavian Astrid, who had been part of a one-hit-wonder dance duo in the nineties. She had reinvented herself as a no-nonsense TV presenter, famed for her direct feedback to the show's participants.

Madison knew, though, that Astrid was a softy underneath the tough exterior. It was Astrid who'd given Madison her 'big break' – her first job as a design assistant on the show, back in her twenties. And it was on that show that she'd met Rich, although he'd been working behind the cameras at that point. A chance on-camera moment of him sanding down a wardrobe door while wearing a sweaty white vest had gone viral. Madison remembered reading the comments to him, back on one of those glorious lazy Saturdays, early on in their relationship before they'd had kids.

Who is this fitty?

He can D-I-Y me any day of the week!

Never wished I was a wardrobe door more than right now.

Rich had initially been embarrassed, but quickly got over it when he was offered a regular slot on the show as the 'Hot Handyman' who demonstrated a variety of household tips and tricks. 'They want me to wear tight T-shirts,' he'd moaned to Madison, although she noticed he quickly got over his reluctance on that front, too.

In fact, she saw he'd taken off his coat right now, despite the freezing December air, and rolled up his sleeves to show his defined forearms. *If this man catches a cold I will not be looking after him*, she thought.

'OK, so what do you want me to say?' he said to Sasha.

'I dunno,' she said excitedly. 'Becca, what do you think?'

Antlers thought for a minute. 'Like, something cheeky for her mum?'

Rich laughed. 'I'll think of something. What's her name?'

'Mandy.'

Sasha leaned into Rich, her best smile on.

'Do you want Antl— Sorry, Becca in shot as well?' said

Madison. 'I'll count you in and then hit play. Three, two, one.'

Rich turned on his mega-watt smile. His voice dropped an octave and became animated and bubbly. 'Hey there, Mandy, this is Rich, the Hot Handyman, although this weather's making it hard to stay warm! I'm sure you can think of a few ways to heat up the home.' He winked. 'Merry Christmas, and a happy new year.'

Madison stopped recording.

'Thank you *so much*,' said Sasha, breathlessly, to Rich, as Madison handed the phone back.

'Absolutely no problem. I hope she likes it, yeah?' said Rich.

Madison cleared her throat. 'Shall we get the kids home?'

'Let's just have a look at that video,' said Rich, taking the phone from Sasha. He watched the screen intently and turned to Madison. 'Babe, I reckon the contrast is off. You should have done it facing the light. Look, you can barely see it's me. Let's just do it again, OK?'

'You sure?' said Sasha.

'Of course,' said Rich. 'Anything for a fan.'

Sasha giggled, and took up her position by Rich's side once again.

Madison flicked on the camera mode. Her hand was getting cold out of the glove she'd been wearing, and the kids were shifting impatiently. 'Three, two, one,' she said, and they were rolling again.

'Hey there . . .' said Rich, and stopped. 'Damn. What's your mum called again?'

'Mandy,' said Sasha.

'Mandy, got it.' He looked at Madison. 'OK to go again?'

She gave a thumbs-up, glancing at the kids, who were looking increasingly bored and chilly. 'Not long,' she mouthed at them.

This time, Rich stumbled over the line about the weather, saying it was hard to stay cool. That meant they had to record it again. He looked flustered.

'It's OK,' Madison said. 'We've got the first one. That's all good.'

'But it needs to be perfect,' Rich said.

They did two more takes. By the end of it, Madison thought that even Antlers and the elf were getting tired.

'YES!' Rich beamed, as they watched the last video. And it was perfect, Madison had to admit. Rich's voice was confident and assured. All trace of fatigue was gone from his face in the golden glow of the fairy lights. His shoulders and arms were strong. He looked – and sounded – like a main player. Not a sidekick any more. And if Madison was a bit annoyed by the amount of time he'd spent charming his fans while her fingers were freezing, and she could swear the kids were turning into icicles, she just had to get used to it. Over the past few years, Rich had been recognized more and more, and that was only going to increase if he *did* get his own show. Change was on the horizon for Rich, for all of them.

2

Once they were in the car on the way home, Rich lapsed into silence. Madison was driving, and focused on the different decorations within each borough they drove through. *Zones One and Two definitely have different budgets*, she thought. She loved London. Yes, it was big, busy and expensive. All the things people said. But to Madison, it was a place of nostalgia, happy times, good memories and, thanks to the vibrant mix of cultures and colours, endless inspiration for her design work. And at Christmas the city felt hopeful, magical and somehow full of possibilities.

She thought of all the versions of herself she'd been in London – a schoolgirl, an art student, a twenty-something desperate to make her way in the world and have as many adventures as she could. Getting her first 'proper' design job on the show. Becoming Rich's girlfriend. And then – a mother. She glanced at the kids in the rear-view mirror. Chloë was nodding off, and Jordan had his earphones in, nodding to some inaudible beat. Despite all the wonderful choices on offer, she was so glad she had ended up like this: her family, her team, all together.

She glanced at Rich, who was staring out of the window,

chewing the side of his thumbnail, lost in thought. 'You OK, babe?' Madison murmured.

He jerked round to look at her. 'I'm thinking about the video,' he said. 'Wondering if I should even be doing that kind of thing any more. Like, imagine if someone took offence at what I'd said. Social-media storm. Career suicide.'

He chewed his thumb some more and sighed. Madison knew how her husband came across to the observer: confident, smart, maybe even a bit cocky at times. But he had a streak of insecurity and, at the moment, it seemed to be getting bigger.

'You're nervous about the new show,' said Madison, soothingly. 'But don't stop being *you*. That's who they want. Someone who is going to be a natural with fans, someone with real warmth.'

'Yeah, but what if—' Rich broke off.

'What if?' said Madison.

He shrugged. 'It doesn't matter.'

'Look, babe. Whatever happens, you'll have us. We've got your back all the way.' She took her hand briefly off the wheel and reached over to squeeze his. There was a moment's pause before he squeezed her hand back, then let go, resuming his stare out of the window.

She reminded herself that she needed to be patient. The suspense over Rich perhaps getting his own show had dominated their lives for the past couple of months. It had lurked as a possibility several times before but never felt concrete until his agent had told him a major streamer wanted to create a new home-makeover show, and was looking for a presenter to front it. These things came and went quickly, but it was what Rich had dreamed of – and if he got the show, it had professional implications for her too.

Madison hadn't returned to the TV show after she'd had Jordan. It often required them to work away from home, at short notice, with long hours, which wasn't compatible with young children. Then Chloë had arrived, and just when they'd been getting back to a new kind of normal, Madison's beloved mum had become ill with terminal cancer. Madison had nursed her until she passed away, then looked after her distraught dad.

In the last year Madison had returned to working part-time, as a design assistant at a hotel chain, but it wasn't her: too rigid and bland. She and Rich had often discussed what it would look like for her to return to working in TV.

'Just imagine,' she said now, 'the two of us working together again. It'd be fun, right?'

'Yeah, sure,' Rich said distractedly.

She tried a different tactic. 'Might even get to misbehave at the Christmas party,' she murmured. She could remember that night like it was yesterday . . .

The production company that made *House Mates* had an annual Christmas party, and it was a big deal. Madison had *loved* Christmas ever since she was little. You could go all out at Christmas – it was a time for excess, for loads of tinsel, for spending a bit more than you should on the perfect gifts for family and friends, for that extra glass, or three, of bubbly. The first Christmas party had been right after she'd started at the company, so she'd been on her best behaviour, and had even felt a little bit left out of her colleagues' closeness. But now, a year in, she'd felt like they were family, and she was ready to let her hair down.

Naturally, it was themed – there was a prize for the best outfit, and this year's theme was Icons. What could be more iconic than Santa? Madison had thought, and she'd bought herself a red dress and was preparing to glue some white fluff along the hem. She'd managed to find a quiet spot in one of the office meeting rooms to do it, and was engrossed in carefully handling the glue gun and applying the finishing bits of fluff when the door flew open, knocked into her and caused glue to splurge everywhere.

'Sorry!' said Magda, another designer, tumbling through the door, holding a glass of fizz, and swiftly followed by Astrid. 'We were looking for somewhere to wrap the Secret Santas.'

'Oh, no worries,' said Madison, eyeing the dollops of glue on the floor. At least they weren't on the dress. She decided she'd put it on, then add any finishing touches. She slipped into the toilets and changed, tugging the red dress over her head, then marching back to Astrid and Magda.

'Ta-da!' she cried, bursting in. 'What's more iconic than Santa?'

Astrid and Magda looked her up and down, their smiles frozen.

'That's what you're wearing?' said Astrid, pointing at the dress.

'There's, umm, a . . . bit of a mark,' said Magda, reaching out with a tissue and dabbing at the front of Madison's dress.

Madison looked down and saw a massive, sticky glue stain. 'Oh, *shit*,' she said.

'You will barely notice it,' said Magda, encouragingly. 'Especially when the lights are down and everyone's drunk.'

Astrid snorted. 'You English, always so polite. Madison, darling, you cannot possibly wear that dress.'

'I mean, it does look like someone . . . overexcited,' said Magda, blushing furiously.

'And I presume that's not the look you're going for,' said Astrid.

'No, it most definitely isn't,' replied Madison, in despair. Why did this stuff always happen to *her*? She didn't want to go to the party in her scruffy old jeans and the jumper that she'd been wearing since six a.m., even if the party was in the boardroom.

'Hang on, Cinderella,' said Magda. 'I've got an idea.'

She beckoned for Madison to follow her through the corridors of the production office, where posters of present and past shows adorned the walls.

Magda unlocked a cupboard. 'Shouldn't really be doing this, but I know they stashed a host of costumes in here on the way back from a promo shoot,' she said. 'Come on, let's see if we can find you another outfit.' She rummaged among the railings, and gasped. 'This! Oh, my God! It's perfect.'

She pulled out a white halterneck dress, with a full skirt, that seemed to shimmer and glow with a life of its own.

'Isn't it too dressy?' said Madison.

But Magda was a woman on a mission. She rummaged further and found a pair of silver high heels. 'Just try it on, Madison,' Magda begged.

Madison went into the loos again, pulled on the white dress and put on the shoes. She took a deep breath before she went out. She was generally OK with how she looked – she sometimes felt nice enough, but she wasn't a knockout like her best friend, Jess. And she was fine with that. Mostly. As long as this looked OK, that was fine.

Madison glanced in the full-length mirror and did a double-take. That couldn't be her! The dress fitted like it had been made for her: it skimmed and showed off her curves in all the right places, and her brown skin gleamed against the bright white fabric. The high heels elongated her legs and she spun round, twirling. She felt *amazing*. She couldn't wait to hit the dance floor in this little number!

'Oh. My. God!' said Magda, bursting through the door. 'Madison, you look absolutely incredible! Where have you been hiding that figure?'

'Thanks, Mags,' said Madison, grinning shyly.

'Madison Monroe,' said Astrid, coming in behind her. 'Phenomenal.'

'Just one finishing touch,' said Magda, pulling out a deep red lipstick and applying it to Madison. 'Perfect. Now let's get in there.'

They walked into the boardroom, which had been transformed for the party, tables pushed back to make a dance floor, flashing disco lights, a buffet laden with beige food – much to Madison's disappointment, it didn't look like they'd splashed out for the end-of-year party. But there were mince pies, and Christmas tunes were blaring.

Some of the staff were already the worse for wear, Elton John's sparkling glasses, Britney's snake, and an array of wigs slipping off as the dance moves got wilder.

'Everyone's checking you out,' murmured Magda, and Madison opened her mouth to protest before she saw it was *true*. Heads were turning to watch her walk into the middle of the room. Her colleagues were smiling and raising drinks to her. She made herself pull back her shoulders and smile too. Her smile was her favourite feature: it showed off her naturally straight white teeth and the dimples she'd inherited from her mum.

She went to get some fizz from the makeshift bar, picking up a glass and reaching for the bottle. 'Please, allow me,' said a smooth voice at her side, and she turned to see Rich in a tuxedo.

Of course she'd noticed him when she'd begun working there – everyone had. They'd been introduced, and he'd once helped her as she struggled to get an awkward box up some stairs, but that was the limit of their interactions. Working on separate teams with different schedules had dashed Madison's hopes of properly connecting with him. Until now.

'Is the name Bond, James Bond?' said Madison, reaching out her glass for Rich to pour her some fizz. The drink, the dress or the mixture of both had boosted her confidence.

Rich laughed. 'Something like that. The name's Rich. Rich Sykers.' He clinked his glass against hers.

Madison had a weird moment of wondering if he really didn't recognize her, if she was *that* forgettable, before shoving it to the back of her mind – maybe she was overthinking it.

'Madison. Madison Monroe,' she said.

'Well, Madison – what can I say? You're an absolute bombshell.'

Madison wanted to grin with delight. Instead she embraced the essence of her icon, and lowered her eyes to the floor, then looked up to meet his. 'I'd better go and greet my adoring fans.' She smiled cheekily and sashayed away, aware that Rich was watching her go.

Madison hit the dance floor in style, working her hips, singing along to the tunes at the top of her voice. She loved dancing, loved the beat working its way through her body, putting her hands over her head and letting pure happiness flow through her. Everyone was dancing in no time, and that was when Madison ducked away to wipe her brow and armpits discreetly with napkins, only to find Rich at her side again.

'I cannot take my eyes off you,' he said, and she noticed again how handsome he was, and felt her stomach flip. 'Can I have the next dance with you?'

'Sure,' said Madison, breezily. She seemed to have acquired an entirely different personality in this dress. 'Just make sure you can keep up, yeah?'

Rich laughed. On top of everything else, it turned out that he was an amazing dancer. He twirled Madison round, and danced up behind her, his arm around her waist, and Madison shut her eyes, leaning into the feeling of them dancing together, their rhythm perfectly matched . . .

'Right, OK, time for a quick speech,' came a droning male voice. Colin, the head of Accounts, pulled the music, to groans from everyone. 'Just a very swift run-down of where we're at this year . . .'

'Colin, put the music back on or I'm leaving!' yelled Astrid, and everyone cheered.

Colin scuttled away and the music resumed, but Madison was the only person who was glad of the interruption – it had been getting a bit heated for the work Christmas party. The last thing she wanted was to be office gossip in the morning. She hurried to the loos and immediately texted Jess, who was much more used to dealing with men who looked like Rich than Madison was.

Jess rang immediately.

'What the hell do I do?' muttered Madison. 'The hottest man in the world appears to be hitting on me. *Me!*'

Jess cackled. 'Play it cool, Mads. He'll be used to getting what he wants. You just bide your time, eh?'

Madison topped up her lipstick and walked back out. She glanced around the room for Rich, trying to look as if she wasn't searching for him.

'Fancy getting out of here?' Rich murmured in her ear, catching her by surprise. 'The music's entering a phase that's a bit too cheesy for me.'

'I'm gonna stay,' said Madison, thinking of what Jess would do. 'But you can take my number and ask me out on a proper date.'

Rich smiled.

'And while Marilyn would probably have scribbled it in lipstick on a napkin,' said Madison, 'I'm going to put it in your phone.'

She tapped in her number, double-checking that it was correct, and saved her contact details as Madison Monroe.

Ten years later, and married, she was still saved in Rich's phone as Madison Monroe.

3

Madison pulled the car into the driveway of their house and sighed with pleasure at the sight of the windows lit up by Christmas lights. She'd gone simple inside and out, hanging strands of lights that flickered in different rhythms – magical. She'd given the kids free rein on the Christmas tree, though, which was embellished with decorations varying from traditional white-painted wooden snowflakes to a glittering slice of pizza and the bells the kids had fashioned from egg boxes cut up and covered haphazardly with tinfoil. Lights flashed from top to bottom and, at their request, Madison had glitter-sprayed the tips of the branches to make them look snow-lined. It worked, but the poor tree was suffocating under all the tinsel.

Sometimes Madison thought back to her carefully co-ordinated Christmas trees and wanted to laugh. Those days were long gone, but she wouldn't have it any other way.

She always loved coming home. Those four walls represented a hell of a lot of hard work from her and Rich – years spent scrimping and saving for a deposit, buying a 'fixer-upper', living in chaos with one small child, then two while they spent hours sanding down and repairing the skirting boards, plastering and repainting the walls, pulling out the bathroom and the kitchen and replacing them with something more modern.

'We should just have got Jess and Michael to swap with us,' Madison had grumbled more than once. 'Done it as part of the show.'

But then, gradually, the house began to look like home. After the bulk of the work was done, Madison put her skills to full use. She designed a cosy living room, with squishy sofas and bean bags for the kids. She turned the boxroom into a tiny DIY space for Rich, storing his tools neatly, and created a beautiful bedroom for the two of them. She knew Rich didn't like it when a design was 'too girly', so she gave herself a dressing-table with a beautiful old-school light-bulb mirror where she did her makeup, then did the rest of the room in a careful blend of their styles. The kids shared a room – and this was getting more difficult as they grew older. The next big project was the attic so they could each have their own space.

'Right, come on, you two,' said Madison, opening her car door, stepping out into the chilly air, then letting the kids out of the back seat. The warmth of the car journey had made them drowsy. 'Whoever's in their pyjamas first gets extra marshmallows.'

If in doubt, promise sugar, and ideally some sense of sibling rivalry. That was parenting 101.

Jordan and Chloë scrambled out of the car and ran to the front door, which Rich unlocked. 'You do pyjamas, I do refreshments?' said Madison, as they entered the cosy hallway.

Rich nodded.

Madison went into the kitchen as she heard the kids bounding upstairs. 'Daddy, he pushed me!' Chloë was saying indignantly, as Jordan protested his innocence.

Madison sensed an argument brewing between the tired kids until she heard Rich speaking, his voice deep. 'Enough of that, both of you. You'll have a quick bath and put your pyjamas on *quietly*. In fact, whoever's the quietest wins most marshmallows.'

Silence instantly fell.

Please, God, let there be marshmallows, thought Madison, opening the cupboards and finding a packet, to her relief, at the back. She pulled out a tiny milk pan – it was a typical small stainless-steel saucepan, nothing special, except it had been her mother Selina's, and was the only saucepan she used to make hot chocolate her way, the Jamaican way.

Miss you, Mum, she thought, as she did a hundred times a day. She heated the milk gently, careful to avoid it boiling, then stirred in the cocoa powder, which she knew her mum would have frowned at. She always used raw cacao that had been dehydrated into a ball. Madison's version was easier to find, plus she kept the other elements in stock. She poured in some thick condensed milk for sweetness, grated some nutmeg, sprinkled in a dash of cinnamon and stirred slowly, taking her time, enjoying the sweet smell.

Then she got down four mugs, each in a pastel colour, and carefully poured hot chocolate into each one.

Right on time, she heard footsteps on the stairs, then pattering along the hallway. Chloë and Jordan came into the kitchen, Chloë in her pink fleece pyjamas, Jordan in a red and black plaid print, a mini version of his dad's.

'Can we make noise yet, Dad?' said Jordan.

Rich smiled. 'I think you just did,' he said, squeezing his son's shoulder. 'I'm going to declare it a draw. You were both very, very quiet when it came to putting on the pyjamas.'

Madison pushed the marshmallows towards them. Chloë and Jordan reached for them, dropping them into the hot chocolate and watching them go gooey. 'Leave some for us!' She laughed, plonking some into Rich's mug. She could tell the kids were tired from skating: instead of their usual chatter, they were sipping their hot chocolate in relative quiet.

She caught Rich's eye and nodded gently towards them. 'Time to brush your teeth and get into bed,' she said.

'Who's doing the story?' said Chloë, with a huge yawn.

'It's my turn. Let's go! Chop-chop,' said Rich, ushering them out of the door again, although Madison suspected they'd be asleep before he had read more than a page or two.

Her hunch was correct: Rich was back downstairs before she'd finished clearing up.

'They're passed out,' he said. 'Listen, I just have to check some emails, OK?'

'Sure,' said Madison. 'Then maybe we can snuggle up with a glass of wine? Watch a film? Chat about everything that's going on?' She raised an eyebrow and tilted her head.

'Sounds good,' said Rich, eyes fixed on his phone.

Madison pressed her lips together. It was one of her bugbears about him – the amount of time he spent on his phone. 'Or we could, you know, rob a bank. Have a threesome. Set fire to the wedding presents your mum gave us that I never really liked? You know, the tablecloth we only use when she comes over?'

'Sounds good,' said Rich again.

Madison sighed and crossed over to him. She put a hand on his arm and he jumped back. 'Babe. You aren't listening to me. Please, let's chat properly,' said Madison, startled by his reaction.

Rich hesitated, then nodded and put his phone into his pocket.

Madison poured them each a glass of wine, and they went into the living room, sitting side by side on the forest green three-seater sofa, which she had upholstered herself to match her Zen vision.

She leaned over and put on some chilled-out music, then pulled her legs under her, getting comfortable. This was what they needed. Some proper time to talk. Madison scanned the room, which they all called the green room because of the array of plants in it, as she tried to find the best way to start the conversation. She gave up and just spat it out.

'So what's going on with the show?' she said. 'That's what's on your mind, right?'

'Yeah,' said Rich, exhaling. 'It's looking really promising. The producer wants to meet with me one more time. But my agent's saying it's pretty much a done deal. Just need to agree on terms. Money.'

'But that's amazing,' said Madison. 'That's a cause for celebration!'

'Yeah . . .' said Rich, looking down and picking at his thumb again.

Why was he so troubled? This was everything they'd been aiming for. They should be popping a bottle! It could be her big break again too – a chance to get back to the excitement of TV, to doing a design job she really wanted. She felt butterflies in her stomach at the thought of it. She just *knew* she had so much more to give as a designer, and loved the idea of working again as part of a brilliant creative team, getting inspired by other people. If that included her husband, well, they were already a great team at home and surely that would be the case at work too . . .

His face was tense. Why wasn't he as excited as she was? Her heart plummeted as a thought occurred to her. She pulled a cushion on to her lap, choosing her next words carefully. 'Babe,' she said gently. 'I know we talked about me working on the show . . . but if it's looking like that won't happen, you can just tell me. Is that what's eating away at you?'

He didn't reply. In fact, it was like he was frozen. The whole atmosphere shifted. Even the soft melody and gentle beat weren't helping. Madison felt disappointment blossom through her, but she squashed it down. 'Rich, look at me,' she said. 'It doesn't matter. There'll be other design jobs I can go for. Maybe I can speak to Astrid again, but any win for you is a win for me, for all of us—'

'Madison, stop,' said Rich, sharply. 'Just *stop*, will you, for once?'

Madison sat back, shocked. The harshness of his words and the bass in his voice reverberated through the room. The Christmas-tree lights flashed, and suddenly seemed ridiculous. She wanted to turn them off. She looked at Rich.

He placed a hand over his face, rubbing his chin, over and over. 'I can't do this any more,' he muttered.

Madison felt an abyss was opening up. She could barely compute the words he was saying. It made no sense. 'Work?' she stuttered.

'Just *all* of it, Madison,' Rich said, his voice close to breaking.

'Explain it to me, please,' Madison said, her heart pounding.

'It's just *everything*. I'm exhausted all the time. I'm trying to provide for the family. I'm trying to be ambitious. I'm trying to make this show come off. I'm trying to be my best self, all the time, and it's exhausting. And—' He stopped, cutting himself off, his chest rising and falling fast.

Madison was stunned. She had known he was stressed but not that he was feeling like this. She reached out a hand to him, laid it on his forearm. He stared at it, as if it was some foreign object. 'Please look at me,' she said, her voice low. 'I had no idea you felt like this. I—'

He moved his arm away from her, folded both across his chest. 'I need a break,' Rich said, his voice completely flat.

'Like, a holiday? We could all use that, I completely agree,' Madison heard herself say, but she felt as if someone else was speaking.

Rich got up and switched off the music, his gestures quick. The silence was deafening. 'It's not that. I need space. I just need some *space*.' He began pacing around the room, nodding to himself. 'Yeah, yeah. That's what I need. Get my head together,' he muttered.

Madison felt as if someone had punched her, hard, in the stomach. She couldn't catch her breath. 'What do you mean, space?'

He stopped pacing, but he kept his eyes down. 'I need to leave. For a bit.'

Madison couldn't take it in. She felt dizzy. '*Leave?*' She forced herself to take a breath. 'Our kids are sleeping upstairs. We've just taken them out. I don't understand why that would make you want to . . .' She couldn't utter the words. 'Please, just sit down,' she said, patting the sofa beside her. 'Sit down.'

He didn't. Instead he was shaking his head. 'I need to get some stuff,' he muttered, as he left the room.

Madison sat frozen while above her she heard drawers opening and closing. She made herself stand and walk up to their bedroom, past the family portraits that lined the staircase. It was hard to move. Her limbs felt heavy and weak.

Inside the bedroom, his case was flung on the floor, open. Part of her felt she could have laughed hysterically – this was like a scene from a film. Rich couldn't just *walk out*. They'd had a lovely evening together with the kids. He'd just put them to bed. They were meant to be downstairs, talking about his new show. She couldn't understand what was going on.

He was pulling shirts out of the wardrobe. She went over to him, placed a hand on his shoulder. 'Just *look* at me, please, Rich.' Somehow she felt that if he *looked* at her, he'd exhale, stop what he was doing and come to his senses. Then they could finally talk. Was this a nervous breakdown? Was this how it looked? Should she be calling the doctor? Or was he playing some kind of practical joke?

He glanced at her for a micro-second, then away.

'Rich, tell me what you need? Tell me what's going on.'

'I told you. I need to get away,' he said, his voice cold and shut down.

'For how long?' she said, her voice rising. 'And where?'

He didn't answer her, just kept putting things in the suitcase.

'What about our kids?' she whispered. 'Our kids, who are sleeping next door, right now.' She pointed in their direction while her eyes remained firmly on his.

That stopped him. 'A few days,' he said quietly. 'I'll go to my cousin's. Just give me a few days.'

He went to the wardrobe again, pulled out his warmest winter coat and put it on. That gesture made this real for Madison. He was going. He was really going. He was going out into the cold winter night, to some uncomfortable sofa-bed at his cousin's, rather than staying with her. Despite the warmth of the house, her whole body felt cold. 'And what am I meant to tell the kids?' she choked out.

Rich's face dropped. 'Just tell them I'm working, OK? Away for a few days.' He picked up his bag.

Madison stared at him. She couldn't process this. 'Please . . .' she said, her voice cracking. 'Please, Rich. Just stay. I'm begging you. Just stay, and let's talk.'

There was a moment, a long moment, when she thought he might put down his bag, take off his coat and sit with her. But he shook his head and zipped up his coat. 'I have to go,' he muttered eventually, and stepped out of their bedroom.

Madison heard the front door open and close.

4

Madison didn't go to bed – she couldn't bear to get into the double that would still smell of Rich, the bedroom she considered their sanctuary. She stayed on the sofa, watching the Christmas lights flicker, for hours as her mind raced, then slowed to total blankness, and started racing again. She stared at her phone, hoping Rich would text her, let her know they'd be OK, but the screen remained blank.

She kept turning over the evening they'd had: had she done something that had upset him enough to leave? When she couldn't find anything, she reached further back, looking at their most recent messages – who was fetching the kids, who was cooking dinner, the occasional funny meme, or suggesting they see friends – usually Jess and her husband Michael.

Eventually, at three o'clock, she got up, turned off the lights and curled up on the sofa, pulling a blanket over herself. She didn't think she would sleep, but she must have dozed off, because the next thing she knew light was struggling through the curtains and Chloë was peering down at her. For a moment, the only thing Madison felt was love for her daughter, pure wonder that this beautiful little human existed. Chloë's face was gently illuminated, her deep brown eyes full of curiosity.

'Why are you sleeping on the sofa, Mum?'

Madison sat up blearily, rubbing her eyes, her throat raw, as the reason she was sleeping down there tumbled back into her conscious thoughts. Rich had left, mysteriously, without explanation. Panic rose in her, and she pushed it down. There was no way she'd let Chloë detect something was wrong.

'Just, umm, making sure Santa doesn't arrive too early,' she croaked.

Chloë frowned. 'Really?'

She *had* to keep things normal for the kids. She cleared her throat and made her voice firmer, smiling at her daughter. 'Yeah, sometimes he gets the day wrong and leaves presents too early.'

Chloë was young enough to believe this but Madison changed the subject just in case – she didn't want Jordan coming down and finding her in this state: he was older and a little more perceptive than his younger sister.

'Do you want Coco Pops for breakfast?'

That was guaranteed to get Chloë beaming. It was Monday, and they were never allowed sugary cereals on a school day.

'*Yesss!*' said Chloë.

'Is your brother up?'

Chloë nodded enthusiastically. Madison knew that Jordan might well be awake, but he definitely wasn't up. He had to be dragged out of bed these days.

'Come on, wash first, then Coco Pops,' she said, leading Chloë up the stairs and into the bathroom, where she helped wash her face, then dressed her in record time.

She marched into Jordan's room and pulled off the covers. 'You have fifteen minutes to get washed, dressed and at the table ready for breakfast,' she told him calmly. He didn't budge, and Madison had to change tack. 'Your time starts . . . NOW!' she barked, like a drill sergeant. He flew out of the bed. Madison smiled to herself.

As Madison went downstairs, her daughter trailing behind her, Chloë asked, 'Can Dad do my hair?'

Madison's heart squeezed painfully. As a proud girl-dad, Rich had always done Chloë's hair. Nothing elaborate, just brushed back into a ponytail or plaits with colourful bobbles at the ends. Some of her most precious moments had been listening to father and daughter chat as he'd worked. It was their bonding time.

Jordan had his time, too, when Rich took him to the barber every three weeks.

'Dad's had to head off very early for work,' Madison said, surprised at how easily the lie came, and how steady her voice was. 'He'll be away for a few days. But I can do your hair.'

Chloë nodded, and Madison felt a weird optimism surge through her. Maybe everything would be OK. Maybe he would just be away for a few days, and she had to keep calm and carry on. Now that it was daylight, now that they were getting ready for the school run, maybe she could almost pretend that things were normal.

On autopilot, Madison pulled down bowls. She took the cereal from the cupboard and milk from the fridge. She began making herself a coffee from the machine, placed a spoon in Chloë's bowl and put Jordan's in front of his empty chair. She knew this morning routine so well. She just had to do one task after another, not think about anything else. Check they had their homework. Check they had lunch. Check they looked neat and— 'Jordan, time's nearly up! You have two minutes to get your butt down here,' she bellowed.

Jordan ran into the kitchen, happy he'd beaten his mum's imaginary stopwatch. He looked so much like Rich sometimes. At ten, he was at a funny stage of wanting to be older than he was, and sometimes still the kid who came into their room for a cuddle if he'd had a bad dream. He idolized his dad, but was also a Mummy's boy, which Madison appreciated. It wouldn't be like that for ever. 'Morning, Mum,' he said, giving her the sweetest hug ever.

Madison squeezed him back as tears welled in her eyes. She half wished she was dealing with a stroppy Jordan that morning – easier than him being so sweet. 'Right, you two, let's not be late for school today, please.' She glanced at the clock. 'Come on, eat up!' She motioned with her hand as she gulped her coffee. 'You need to be by that front door, packed lunches in hand, ready to go in the next five minutes, yes?'

'Yes, Mum,' they groaned.

Madison used those minutes rounding up half-finished homework, overseeing teeth cleaning, adding fruit to their lunch boxes, then ushering them out of the door and into the car. Usually they would walk to school, but today Madison wanted to get there as quickly as possible.

Everything is fine. Everything is fine, she told herself. *Focus on what is happening right now.*

She breathed in and out slowly to steady herself, turning on the radio to drown out the kids' squabbling. As she parked at the school, she glanced at her watch. They were actually early, for once.

'Come on, then,' she said, her voice bright. 'Let's go, team!'

'There's Sienna!' said Chloë, beaming as she spotted Jess and her daughter arriving at the school gates.

Jess was looking gorgeous, as always, her skin glowing. She

was dressed in a classic high-street Chanel-esque style and looked like a powerful boss. 'Hey, babe!' she said, coming up to Madison and giving her a hug.

'Hey,' Madison said, squeezing her back.

'I'll never get tired of watching them head into school together,' said Jess, smiling fondly as the kids walked in, turning back to wave at their mums. 'Soon they'll be moody teenagers and won't want *anything* to do with us. Remember how we could be sometimes?'

Madison sighed. 'Well, you were OK, actually. I had my moments but it was Ladene who was the worst of us.'

Jess loved reminiscing about their gang of friends in school. There'd been four of them – Madison, Jess, Ladene and Abiola – and they'd added Finn to their little crew when he'd joined in the sixth form. They might have changed over the years, but the love, the jokes and the dynamics remained the same.

Madison tried to think of an example of when they'd been stroppy teenagers, but it was like her brain wasn't working properly. She kept having waves of emotion: sometimes it could all feel *normal*, then she'd remember last night and her stomach would drop. 'You OK?' Jess said.

Now was the moment to tell her. This was her best friend. She'd been there for Madison through thick and thin. 'Didn't sleep that well,' began Madison. What should come next? *Rich has walked out? Rich has gone away for a few days? Rich has left us?* She couldn't find the words to express herself, and the moment passed.

Jess dived back into the conversation. 'Oh, babe, it's the time of year – so much on! Listen, I was wanting to chat to you about the nativity.'

'Right, yeah,' said Madison, trying to work out how she

could raise the subject of Rich. She couldn't make sense of anything or take anything in, and . . . 'You know what, Jess, do you mind if we chat some other time? Think the lack of sleep is bringing on a headache.' She touched her forehead.

'Oh, of course,' said Jess, her face full of sympathy. 'Sorry. There I am, banging on. Do you want me to bring anything round? Pick the kids up later?'

'Actually, that would be amazing, thanks so much.'

Jess squeezed her arm. 'No problem. Make sure you take it easy today, hon, OK?'

Madison smiled and nodded gratefully.

Madison arrived back to a silent house. After sending a quick email to her boss to say she wouldn't be in today – there was no way she was making it into the office – she sat at the kitchen table and stared into space, the hours passing. Now that she was away from the distraction of the kids, aspects of last night swirled in her mind. She kept replaying the conversation with Rich, his words causing more pain and confusion each time she thought of them. *I have to go. I need space.*

What did it *mean*?

She kept looking at her phone, but there was no word from him. She started typing out text messages: *Hey, babe, just wondering if you're OK?*, *Hey, did you get to your cousin's?*, *Hon, please, can you tell me what's going on? I love you.*

She put down her phone. If he'd asked for space, maybe she needed to respect that. Slowly, the shock gave way to tears.

'Oh, Mum,' she whispered. 'What do I do?'

Madison missed her mum so much. Selina had passed away four years ago, from a fast-moving cancer. It had been only a few months from her diagnosis that she'd finally transitioned.

Madison had been heartbroken, and, truth be told, she still was. It had all happened so fast. How was Selina no longer here? Madison had felt like a walking zombie for weeks afterwards, but within the rollercoaster ride of grief she found comfort in knowing her mum was pain free, at peace and, as a devout Christian, had most definitely made it through the pearly white gates of Heaven. Her mum had been her anchor, her dad's too. She had been desperately worried about how he would cope without Selina – emotionally and practically. They'd been married for more than fifty years.

Madison had been thinking at that point about going back to work, but when her mum was diagnosed, she wanted to spend every possible moment with her. After she died, her spare energy went to her dad. She cooked batch meals for him, spent as much time with him as she could, encouraged him to see his friends. Thank God for the kids – their high spirits and joy brought random moments of laughter that penetrated the thick dark rain clouds above their heads.

Madison had been raised as a Christian and believed in God but didn't go to church as often as Selina would have liked. In fact, she was ashamed to realize, her mum's funeral had been the first time in years she'd set foot in a church. But she always wore a small Angel Gabriel necklace, a gift from Selina several years before, to remind her of her religion and her mum. Sometimes she could have sworn she felt her mum's presence near her.

She clamped her eyes shut and willed her mum to help her if she was there. But when she opened her eyes, she felt more alone than ever.

She spotted a photo of the family – her, Rich, Jordan and Chloë – arms wrapped around each other, huge smiles. She picked up the frame and stared at the image for a long time. He couldn't want to leave this. He couldn't. It was impossible. Rich loved having a family. Madison had fallen pregnant a bit sooner than they'd planned, while they were still enjoying the heady days of being a couple, and even though they'd vaguely talked about kids in an abstract sense, her being pregnant was another thing altogether. But Rich had *loved* the news. He'd always wanted to be a dad.

Nine months later, Jordan was born, and Rich was smitten. He and Madison *were* amazing parents. Of course, he was working and, given his long hours, Madison did the bulk of the childcare, but as often as he was able, Rich took charge of Jordan and encouraged Madison to rest or see her friends. They were lucky in that they had two sets of grandparents who were happy to pitch in and offer support, even if Madison did find Rich's mum's advice a little overpowering at times.

Memories of how Rich had been after the arrival of Jordan, then Chloë, strengthened Madison's resolve. Of course Rich didn't want to leave. He was clearly going through something, and his mental health might have been affected by all the recent work pressure. But that still left the question of what she should *do*. Madison wasn't very good at doing nothing: if there was a problem, she liked to fix it. Should she look up therapists, insist that he come back and talk to her, or head round to his cousin's? Should she call him? Was this some kind of test of how much she'd be there for him?

She pulled out a notepad and began writing down her thoughts:

Feeling so lost after last night. I need to do something but I don't know what to do . . . Can't believe he's not going to walk in after work like normal. I'm alone in bed for the first time in years. This all just feels so surreal and I feel so sad, so sad that he's had to do this, that he felt leaving was his best option rather than telling me what the actual problem is. Is it the job stuff? Family pressure? Sex? Me?

She chewed the pen as emotions spiralled through her.

This wasn't helping. She just felt like a tangle of confusion. She pulled out the to-do list of Christmas tasks, and ordered presents for the kids, then looked for a gift online for Rich. She scrolled through expensive sweatshirts and hoodies, a pair of trainers she knew he'd had his eye on for ages. But maybe she needed to do something more special. She racked her brains, then got up and began to clean the kitchen from top to bottom. She planned dinner for the kids that night, nothing complicated. Although she had no appetite, she made herself some toast and tried to force it down.

She lay on the sofa and fell into a shallow sleep, woken by a tap on the door.

'Rich?' she called, happy, getting to her feet, then realizing that if it was him, he'd have used his key.

It was Jess, with the kids and Sienna. 'Special delivery!' she called, as Madison opened the door.

'Wow! Is it that time already?' said Madison, rubbing her forehead. She was completely disorientated.

Jess frowned, in an expression of concern. 'You sure you're not coming down with something?'

'Just tired,' said Madison.

Jess came in and shut the door behind her. 'You kids go and chill in the living room,' she told them. 'I'll bring you a snack, OK?'

She and Jess were godparents, almost like second mums, to each other's children, and Madison loved how close they all were. Jess ushered her into the kitchen and put the kettle on. 'You look a bit worn out. I'm not sure if tea is going to fix it, but let's see what you've got.'

Jess reached into the cupboards and made Madison a cup of camomile tea, then found some packets of nuts and raisins for the kids. 'Catch! she shouted, from the living-room door, as she threw over the healthy snacks. They were met with groans, and protests from Chloë that she wanted chocolate.

'What time is Rich back?' Jess asked, as she re-entered the kitchen. 'Can he be on parent duty tonight? You need a bath and an early night, that's for sure.'

Madison swallowed. 'I'm, uh, not sure,' she said quietly.

Jess rolled her eyes. 'Honestly, that job!'

'I know,' muttered Madison.

'So where is he this time?'

Madison buried her face in her hands.

'Madison?' said Jess, coming to sit by her. 'Hey, what's wrong?'

Madison shook her head. 'I don't know when he's coming back, Jess.' She glanced at her best friend, whose face was full of confusion, a mirror of Madison's own feelings.

'What do you mean?' Jess said slowly.

Madison exhaled and forced out the words. 'Last night. We'd just had a great time out with the kids. We got home, he put them to bed. And then it was like he just *freaked out*. Like it wasn't him. He was saying how he's under so much stress, and how he just needs some time away, and how he's going to stay at his cousin's for a few days.'

Jess looked stunned, her mouth dropping open. 'Are you serious?'

Madison nodded miserably.

'OK,' Jess murmured. 'OK. Let me get my head around this.'

'I feel like I'm going crazy,' said Madison. 'It's not even been twenty-four hours since he left.'

'Have you heard from him today?'

'No.'

'Do the kids know?'

'They think he's away working. It's not that unusual for them, and I want to keep it normal.'

'Yeah, of course,' said Jess, her face creased with worry.

'I just don't know what to do, Jess. One minute I'm gutted. The next I'm numb. Then I have these weird moments when everything seems normal. Should I be going round there, insisting he talks to me, to show how much I care? Or do I just wait and give him the space he asked for? Like, what am I meant to be doing? How long am I expected to wait?' Madison felt helpless.

Jess was lost in thought, tapping her thumb against her lower lip. 'Let him do this,' she said quietly. 'Do not contact him. Let him have his space.' She reached for Madison's hand. 'It sounds to me like he's just flipped out. Stress. A few nights away from your cooking, away from home, he'll come to his senses. Realize that this is the best place for him to deal with whatever's going on.'

'Do you think?' said Madison.

'Yeah,' said Jess, and smiled. 'It's just men being useless and not managing emotions well, isn't it?'

Madison wasn't sure. She and Rich had gone through periods of stress and difficulty together in the past and he had never reacted like this before. 'I dunno. Isn't that just an excuse for them?' She glanced at her phone. 'I feel like ringing him up and having a go. I'm the one who's left here, keeping things together.'

'Babe, I can see you're angry, and I don't blame you, but don't do anything that might make the situation worse. You've got to rise above it and give this some time. If you ring him up and have a go, it's just bringing more conflict into the situation, which may push him further away.'

Madison sighed. 'I get what you're saying. I still don't get why he had to leave.'

'You don't have to get it,' said Jess. 'Look, just hold tight. Imagine he *is* away on that work trip, and he'll be back before you know it. Probably contrite and saying what an idiot he's been.'

Madison picked at her nails. 'Maybe you're right.'

Jess glanced at her phone. 'Sorry, babe, I have to get back and sort Sienna out. But listen – just try not to worry. He'll be back soon. This is *Rich* we're talking about, not some random guy.'

Madison nodded slowly. 'Don't say anything to the rest of the gang.'

'Of course not.' Jess gave Madison a huge hug. 'Get a takeaway tonight. And I'm on the end of the phone if you need me. But I reckon, by Christmas, it'll be like this never happened.'

Two more days crawled past. Rich texted Madison once, saying he hoped the kids were OK and that he loved them. Madison hadn't been sure how to respond and had found herself repeatedly typing out long paragraphs full of questions, then deleting them. Eventually, scared of getting no reply, she sent a heart emoji instead.

*

41

Madison felt as if she was trying on different responses to the situation, like different outfits. The easiest moments were when she was on autopilot with the kids, during those busy times of the day – getting ready for school in the morning, picking them up in the afternoon, making dinner and doing bedtime in the evening. Then, things almost felt normal.

The gaps between those times were more difficult: she had one day working from home in her part-time design job, but she could barely focus on emails. The worst moments were when her mind felt like a washing-machine: churning the same thoughts around and around, accompanied by different emotions. Why had he left? Had she done something wrong? Was there something he wasn't telling her? When would he be back?

Sometimes she felt panicked by the uncertainty, and by how much his leaving had blindsided her. Never in a million years had she thought Rich would be capable of something like this. She prided herself on being able to read people well, but she'd clearly missed something in relation to her own husband. *Had* she been putting him under more pressure than she'd known? Then she'd remember *she* was now holding everything together, looking after the kids, *lying* to the kids – that was the bit she resented most – and then she'd feel a wave of anger that swelled to become sadness that *this* was how things were, when all around her other families were getting ready for Christmas. But after the tears, she would dry her eyes and remember Jess's words: soon things would be back to normal.

But even those reassuring words had started to feel like added pressure. What if things weren't sorted by Christmas? She kept going round on this emotional rollercoaster, getting nowhere but feeling completely exhausted by the end of it. It felt like running on the spot.

It was at lunchtime on the third day after Rich had left that her phone pinged with a notification from him. Her heart was in her mouth as she read it:

Hey, just remembered it's Mum's birthday tomorrow. We need to be round there for 6!

Her mouth hung open in disbelief. Was that it? It was the type of hastily dashed off message she normally got from Rich when he was frantically busy. He'd never been one for lengthy comms. But this was like nothing had happened. This was like they hadn't spent the last three days apart.

Madison stared at the ceiling, unsure how to reply. She typed, *Yeah, we're fine, thanks for asking*, then deleted it. She typed, *Are you OK?* and deleted that too. If she was honest, the last thing she wanted to do was put on a brave face for Rich's mum, Tina. But maybe this was a chance to show Rich what he was missing out on. He'd said he'd be away for a few days, so maybe tomorrow he'd be back. She tried to strike the right balance of showing him she cared and giving him space in her reply:

Hey. Hope you're OK. Yes, that's fine x

She waited with sweaty palms. Rich sent a thumbs-up.

She began typing a variety of replies, fast and frenetic, then paused. She needed to show him that she was still on his team, but to respect his need for space.

Should I get your mum a card?

Yeah, that would be amazing. Thanks, babe. Maybe some flowers too.

He'd called her 'babe'! Like nothing had changed! It was stupid to feel like this on the basis of a single word, but hope flooded through her. She needed them to have a great night tomorrow. For him to be reminded that his family had his back, that he didn't need to prove anything to her – just come home.

She made an appointment at the salon, then dashed upstairs and delved into the back of the wardrobe, pulling out clothes she hadn't worn for ages, and appraising herself in the mirror. OK, she'd changed shape since the birth of the kids, but Rich had always reassured her that he loved her figure. Tomorrow, though, she'd make an extra effort. They needed to reconnect. She inhaled and exhaled, finally feeling she knew what to do. She was a woman on a mission. Get Rich home for Christmas.

5

The next day, waiting for Rich to arrive at the house, Madison felt as nervous as she had before their very first date.

The previous day she'd had her hair blow-dried and straightened. She'd served up an easy meal of chicken nuggets and chips to the kids and, to their delight, plonked them in front of the TV so that she could indulge in an evening of pampering. Exhausted from all that had been going on, she'd slept relatively well. She'd changed the sheets that morning, to the very best linen, which smelt like a fresh spring day, thanks to her favourite fabric softener. As she straightened the bed and plumped the pillows, she hoped she and Rich would be rolling around in these sheets that very night. Making-up sex could work wonders.

She picked up the kids from school, and set them to work making birthday cards for Tina, known to them as Nanny T. She'd bought a beautiful bouquet of flowers, wincing at the cost and feeling a flash of irritation at Rich – why couldn't *he* sort this out for his mum? – that she tried to suppress.

She ironed a shirt for Jordan, and cajoled him into wearing it, and a dress for Chloë, who wanted to pair it with her wellies. Madison spent twenty minutes negotiating with Chloë over her shoes when that time could have been spent prepping her tired face. She normally let the kids choose what they wanted to wear, within reason, but she knew Nanny T appreciated them being dressed up. She knew, too, how much his mum's opinion mattered to Rich.

'Right! I need you both to keep your clothes clean, please,' she warned. She looked down at their shining brown eyes and felt her heart melt. She was so proud of them, standing there in their best outfits. 'Come here and give me a hug. You both look absolutely lovely. You do every day, but Nanny T will be so pleased.' She embraced them tightly and went upstairs, tears welling in her eyes. She wanted the kids to be happy. She didn't want them ever to question that their parents loved them more than anything on the planet.

Now's the time to be strong, Madison, she told herself. *Big happy smile on.*

She walked into the bedroom and shut the door. She needed this time. She put some soft R & B classics through the speaker on the dressing-table, and switched on the light bulbs around the mirror. Madison had always believed in the power of a good makeover. She'd seen it a thousand times on the show. People fell back in love with the same room once it had been shown some love and appeared to them in a different light.

With one hand in the air, she dipped her knees low and sashayed her hips from left to right. She closed her eyes, losing herself momentarily, and when she opened them, she met them in the mirror and smiled. *Yes, girl, you got this; yes, you do, yep, yep.* She broke out into a routine: twerk, twerk, whine the waist, whine the waist, two-step, two-step, shuffle, shuffle, shuffle, krunk, and krunk, drop it low and take it up slow.

Exhaling, Madison felt a little more like herself. She'd always loved to dance, from making up routines with the girls and Finn at school, to getting sweaty in nightclubs, to dancing around the kitchen with the kids. As she settled into the movement, she felt the familiar joy return to her – she needed to do this more. As the song ended, she pulled out the rest of her makeup, applying Shine the Light highlighter, Deep Black mascara, then finishing off with Nude Brown Boss lips and Let It Glow makeup-setting mist.

She went to her wardrobe and contemplated the clothing within. An abundance of comfortable leggings and sweatshirts, the plain trousers and shirts she wore to work . . . She rummaged further back. Here were her 'old' clothes – the sequined dresses, the colourful jumpers, the leather trousers. She smiled. And there was the dress she was planning to wear. She pulled it out, marvelling at the beautiful camel shade. It was a stunning bodycon jersey dress, with a draped cowl neck, long sleeves, and it hit just the right point on her thighs. She reached even further back in the wardrobe and found the brown suede boots she'd team it with, the ones that revealed just the right amount of skin to drive Rich crazy.

The last time she'd worn this outfit was before Jordan was born. Rich had taken her on a last-minute surprise trip to Paris, where they'd stayed in a sumptuous hotel. Madison could close her eyes even now and see the gold and cream décor, the rose petals scattered over the bed, which, yes, had been cheesy but they'd both loved it. Madison had worn this dress out for dinner, loving the way it clung to the curves of her pregnant body, feeling sexy, knowing that Rich couldn't get enough of her.

Later that night, he'd got down on one knee, holding out a beautiful diamond ring to her . . .

The memory blazed across Madison's mind as she got ready. The dress was as gorgeous as she remembered, the fabric still soft. Rich would remember it, she just knew. She studied herself in the mirror, liking the way she looked. The shrieks of the children jolted her out of her reverie – that was the sound of Rich's keys in the door. Her heart rate went up. She reminded herself of the plan: she was going to make this a great evening.

'Dad!' she heard the kids yell, and Rich greeted them, requesting a hug from each of them. She held out her hand and looked at her engagement ring, noticing that her fingers were trembling.

Stop it, Madison, she told herself. *You both made vows. Good times and bad. This is just a bad time. It can be worked through.*

She stepped out of their bedroom, spritzing perfume as she went, and headed down the stairs.

Rich stood in the hallway. He was dressed smartly, in a white shirt, tie and a plum-coloured jumper. His parents had always been quite traditional and liked their kids to dress a bit more conservatively. As they weren't around them all the time, Madison was happy to oblige. She felt her heart jump into her throat. All she wanted to do was kiss him. She'd never lost that butterflies feeling around Rich. He could still make her go weak at the knees.

'Mum, you look so pretty!' said Chloë.

'Thank you, darling,' said Madison, giving her daughter a kiss. She glanced at Rich. Normally they'd hug when he got back in, but was that OK now? 'Welcome home,' she said.

He smiled, but she felt it didn't reach his eyes.

'Thanks. You look good.' He hesitated, then leaned in and gave her a peck on the cheek that almost, but not quite, reached the corner of her mouth, leaving Madison feeling even more confused.

6

As Rich pulled into his mum's distinctive purple-gravel drive-way, Madison's nerves were churning. The kids had chatted all the way there, which was a relief, as the atmosphere between her and Rich was as awkward as hell. She'd asked how he'd been, and he'd just muttered 'Fine' and that was it. Maybe she was expecting too much, but her ideal fantasy had been of him arriving, pulling her into his arms and saying he was so, so pleased to be back. And that wasn't happening. *Yet*, she reminded herself.

She pulled down the sun visor and inspected her face in the mirror. She plastered on a smile, willing it to stay in place for the next couple of hours. Had it been a mistake to come? Tina was perceptive, and outspoken with her opinions, and Madison had had to grit her teeth on several occasions as Tina held forth, telling herself that her mother-in-law always meant well. If Tina thought there was a problem between them, she would say something. Madison applied another layer of lip gloss and shut the visor as Rich turned off the engine.

'Right!' She sprang into action, turning to her children. 'What do you both need to remember?'

'That we are raised up, not dragged up.' Chloë spoke on behalf of them both.

'Which means?'

'We got to be good for Granddad D and Nanny T,' Jordan shouted.

'You make us say this every time, Mum,' Chloë said. 'Why?'

'Why?' Rich looked at Madison, and she adjusted her tone. 'Because you never remember. Come on, let's go.'

She urged everyone out of the car. Tina opened the door and smiled before Jordan made it up the steps to knock. She looked beautiful, radiant even. Her long silver hair was pinned into a flower-adorned up-do, reminiscent of Billie Holiday. A silver sequin-embellished bolero shrug covered her arms and perfectly complemented her black velvet dress, which fell to the floor. When she looked as glamorous as that, Madison questioned why she wanted her birthday at home, and then she remembered. Tina always said that it didn't matter where you were, it always paid to look expensive.

'Nanny T!' he shouted excitedly, as he hugged her. Madison couldn't help but smile. Jordan loved his grandma – they definitely shared a determined temperament.

'Ooof, steady on, Jordan. Good to see you, baby. It's good to see you all. Come in, come in. It's cold out here.' She greeted each of them with a hug and ushered them into the house. Strong and firm, but also kind, nurturing and wise, Tina had stepped into the role of matriarch in recent years – on both sides of the family.

Having lost her husband, Hamilton, eighteen years ago when Rich was only twenty-two, Tina understood better than anyone what the family was going through when Madison's mum had died . . . Tina had been a great support for the whole family when they needed it most, but especially to Madison's dad, Devon. After Selina's death Tina had convinced Devon to attend her church as well as his own. Both had a robust community, and Devon had been warmly welcomed into the tight-knit group at Tina's and often now went on church-organized outings with them. In return, he had persuaded Tina to go with him to a couple of comedy nights. He'd told Tina, 'At this age life is too short to be serious all the time,' although he'd secretly informed Madison it was to help lighten Tina up a bit. Whether the comedians were good or awful, Devon said they always laughed.

Madison found their new closeness reassuring: she was comforted in the knowledge that her dad hadn't shut himself off from the world after her mum's death. Due to Tina's perfection, Madison might occasionally, and discreetly, roll her eyes at her mother-in-law's exacting standards, but she had been grateful for her strong presence more times than she cared to count.

As soon as Tina closed the door, Madison felt the warmth from the fireplace and the smell of home-cooked food wrap around her, and smiled at the familiar voices coming from the living room.

'Is that my grandson and granddaughter I can hear? Come and show me love, nah man?' shouted Madison's dad from the front room. He was sitting in his favourite chair playing dominoes with Rich's older brother, Lloyd, who was sporting a cap, jumper and jeans. Madison immediately clocked that Lloyd looked more casual than everyone else. The favourite son was allowed to be a rebel, while everyone else had to fall in line for peace. And Lloyd knew it. His charm and cockiness allowed him to push people's boundaries, and if he looked and smelled expensive, and carried himself in a certain way, he got away with it. 'Looking good, Madison,' said Lloyd, taking her in. 'That brother of mine behaving himself?'

Madison bit her tongue. There was just something about Lloyd that always made her hackles rise. He was the stereotypical older brother – tall, good-looking and successful – and he always found a way to let you know it.

'Granddad Devon, Uncle Lloyd!' shouted Jordan. As he ran towards his granddad, he tripped and landed on the dominoes, shifting all the white plastic pieces.

Everyone laughed, except Madison. 'It's taken you all of two minutes to cause chaos. How?' Madison asked, in a low, firm voice.

Lloyd chuckled. 'Madison, it's cool. I was winning anyway.' He grabbed and tickled Jordan. 'Do you wanna see the new car I'm buying? It's a beauty.'

Jordan nodded vigorously, eyes wide, and Madison tried to suppress an unreasonable irritation at Lloyd showing them his Tesla before he'd asked anything about their lives. Rich had grown up in Lloyd's shadow.

Madison sat next to her dad. 'How are you, Dad?' she asked, knowing what his response would be.

'I'm as well as I can be.'

Madison looked at her father, who turned away. She touched his arm, and again he gave her his standard response. 'This blasted leaky eye.' He wiped away his 'eye water' with his initial-embossed handkerchief.

Madison squeezed his hand. Grief came in waves, Madison knew. Some days were bearable, others overwhelming. Four years ago could feel like yesterday or today. Important dates, such as birthdays, anniversaries and Christmas, were difficult, but family get-togethers could be hard too. In a world full of words, finding the right ones took a level of clarity that the black fog of grief wouldn't allow. And when the one grieving was a proud Jamaican man, you'd never know the full truth of how he was feeling. His motto – 'I'm as well as I can be' – was enough, more than enough.

Madison put on a big smile. 'We'll have a good time tonight, celebrating Tina.'

Devon brightened, patted her knee and turned to the door as Rich came in. He reached out his hand and shook Rich's.

'Good to see you, Devon,' said Rich. 'Looking very dapper in that navy suit. Is it re-match time with the dominoes?' he said, rubbing his hands together.

Madison could almost believe things were normal. She headed into the kitchen to ask if Tina needed any help.

'It's nearly ready,' Tina said. 'Nothing to do.'

'I feel bad you cooking on your birthday,' said Madison, but Tina shooed her away. 'Are you sure there's nothing I can do?' she stressed.

'OK . . . Erm, you can cut up those tomatoes for the salad . . . in quarters, please.'

Madison picked up the knife from the counter and made the first cut through the beefy red tomato. 'Hold on, no, no.' Tina hurried over.

Madison was confused.

'The first cut should be vertical, not horizontal,' explained Tina, taking the knife from Madison's hand and demonstrating. 'Honestly, who taught you to cut like that?' It took everything Madison had not to explode.

'Does it matter how a quarter becomes a quarter? Vertical or horizontal first doesn't matter as the outcome is the same, no?' she said as breezily as she could. Tina shook her head, and continued the task she had given to Madison, who watched with silent, controlled breathing while giving herself a pep talk:

Don't take it personally. This is how she is. Just accept all of her.

'Please can you add glasses to the table and the Sorrel?' Tina eventually said, gesturing towards the fridge.

'Any particular one?' Madison asked, as she looked at the unlabelled wine bottles on the shelf, which of course no longer contained wine. In Jamaican households, nothing ever contains what the label says. Madison had never quite forgotten the childhood disappointment of opening an ice-cream container to find rice or stew. Now, she always bought and kept clear containers to store food and recycled the branded ones.

'Take both. The gold top has rum, the green top doesn't.'

Madison did as instructed and returned to the kitchen, past Chloë, who was hovering in the doorway. 'You OK, Chlo?' said Madison.

'Yeah,' said Chloë, looking at the floor.

Tina bustled past. 'Children, wash your hands and get to the table, please!'

'We already washed them at home,' whispered Chloë.

Madison sighed. 'I know, baby. Just do them again.' She was already feeling this might be a long evening.

She sat beside Rich, willing her kids not to put their elbows on the table. Lloyd and Devon also took their seats.

Devon closed his eyes and bowed his head. Everyone followed as he said the family prayer, ending with 'Amen' in unison, the cue for everyone to help themselves. Once all the plates had been filled, Lloyd stood up. 'I wanted to make a toast to you, Mum,' he said. 'The best mother we could ever wish for, and a truly amazing woman. Thank you for everything you've done for us.'

They all clinked glasses, and Tina's eyes shone with pride as she looked at Lloyd. Madison felt Rich twitch by her side. She needed to put her plan into practice. She cleared her throat. 'It's always such a special time of year,' Madison said. 'Your birthday, Christmas – and the time when me and Rich got together.'

She turned to him. He glanced at her and gave a small smile.

'I couldn't believe he'd finally managed to get such a beautiful woman,' said Lloyd, laughing. 'Still can't believe it. Nice work, little bro.'

Rich gave a forced laugh.

'How's things with you anyway?' Lloyd continued. 'Jamila' – she was his beautiful wife, who always found an excuse to wriggle out of family occasions – 'said she'd been watching a few episodes of the show recently. Very amusing, she said.'

'Have you watched any, Lloyd?' said Madison. She knew she was pushing it.

Lloyd shook his head. 'I'd love to have time to watch TV, but work is way too busy.'

'Did he tell you he's moving up again?' said Tina. 'My son, a company director.' She shook her head in happy disbelief.

'Congratulations,' said Rich, his eyes lowered.

'Mum, stop it,' said Lloyd, with a wide grin on his face. 'She'd told half the church before the announcement was even official.'

'It's nice to share good news,' said Tina.

'And even nicer if it makes your friends a little bit jealous!' laughed Lloyd, reaching over confidently to refill his glass. 'Touch more to drink, Rich?'

'Trying to cut down at the moment,' said Rich, his voice curt.

'Good idea,' said Lloyd. 'Me, I'm planning on doing that in the new year when the marathon training kicks in.'

'I didn't know you were taking part,' said Rich.

'Yeah,' said Lloyd. 'Want to see if I can get a better time.' He turned to Jordan. 'You much of a runner at school? I think I was on the youth squad at your age.'

Jordan glanced at his mum, as if he was unsure how to answer.

Madison was irritated. She wasn't having Jordan dragged into this competition, and why wouldn't Lloyd ask Chloë about *her* athletic abilities? It was one thing understanding the family dynamics in abstract, but she found it even more demoralizing to see the competition between Rich and Lloyd in person. Rich always felt one down from his brother. She just wanted Lloyd to see what *he* had. Two amazing kids, a fantastic career, and *her*. That had to be worth something, right?

She cut in: 'They both enjoy their sports, Chloë too.' She took a sip from her glass. 'Rich has some really exciting job news as well,' she said, hoping to nudge him into action.

'Yes?' said Tina, her eyes bright.

Rich looked down. 'Nothing definite to report yet,' he mumbled.

Lloyd tutted. 'This showbiz world, you never know if you're coming or going in it. Look, bro, if you ever want in, just say the word to me, OK? Bring you in at a decent level. Company car.' He glanced at Madison. 'Good money. Mean you don't have to work if you don't want to, Madison.'

Madison could feel a stress headache coming on. This was not going as planned. She'd wanted to talk about happy family memories, to remind Rich of just how good they were as a family unit. Instead they seemed to be on the receiving end of a careers chat from Lloyd. It wasn't setting the vibe she wanted, especially not for a planned seduction once they'd got home.

'How's Christmas preparation coming along?' she asked Tina, which – as she'd expected – led Tina to launch into a long and detailed explanation of how everything was in hand, which was safer territory, if not the most inspiring.

'You off your food?' Rich asked Chloë, who was pushing her dinner round her plate.

Chloë didn't answer. Rich gently patted her on the back. 'Try to eat a bit more, baby.'

After a few more mouthfuls, Chloë leaned into Madison. 'Mum,' she said, dragging out the word in a way that normally meant she wanted something. 'Were you popular at school? Like . . . did you have many friends?'

Madison frowned. She wanted to cut to the chase and find out why Chloë was asking this, but she remembered Jess saying she needed to be more patient when it came to these things. She always said parents had to act normal, not let the kids know you'd seen a potential red flag. Madison leaned in closer to her daughter. 'I knew everyone in my year, but I had four close friends.' She smiled. 'Was I liked? Not by everyone. But I didn't care. I only cared that my close friends liked me. And we're still friends to this day. Auntie Jess, she's still my best mate. And then you know the rest: Ladene, Abiola, Finn.' She was hoping that Chloë would say more, but the little girl shrugged and returned to her plate. At least she was eating, noted Madison. Maybe it had been a general question.

The chit-chat drifted on: Christmas, the neighbours, and then the kids were having a spirited argument about what superpower they would have. Jordan was insistent on flying. Chloë wanted to breathe underwater.

'What about you, Mum?' said Chloë.

Madison hesitated. 'I'd like to be able to time-travel,' she said. 'Especially back in time.'

'Where would you go to?' said Tina.

'I'd love to travel to when the kids were babies,' she said. 'Those days are so intense, you feel like it'll never get easier. But I'd like to go back and appreciate the moments when they were so little.'

She held her breath and tried to make eye contact with Rich. Had he even noticed the dress she was wearing?

'And sometimes I'd like to go back even further. To when me and Rich met. They were happy days.' She needed Rich to remember how good things had been. How right it had always felt between them.

'What's for dessert, Mum?' Rich asked, changing the subject. Madison's heart sank.

'It's apple crumble and custard,' Tina said. The kids cheered. 'You'd better help me clear the table first. Come on, all hands on deck.'

Madison remained seated as everyone else rushed to get up, apart from her dad.

'I understand what you mean about travelling back in time.' Her dad sighed. There was no need for him to voice what he was thinking.

'Bad day with it, Dad?' Madison asked softly.

He nodded. 'Sometimes I just . . . *miss* her. And sometimes when we're all together and she's not here . . .'

'It makes it all the more apparent,' finished Madison, and her dad nodded.

'But I have you, and your lovely family,' he said. 'And that keeps me going.'

Madison pressed her lips together. She wished she could

confide in her father about what was going on, but they'd never really had that kind of relationship. It had always been her mum she'd talked to about emotional stuff. And there was no way she could destroy her dad's impression that she had a happy family life: he'd worry. Whatever this bump was in her relationship with Rich, she had to tough it out alone.

As fast as the others had left for the kitchen, they piled back in with piping hot bowls of goodness. Madison sat back in her chair. She couldn't eat another mouthful, even though the apple with nutmeg and cinnamon smelt delicious. She rubbed her belly under the table and excused herself to make some peppermint tea, craving a moment of solitude.

'Seconds are calling and I'm giving in,' Tina announced, as she walked into the kitchen a few minutes later. She piled more apple crumble into her bowl, then turned to Madison. 'So how are things? I know something's up.'

Her question threw Madison off guard. That was not how she'd envisaged this going. The last thing she wanted was her mother-in-law sensing something wasn't right.

'It's just a busy time. I'm tired, Rich is tired . . .'

Tina narrowed her eyes and tilted her head to one side, clearly seeing through her evasion. Madison wondered if Tina could shed some light on what was going on with Rich. Maybe he'd confided in her.

'Well,' she began carefully, 'Rich has been acting a little weird—'

Before she could go on, Tina held up her hand and interrupted. 'He works hard for his family. Of course he's tired.'

'We're a team when it comes to the family,' Madison said, trying not to sound too defensive but inwardly fuming at Tina's implication that *she* didn't work hard for the family too. She was the one who did most of the school runs and meals, and she was *always* the one who had to flex around Rich's work schedule. She almost wanted to lash out and say that Rich had walked out a few days ago. 'Rich isn't the only one who makes sacrifices, you know.'

Tina didn't respond, and Madison felt her neck grow hot as an uneasy silence settled on the room. She cleared her throat. 'Has he . . . said anything to you?' Madison couldn't believe she was being so bold.

'You said it yourself, Madison. He's tired.' Tina stepped forward and took one of Madison's hands in hers. 'Don't look for problems that aren't there.'

So she didn't know, Madison thought. *Was that a good sign? Did it mean Rich was planning on coming home imminently?*

Madison's eyes pricked with tears, and the fight left her. She wanted to believe Tina, that there weren't any real problems.

'I know he loves me, it's just that . . .' Unable to find the right words, she tailed off.

'Marriage isn't always perfect.' Tina gently squeezed her arm. 'You know this. There will be downs as well as ups. And he's always wanting to prove he's enough, that he's a success. That takes its toll. But it's good he's a hard worker.' She smiled and returned to the table, leaving Madison with the residue of good old Jamaican tough love. She looked to the ceiling and tried to blink away the building tears, wiping her cheeks with her sleeves.

She took a few deep breaths and held her tea for comfort, savouring its warmth. She had a fleeting sense that her mum would have given her the same advice as Tina, but perhaps in a softer, more understanding way. She smiled and shook her head sadly, staring into her cup, and watched, in a daze, as the water turned to a darker shade of green. As it continued to brew, memories of chatting with her mum over a cuppa flicked through her mind.

Mum, I wish you were here.

After they'd sung 'Happy Birthday' to Tina, and watched her blow out her candles, aided by Jordan and Chloë, the family took pictures, wrapped cake in napkins and said their fare-wells. They got back into the car and drove home, Madison's heart thudding.

'Upstairs and do your teeth,' Rich said to the kids, as they went in. 'Come on, you two. Enough excitement for one evening.'

They scrambled upstairs and left Rich and Madison in the hallway.

'Are you heading off, then?' Madison said. She was half sur-prised at the directness of her question, but waiting for him to say something was making her anxious, and also annoyed.

Rich shifted. 'I can stick around for a bit,' he mumbled. 'I'll put the kids to bed.'

'Maybe afterwards we could have a glass of wine,' said Madison. 'Watch something?'

'Yeah, maybe,' said Rich, his gaze meeting hers for a second, then dropping away. He was like a stranger, Madison noted miserably. It felt so awkward between them. But he was here and he was going to stay for a bit. Maybe that was when they could clear the air and reconnect.

Rich disappeared upstairs with the kids. She listened for a few moments, as the familiar sounds of Rich overseeing teeth-brushing filtered down the stairs. Moving quietly, she padded into their bedroom, preparing to get changed and take off her makeup, when she paused at the mirror, turning her head this way and that. She decided she'd stay looking glam for a little longer.

Instead of reaching for her makeup remover, Madison reached for her Vinyl Black eyeliner and reapplied flicks to the corners of her eyes. That was better. She put on the R & B classics again in their bedroom. Her thoughts skipped ahead. With the kids tucked up and asleep, maybe she and Rich could cosy up over some wine, a film playing in the background. They could chat about whatever was worrying him, and maybe, just maybe . . . Madison found herself half smiling in the mirror. Sex was way less frequent these days than it had once been, but that was normal with two kids, right? And she still found her husband completely gorgeous. Maybe they just needed to rekindle the spark.

Madison began to dance in the mirror, nothing too out there, just feeling her body move to the music, and the smile spread across her face. She decided to stick with the electric slide – yes, partly to be kind to her knees. She pivoted on the spot, looked up and nearly screamed. 'How long have you been standing there?' she said to Rich. 'You gave me a shock!'

Rich frowned. 'I just got here. I was looking for Chloë's teddy.'

'You wanna come dance with me?' Madison beckoned him towards her and continued the famous routine.

'I should get back to the kids . . .' said Rich, but his voice was hesitant.

Madison grabbed his hand and pulled him towards her. She whined her waist in response to the track, teasing him with her moves, trying to reel him in with her eyes. For the first time, she felt him look at her properly. His hands slowly moved to her waist, and he began to move to the music as well, shutting his eyes briefly. Madison could have sworn she saw the tension drain from his face. Was this it? Was this all they'd needed to do more of?

The music moved on, and she felt Rich step into her, close enough that she could smell his familiar aftershave. She stepped back into him, and then—

'Daaaad?'

Chloë appeared in the doorframe.

Rich leaped back as though he'd been scalded.

'Where's my bear?' said Chloë. 'You said you were going to find her.'

'Sorry, baby,' said Rich. 'She's not in here. I'll go and look downstairs.'

He scuttled out of the door without so much as a back-wards glance at Madison. She sighed, snapped off the music and picked up a hoodie. She had no clue what to think. Rich had been relaxing into the moment with her, but then he'd jumped away like he was doing something he shouldn't. When their kids had interrupted romantic moments before – hey, it happened – he'd always been sure to give her some kind of re-assuring gesture – a wink, a lingering touch on the arm – that let her know he couldn't wait to get back to her later. Not this time.

She headed downstairs and into the kitchen. She took out two glasses and a bottle of wine, pouring a generous measure into each.

'In here,' she called softly, hearing Rich's footsteps in the hallway outside. 'Thought you might need this,' she added, as he came in, pushing the wine glass towards him.

'Thanks,' he muttered. He took the glass but didn't meet her gaze. If anything, the atmosphere was even more awkward.

'I was thinking we should talk about the kids' Christmas presents,' began Rich.

'Oh, yeah, sure,' said Madison, surprised. 'They did their lists last weekend.'

He nodded. 'Obviously we'll still get them presents from both of us.'

Her heart was thudding. 'I hadn't thought otherwise.' She took a huge gulp of wine. 'What are you trying to say?' An awful thought occurred to her. 'Are you saying you won't even *be* here for Christmas?'

Rich looked up, shocked. 'Of course I'll be here for Christmas. The day, at least.' He pressed his knuckles into his temples.

'Are you even staying here tonight?' Madison said, voice trembling, but the wine making her braver.

He didn't answer for what felt like a million years. 'No,' he whispered. 'No. You know it's best. It's what we agreed on.'

What you told me was happening, screamed a voice inside Madison's head, but she nodded mutely. 'Why did you come back with us?' she asked, her voice flat.

'To put the kids to bed.' He swallowed. 'To get a bit more stuff.'

Madison's heart plunged still further. She poured more wine. 'I don't even know where you're staying.'

'With my cousin Marvin. Over in Bethnal Green.'

Madison couldn't speak. She nodded mutely again. She felt as if she'd fallen into some strange parallel universe where she didn't understand the person she had thought she knew best.

'I just need some time,' Rich was saying, his voice pleading again. 'Just a bit of time to get my head straight, especially with everything that's going on.'

He squeezed her arm and walked out of the kitchen. It occurred to Madison that there had been a time when they'd straightened out their heads together. She'd thought there was no problem or stress they couldn't navigate. Clearly, she had been wrong.

7

'Sorry I'm late!' Madison rushed in and dropped her bag and coat on a spare chair at the back of the church hall. She'd left the kids with her dad, then got stuck in traffic.

'We haven't started yet,' said Jess, soothingly, looking gorgeous and serene in a grey tracksuit with retro trainers. Jess somehow always managed to look high end, even when she was dressed casually.

Valerie, the choir leader, gave Madison a raised eyebrow and a telling-off: 'But we *may well* have started. I tried to impress upon you girls the importance of punctuality.'

Even though Madison was almost forty, she cringed at Valerie's words. It was an effort not to reply, 'Yes, miss,' and from the expressions of her friends, she knew they were feeling it too.

Valerie had been their music teacher at school. She had looked exactly the same more than twenty years ago. It was impossible to age her, and Madison could have sworn she wore exactly the same outfits. There was a little more grey in her hair, but Miss Valerie Campbell was a fixture in their lives that they couldn't imagine changing. When they'd all joined the community choir as adults, she'd told them they could call her Valerie, but 'Miss Campbell' still tripped off Madison's tongue now and again.

'Sorry, Mi— Valerie,' said Madison, as they all moved forward to form rows.

Along with Jess were Abiola and Ladene. They'd all been friends since they were thirteen. Ladene was tall and elegant, her hair cropped short, her eyes framed by bold statement glasses. She was a real culture vulture, always out at the latest play or exhibition, but her real passion was music and she worked part-time programming a festival that took place annually, focusing on booking up-and-coming bands. Ladene had definitely been the cool one of their bunch in school, the one the boys were ever so slightly scared of, and indeed Madison had been too – until she realized that, below the tough exterior, Ladene had a heart of gold. Still, you didn't always want to hear Ladene's blunt truths aimed at you – she had a habit of speaking her mind before she'd thought how to soften her words, and Madison had sometimes cringed at her outspoken opinions.

Abiola was the smart one, though she was always too modest about it. Straight As in school, and she'd been set to study history at university when her brother had been tragically diagnosed with a brain tumour. He'd died only a few months later and Abiola had been devastated. They all had. Abiola had always been the strictly organized one, who kept them all on the straight and narrow and reminded them to do some revision once in a while. Seeing their competent, sorted friend grieving so deeply had affected them all. Abiola had taken a year out, spent time with her wider family and come back with a decision. She was going to study medicine. She was going to be the best damn doctor the world had ever known.

She did study medicine, but decided to specialize in obstetrics and gynaecology. 'It's nice to be bringing life into the world,' she once said to Madison, who understood completely. Now, Abiola was a senior doctor at a London hospital, but – as often as time allowed – she still came to choir rehearsal. If Ladene was outspoken, Abiola was reserved, but her instincts were rarely wrong and the girls all listened carefully whenever she offered an opinion.

'Madison, come next to me,' whispered Jess, as they took up their positions, which just happened to be in the order they'd had since they were kids, Jess and Madison in the middle, Ladene and Abiola to either side.

Ladene rolled her eyes. 'This is just like assembly in Year Nine. Would it kill you to be apart for half an hour?'

But Madison knew she was just joking. Ladene and Abiola got on fiercely well, respecting each other's independence and drive. Ladene always said that Abiola made her think twice before she opened her mouth. Abiola said that Ladene helped her open up and actually *say* what she was thinking.

'Would you ladies kindly behave yourselves for once?' said a softly spoken Irish man, raising a perfectly shaped eyebrow, as he bustled up to them with the song sheets. Madison and Ladene had both suggested to Valerie Campbell they could find the lyrics via their phones, but she had insisted everyone stuck to song sheets. Madison felt herself properly smile for the first time since Rich had left. That was down to Finn. One of life's sunshines.

He'd joined their school in the final year of GCSEs, a skinny, nervous boy from Dublin, who'd come to the UK thanks to his dad's job. Madison could remember his first day so vividly: she'd noticed him nervously trying to find his way around the school's boisterous corridors, in a school uniform that swamped his gangly frame, his brown hair carefully styled with gel. It turned out they were in the same class, and they'd quickly bonded over the awfulness of the school uniform – it was mustard yellow and black, which made them look like wasps buzzing around. Finn hadn't been out as gay then, and had received taunts from some of the pupils. Madison couldn't bear it: she stood up to one particular bully who was making comments to Finn and shut him down. From then on, he'd been part of her crew, and when Madison and the rest of the girls were talking about which boy band they found the hottest a few weeks later, Finn simply joined in with what he thought, and nothing more needed to be said. As the only boy among four Black girls, he definitely stood out but they didn't care. And if anyone else did, that was their problem.

Now, twenty years later, Finn had just a little bit of a belly, his hair was beginning to recede, which he denied, and he was happily married to Andrew, but – as with all of Madison's friends – it felt like barely five minutes had passed since that first meeting at school. Finn had appointed himself unofficial sidekick to Valerie as soon as he'd discovered that all of the girls were in the choir, proclaiming, 'I can't have my girls meeting without me!' In recent years, he'd taught himself to play the piano and offered his services to Valerie, who was delighted. 'Looking fabulous,' Finn mouthed to her, with a wink, as he continued down the line of choir members. Madison wasn't sure that was true – her skin was suffering from the stress and she had dark circles under her eyes, but she appreciated his cheerleading.

'Our first song is "Silent Night",' Valerie said, clapping her hands to call them to attention. 'Now, this is a classic, which you should all know by now, and if you don't, well, look at the sheet. There's nothing worse than beautiful voices singing the wrong words.'

Madison spotted Finn standing by Valerie, arms folded, nodding along, like her enforcer, and made a mental note to take the piss out of him later.

'Let's give it a go,' Valerie went on. 'And, Madison, are you set to do the harmonies? This is a classic, so no riffs.'

Madison didn't feel up to standing out today. She just wasn't herself. She centred her thoughts on her mum, who'd had a beautiful singing voice, powerful, yet soft. She had been a star of the choir, and Madison had seen how Selina came alive when she began to sing. She hadn't been a showy woman, but when she'd stepped into that spotlight and sung, she was confident, her voice naturally commanding attention. Madison tried to channel that energy. *Imagine you're singing with her now*, Madison willed herself.

Valerie started them off. '"Silent night, holy night . . ."'

The familiar words rang out. Madison could hear her friends' sweet voices around her. Her throat felt raspy and dry.

Valerie signalled that she should harmonize in a higher key. Madison opened her mouth. '"All is calm, all is bright,"' she sang, and felt Jess shudder next to her – Madison knew she was out of tune. She pressed on, but Valerie waved her hands to stop the singing.

'From the top, girls,' Valerie said briskly. Madison was grateful not to be singled out as having caused them to start again. She took a sip of water from her bottle. *Come on, girl. You've got this*. She waited until her cue, shut her eyes and began. Her voice stuck in her throat. Nothing was flowing. She couldn't even remember the main melody of the song.

What is wrong with me? Tears pricked her eyes. *Why is everything going wrong?*

Valerie rapped on the lectern and the singing halted. Madison closed her eyes and braced herself.

'Madison,' said Valerie, and Madison was straight back in Year Nine. 'Is there a problem?'

'Sorry, I – I'm not feeling too great today,' said Madison, her voice wobbling.

'Shall we ask someone else to take over?' asked Valerie.

Madison touched her neck and gently massaged her throat. 'Maybe. Just for this rehearsal. I'm sure next week I'll be back on it.'

Abiola put up her hand to take Madison's spot, and they set off again. With no attention on her now, Madison was soothed by the familiar melody. She loved weekly choir practice. It gave her space away from the kids, work, schedules and chores, and allowed her to switch off and connect with her friends. Singing her heart out was her escape. But now her mind was swirling. Could she have handled the conversation with Rich better? Maybe she should have screamed at him, turned on the drama, sobbed and cried. But that wasn't her. And where exactly was he staying? He had a multitude of cousins. She hoped he really was with a good influence, like Marvin, who would talk some sense into him.

Madison began yet another conversation in her head with Rich, then wondered if she should text him, or call him, or—

'We've stopped singing, hon,' murmured Jess. Her eyes were brimming with concern. 'You were still singing the chorus.'

Madison flushed with embarrassment. She turned to Abiola and mouthed, 'Sorry.'

'It's fine,' Abiola mouthed back, with a smile.

'I'd like to remind you, ladies,' said Valerie severely, 'that we are fast approaching our Christmas concert. And we've been invited to sing this song at the shopping centre.'

'On their main stage, no less,' chimed in Finn. 'The one by the piercing salon, and the phone shop.'

'Indeed,' said Valerie. 'And we really need to be on top form for the performance.'

Madison rolled her eyes at the thought of the shopping centre's tiny stage. 'You'd think it was Wembley Stadium,' she muttered to Jess, but then she saw Valerie's and Finn's serious faces and felt guilty. A stage is a stage, she reminded herself.

'Let's take a break and come back strong,' said Finn.

Madison grabbed her bag and scuttled outside. Normally the break was one of the highlights of choir practice – a time to have quick catch-ups with her friends, to crack jokes they'd had since they were teenagers, and to find out how their weeks had been – but how could she pretend everything was normal? She took a few breaths in the freezing air and pulled out her phone.

A notification from Rich.

Her heart pounded. Maybe it would say he was back home right now. That he was making her dinner, and did she want to watch a film when she got in? She opened it.

Hey, the message read, *could we have a call tonight to go through childcare for the week? I need to let Amber know when she can book meetings.*

Amber was his agent's assistant.

How was Madison meant to interpret it? She was relieved that at least she'd see him, at some point, that maybe there would be other opportunities to connect with him. But the message also meant he wasn't coming back any time soon.

Sure, she typed back. *Just at choir now but can call you after?*

A few seconds and Rich was typing. She held her breath as the dots flickered and stopped, then began again. A large thumbs-up appeared.

Madison sighed and shoved away her phone.

'We're set to start,' said Finn, sticking his head out of the door. 'Jesus, it's freezing out here. Colder than a polar bear's bollock.'

Madison couldn't help but smile. 'Coming,' she said.

'You OK?' said Finn, holding the door for her.

'Yeah,' she said. 'Felt a bit faint. Thought the fresh air might help.'

'Get that husband of yours to look after you when you get home, eh,' said Finn. 'I'm not having you run yourself ragged at this time of year.' He looked at her. 'You're already *worryingly thin*, Madison.'

This was one of their jokes that had been running as long as their friendship. Both of them had gone through various diet fads over the year, sometimes determined to starve themselves into another shape entirely, and it was one of the advantages of getting just a *little* bit older that they were much happier in their skins. Whenever they went out for food, they'd implore the other to treat themselves – 'Have that doughnut,' Madison would frequently say to Finn, who couldn't resist a pastry. 'Honestly, you're wasting away to practically nothing.'

The joke originally came from Madison's mother. When Finn had first come to the house, Selina had kept trying to feed the *mawga*, to 'fatten him up', saying this directly to Finn, which made Madison cringe. She explained that *mawga* meant 'meagre and lanky', and although rude, it came from a place of love. Finn received it as such. Staying for dinner quickly became a regular thing and Finn's taste buds were exposed to a variety of Jamaican dishes. Jerk chicken, plantain, corned bully beef and cabbage with rice were his favourites. On her lazy days, when she wanted to make something quick, Selina made baked beans more flavoursome with added onions, cherry tomatoes, paprika, chilli flakes and black pepper. Finn loved it. Jacket potato, cheese and beans had never tasted so good. While spinach was the source of Popeye's strength, Madison's mum and dad were convinced it was Guinness punch, and Selina would make an extra batch weekly for Finn 'to help build you up'.

Finn had adored Madison's mum. Sometimes when Madison visited her grave, she'd find fresh flowers there from Finn. He'd loved the warmth and love in her household, saying he always felt accepted there, and it was very different from his own family home.

Madison cleared her throat and returned the joke. 'Honestly, I can barely see you from sideways on, Finn.'

He grinned at her, and they returned to the hall.

She hated keeping anything from her friends. It just felt wrong. But here, at least, she could pretend that Rich *was* waiting for her when she got home.

The second half of practice passed more smoothly than the first, but Madison still felt as if she was in a trance.

'Same time next week,' called Finn, as the practice ended. 'Please do let me know well in advance if you *cannot* attend, and I will make a note accordingly.' He wafted a clipboard in the air.

Madison was glad it was over. She pulled on her coat and wrapped her scarf around her neck.

'Not so fast,' said Ladene. 'What's up with you?'

That was Ladene: straight to the point. 'Nothing,' said Madison. 'Just a bit tired.'

Ladene shook her head. 'I'm not buying it. You could be dead on your feet and you'd still be wanting to run the riffs.'

'Ladene, I'm just knackered. Christmas coming up. Life.' Madison tried to avoid her friend's intense gaze.

'What she means,' chimed in Abiola, 'is that you were perhaps not *quite* as present for choir practice as you'd usually be, and we were wondering if there is any particular reason for that.'

Madison clocked that Abiola had one foot pressing on Ladene's trainer, clearly imploring her to keep her mouth shut. 'No particular reason,' she said. 'Maybe I'm a bit run-down.'

'Sore throat?' said Abiola. 'Say aah.'

Next thing she knew, she was saying 'aah' and Abiola was kneading the side of her neck. 'Looks OK,' said Abiola. 'And your glands don't feel swollen or anything.'

Madison gently batted away her hands. 'I'm sure I'm fine. I just need a good night's sleep.'

'I can give you a lift back,' said Jess, eyes wide, face stricken. 'We could go right now.'

Madison knew that Jess was trying to get her out of there.

'Is something else going on?' Finn said slowly. 'It's not just tiredness, this.'

Madison looked at their faces, at the friends who'd known her longer than anyone else, and she couldn't keep it in any longer. She buried her face in her hands.

'Oh! There's tears,' she heard Finn say. 'Crisis! She's having a meltdown! Action stations, everyone, we can handle this! Madison, we're all here!'

'Come and sit down,' Abiola was saying, calm as always,

pulling down a chair from where they'd been stacked and guiding Madison gently to it.

'You'll feel better just getting it out,' Ladene chimed in, and she felt Jess's hand on her shoulder, gently squeezing, letting her know she was there.

'Chocolate!' Finn was saying. 'Does anyone have any chocolate? We need chocolate now, please!'

Next thing Madison knew, half a Twix was being wafted under her nose and she wanted to laugh, momentarily, before the tears flooded out again. 'I'm OK for chocolate,' she managed to say, wiping her cheeks.

'What's going on?' said Finn, gently.

She exhaled and looked at the ceiling. 'Rich has left.'

There was a moment of complete silence.

'*Left?*' said Finn. 'What do you mean, left?'

'I don't even know,' said Madison. 'One minute we're skating with the kids. The next he's saying he's under pressure and is confused and just needs some space. Then he's *gone.*'

Another stunned silence.

'He can't just go,' said Ladene. 'I mean, no. That's mad. Where is he?'

'At his cousin's.'

'And what about the kids?'

'He's still seeing them. He wants to organize arrangements for this week.'

Ladene tutted. 'Just not sleeping under the same roof as them. And expecting you to fit in with him.'

'Ladene . . .' Madison raised a hand in warning. She couldn't cope with Ladene's pronouncements right now, even though part of her agreed with what she was saying.

'OK,' said Abiola. 'So he's under pressure. He's reacting in a certain way. Not the best way, sure, but maybe he just needs time to process what's going on. The job has to bring pressures, and people react to stress in a certain way . . .'

'Yeah, but meanwhile she's just left on her own!' said Ladene, indignantly.

'I think it's a midlife crisis,' said Finn. 'Andrew was a nightmare when he hit forty. Has he been buying a lot of unusual clothes? A glittery thread or a nifty detail that's really suited to a far younger man? Not that Rich isn't drop-dead gorgeous. Sorry, that's not the point here.' Finn gulped. 'I'm nervous. I always talk too much when I'm nervous and I don't know what to do—' He bit into the Twix and chewed furiously.

Madison frowned. 'I literally hadn't noticed anything was that different. Rich has always liked clothes.' That was true. 'To be honest, I think I should have been more attentive to him. We went through Mum dying, two young kids . . . His work is stressful. It's always been a struggle to have enough time, just us. And now I'm wondering what I missed. What could I have done differently?'

'All of us struggle with those things. It's so difficult to make time,' said Jess, soothingly, although Madison knew that wasn't true. Jess's Instagram was a non-stop stream of gorgeous things she was doing with her husband. 'Look, Rich *loves* you. You're married. You just have to trust in those vows, and he'll be back. Maybe it's just a bad time, and you'll be back on track before you know it.'

Madison nodded slowly.

'Is no one going to say it?' said Ladene, looking around. 'Madison, what if he's cheating on you? What if there's another woman?'

Madison felt she might throw up there and then.

77

'Ladene,' hissed Abiola, but to no effect.

'No way,' said Jess. 'What Abiola says is right. This is *Rich* we're talking about. He would never do that.'

'I know you don't wanna hear it,' said Ladene, 'but, honestly, man leaves out of the blue from a happy home? I don't buy it. What if he's got someone else on the go?'

Finn glanced nervously from side to side. 'My friend's husband left, saying what Rich said, and six months later she discovered he was shacked up with another woman. They'd met on his cycling route when he was allegedly training for a triathlon and . . .' He trailed off, his face scarlet. 'Sorry, Madison. I'm repeating workplace gossip. I don't think that's the case with Rich.'

But was it just Madison, or did he sound less than convinced?

'Abiola?' croaked Madison.

'I go on the evidence,' she said. 'At the moment, there's no evidence to suggest that's the case.'

'Abiola, are you kidding? He's just walked out on her! And the kids!' Ladene was getting herself worked up, and then Finn was trying to intervene and smooth things over between them, and Madison just wanted to be at home, in her bed, not having to think about any of this.

'Stop it, all of you!' said Jess. It was so rare she raised her voice that everyone quietened. Jess was shaking. 'Just stop it. Stop this gossip, now. Come on, Madison. I'll give you a lift home.'

Madison followed Jess outside to her car. They got in and Jess switched on the radio. Madison didn't want to talk about anything. As they pulled away, she acknowledged that having friends to confide in was great, but navigating all their thoughts, feelings and fears on top of her own, not so much. She leaned back and gazed out of the passenger window.

'Here you go,' said Jess, as they pulled up outside Madison's house. 'Just try to trust it's all going to be OK. It's you and Rich. At the end of the day, that's all that matters.'

'Thanks, Jess.'

The two women embraced briefly and Madison got out of the car. The house was empty and quiet when she got in. The kids were round at her dad's – he generally babysat them while she was at choir, dropping them back later. Madison shivered in the hallway. It was dark and she didn't fancy putting on the Christmas-tree lights. Her warm, loving home seemed lack-lustre and empty. Suddenly it didn't feel like home.

Her phone pinged. A message from Jess: *You need to look after yourself. Some pampering! I've booked you a massage for tomorrow xoxo*

Madison smiled. Typical Jess. Maybe she was right: maybe Madison just needed to trust that everything would be OK.

8

Madison walked up the steps of the spa where Jess had made her appointment, already soothed by the hushed environment, the flattering golden lighting and the soft scent of aromatherapy oils. She had dropped the kids off at their Saturday morning clubs – football for Jordan, gymnastics for Chloë – as she did every week. She had the whole morning to herself and was definitely going to make the most of it.

She gave her name to the receptionist, whose eyes lit up. 'You're a friend of Jess,' she said. 'She's one of our best customers.' She handed Madison a white robe and slippers, directing her to get changed and leave her things in a locker.

Why didn't she do this more often, Madison wondered. The words 'time' and 'money' popped straight into her mind, but she pushed them away and resolved to enjoy her treat.

When she was ready, she walked along a plush corridor to the treatment room. The door opened, and a masseuse, face pulled tight either by a high ponytail or by some judicious Botox, beckoned her through. 'Madison?' she said. 'Do take a seat. I'll just run through a few questions, some physical, some emotional, some spiritual.'

Madison perched on the edge of a fuchsia-pink chair, feeling oddly as if she was about to take an exam. Could they not just shortcut to the relaxing bit?

'In terms of your general well-being at the moment, how would you rate yourself out of ten?'

'Well, er, I don't know. I mean, things have been tough recently but—'

'A three?'

Madison screwed up her face. 'I don't know if things are *that* bad. There's so much I'm grateful for in life, and my mum taught me how to look on the positive side . . .'

The masseuse was looking at her, one eyebrow perma-arched, and tapping a pen on a clipboard. 'I'm picking up on a lot of blocked energy. Would you say that you're struggling predominantly with guilt, sadness, anger or a sense of hope-lessness?'

'All of the above?' said Madison.

The masseuse didn't pick up on the joke. 'I can only tick one.'

'Is this really necessary just for me to have a massage?' Madison wasn't enjoying the woman's piercing gaze.

'Oh, yes. It'll really help us pick the best oil for you. We've got some signature blends.'

If only things could be sorted out by a nice-smelling oil, Madison thought wearily.

She shrugged. 'I guess I'm a bit . . . sad.'

The masseuse nodded and stabbed her pen against the page several times.

'I also have a bit of lower back pain.'

'That'll be the sadness.'

Madison frowned. 'Well, I think it was carrying the shopping in and twisting at a funny angle . . .'

'You'd be surprised,' said the masseuse, gleefully. 'The body expresses itself in different ways.'

Now her body was beginning to express itself with a tension headache, Madison thought.

'I think I've got enough to go on,' said the masseuse, and directed Madison to lie on the table, face down, eyes closed, her bits covered with a large white towel. A deeply scented oil wafted under her nose, and large hot stones were placed on her acupressure points. Madison began to feel the tightness in her muscles melt away, and the buzz in her brain quieten.

A few minutes later the masseuse began to speak. 'Follow my voice and just relax. Your toes are relaxed, your calves are relaxed . . .'

Madison tried to focus on each area she named, but that didn't last long. She suddenly remembered going to a spa with Rich on their honeymoon: they were covered with a foamy white lather and looking like giant marshmallows at a hammam bath and spa in Turkey, a wedding gift from their hotel. She pushed away the memory.

Come on, Madison, try to relax, she willed herself, but the more she tried, the less relaxed she became. *God, I can't even get this right.*

Thoughts about Rich began to spiral.

'Your shoulders are even more tense,' said the masseuse, sounding disappointed. 'Do try to relax.'

'I *am* trying,' hissed Madison, earning herself a particularly painful tweak as the masseuse dug into a muscle in her shoulder.

'Ow!'

'Try to breathe through it, and think of how well you'll sleep tonight.'

Just as Madison was about to say something else, the masseuse decreased her pressure and gave her a gentle back-to-toe massage. 'That's you done,' she said, handing Madison a glass of water as she sat upright. 'Now, don't you feel better?'

'Kind of,' said Madison, grudgingly.

'Drink a lot of water,' said the masseuse. 'It always helps.'

Madison thought that a large rum with ginger beer might help more, but bit her lip. She wrapped the robe around her and headed into the thermal baths, which were composed of a steam room, two hot rooms of different temperatures and a chilly plunge pool.

Madison decided to give the steam room a miss – she couldn't 'wash and go' when she needed at least five different products and half a day for her hair. She headed to the first hot room – then realized she'd forgotten her swimsuit. *Damn.* Yes, it was female-only, and nudity was allowed, but she felt more comfortable with a teeny scrap of fabric between her and the world. Maybe she could keep the towel on.

She headed into the sauna, pulled open the door and was greeted by heat as intense as Jamaican sunshine. She shut the door behind her, and concentrated on trying to arrange the towel so that it covered her boobs, but came down far enough that she could sit on part of it to protect her bum and thighs from the heat of the wood. This soon proved to be physically impossible, given that the towel was the size of a postage stamp.

'You might find it easier just to let it all hang out,' said an amused voice.

Madison jumped – and didn't know *where* to look. She admired anyone who could feel comfortable and confident sitting in their nakedness. She just wasn't expecting to see anyone here, let alone someone with *everything* on show. 'Sorry,' she said automatically.

'What for?' said the woman, raising an eyebrow. 'Here, you can use my spare towel – it's hanging by the door – to sit on, if you're really uncomfortable.'

Madison took the towel and sat primly on it, lowering her own towel to reveal a bit more cleavage and hoping this would indicate she was fine with the situation. She shut her eyes and practised a Zen-like expression. In her experience, and from Jess's stories, there were three types of spa-goers: the chatty ones; the silent listeners; and the Zen masters, able to block out everything around them. *I'm on the beach, the sun is blazing and topping up my melanin,* Madison told herself, hoping the stranger would read the room and keep quiet.

'What treatment did you have?'

Madison caught a deep sigh and pushed it down. *Chatty, nosy* and *naked! Why?* With no one else around, she was in a hostage situation. She opened her eyes and looked at the stranger. 'I had the hot stone and Swedish massage.' She rolled her shoulders back and grimaced.

The woman chuckled. 'Did she offer some fairly strong opinions on your emotional state?'

Madison relented and smiled. 'Yeah.'

The other woman rolled her eyes. 'It's in here where I get the pure relaxation. Especially if I've had a tough day at work . . .'

Madison softened, as the woman continued to talk, and took in her whole face. She must be in her fifties, Madison thought. Her short black hair really suited her, highlighting her amazing cheekbones and full lips.

'. . . because I deserve some soft life, some luxury. In fact the only thing missing is a glass of champagne on arrival. Right?'

'Sounds like my type of vibe.' Madison laughed. Maybe it was being poked about by the masseuse, but waves of sadness and panic were descending over her again.

'So, how has your day been?' the stranger asked chirpily.

Trust me to find a chatty Londoner. Madison mustered the energy to remove her frown of irritation. 'Well, Saturday is Saturday-ing.' One at a time she stretched out her legs on the bench and shuffled backwards until her spine met the hot wooden wall.

'Are you all ready for Christmas?' the woman asked.

The mention of Christmas made Madison crumple. What kind of Christmas were they heading for? It was only weeks away, and it had always been a highlight of the year . . . She shut her eyes and a tear rolled down her cheek.

'I'm not sure if you're sweating or crying,' said the stranger, her voice softer.

Madison forced a smile. 'I think it's both.'

'Want to talk? I'm a good listener, and I know what it's like going through a difficult time.'

Madison hesitated. This situation felt crazy. She was in a low-lit, sweaty room with a total stranger. Why did she want to tell her what was going on?

'It's my husband,' Madison burst out. 'I thought things were perfect, more or less, and he's just . . . left.'

She waited for a shocked outburst from the woman, but she just nodded slowly. 'Carry on,' she said, after a pause.

There was something about the calm and power she exuded that Madison was finding even more beneficial than the massage. She inhaled deeply and gathered her thoughts. 'I knew he was a bit stressed,' Madison said. 'Who isn't?'

'Kids?'

She nodded. 'Two. And then, out of the blue, he says he needs space. He moves out, goes to his cousin's.'

'No word on when he's definitely coming back?'

Madison shook her head. 'I feel like I could either arrive back tonight and he's home, like nothing has changed, or . . .' She swallowed, unable to voice the alternative.

'He's gone for good?'

Madison gulped. 'And my head is just . . . out of control. I'm trying to understand where the hell he's at. If . . .'

'If you missed something, if you could have done more, if you could have been more?'

Madison let out a low laugh. 'Are you reading my mind?'

'Speaking from experience,' the woman said, raising an eyebrow. 'I'm Savine, by the way.'

'Madison.'

'So, Madison, what do you want?'

Madison opened her mouth to answer, and found that her mind had gone completely blank. No one had asked her that in a very long while. She allowed the question to settle, before the answer rose. 'I want life to go back to how it was before.'

Savine shook her head sympathetically. 'Of course you do. But I hate to break it to you – that is the one thing that is not going to happen.'

Madison felt the tears come again.

'I'm sorry,' said Savine, 'but you have to realize that. Whatever happens, things won't be like they were before. And I'd rather you know that now than do what I did, and try desperately to make things work again.'

Madison flinched. 'But I'm trying because we're going to fix this,' she said, her voice wobbling, then becoming steadier. 'And that's what Rich wants too.'

Savine regarded her for a long moment. 'How long have you been married?'

'Ten years,' said Madison. 'And we were happy. Like, really happy. We've had our share of troubles, sure, but I always thought we were a team.'

Savine nodded. 'I thought the same. That was the worst part.'

Madison was torn. She wanted to know more of Savine's story, and liked talking and being heard by someone who had been through something similar, but she wasn't going to accept that what had happened to Savine's marriage was happening to hers.

'Can I ask what happened?'

'Tale as old as time,' said Savine, rolling her shoulders back. 'He fell in love' – she put quote marks round the phrase – 'with someone else. Who just happened to be twenty years younger and his secretary.' She snorted with genuine laughter.

'I'm sorry,' said Madison. She felt sick. *This is her situation, not yours. Separate it,* she told herself, but her thoughts were spiralling. Savine had thought she knew her husband, and he'd been capable of this. Was Rich capable of something so awful? Did she really know, beyond any doubt, what he would and wouldn't do? She would never have thought he'd leave his family, even for a short time, and that had been proved completely wrong. She had a heavy feeling of dread in the pit of her stomach. But when she glanced up again at Savine, expecting to see tears or the stricken face of a devastated woman as she relived the memory, Savine was relaxed and . . . half smiling?

'You know what, hon?' said Savine. 'I'm not sorry any more. At the time, it blew my world apart. I knew something was off for months. Your gut doesn't lie. So I became more observant and I followed the crumbs. Receipts in the bin for gifts I never received. He started coming home smelling shower fresh but hadn't been to the gym. We barely ever had sex.' She chuckled again. 'Oh, I still can't believe it either. I just don't understand how someone can risk it all for . . . for a good time. I don't know what else to call it because they're not together now. And the pain, when I found out, was like nothing else. But now I'm grateful for it.'

'How?' whispered Madison. What Savine was describing was her worst nightmare. She was feeling dizzy – she wasn't sure if it was the heat from the sauna or Savine's story.

'I was sleepwalking,' said Savine. 'I'd given so much to that marriage, to propping up my husband, to raising our son – which I don't regret a moment of, he's my world – that I'd forgotten who *I* was. And when I got over the hurt, when we'd dealt with the separation, I lifted my head up and looked around, and it was like the sun came out. I travelled, I saw friends, I dated a bit – mostly younger men.' She cackled. 'I got back in touch with friends my ex had thought were "a bit much". And honestly, now, life is good. Better than good.'

Better than good. Madison forced herself to focus on what Savine was saying. She'd come through the nightmare and things were better than ever. Maybe that was the message to take home. She and Rich weren't breaking up, no way, but maybe after they'd made their way through this, they'd be stronger than ever.

She watched as Savine uncrossed her legs and leaned forwards. With her forearms resting on her thighs, she clasped her hands together and lowered her head. Madison admired her sprawled-out naked truth. *She's literally not hiding anything.*

She knows herself and her worth. The woman looked up again, and their eyes met.

'Sorry,' Savine said, sitting back again. 'We were talking about you, and I've been going on about myself. It's just hard seeing someone in the same situation I was in.'

Madison felt heat rise in her cheeks. This was too much. Rich wasn't a cheater. Just because this woman, this *stranger*, had gone through stuff, that didn't mean their situations were the same. 'No, you've got it wrong,' she said, trying to gather her towel around her. 'Rich isn't a cheat. He just needs some time out. He'll probably be back by the weekend. Then it's Christmas, then we're into a whole new year, and this will be long forgotten.'

The silence that followed spoke volumes.

'You honestly don't know him,' Madison began again, but Savine raised a hand.

'I don't need to know him.' She leaned in. 'Listen to me. I've been exactly where you are now. Denial. You don't know which way is up, which is down. But I'll say this. Don't be a fool. You're a strong woman. Act like it. Don't sit back and wait for him to tell you what's going on.'

Madison was electrified. How could this woman be saying such things to her? She appreciated people being direct and straightforward, but this was a whole other level and she couldn't quite believe she'd sat through it all. But she wasn't storming out. Instead she was asking, 'So what *do* I do?'

'Find out what's going on. Look for clues. Find out if there *is* someone else. I know you don't want to hear it but, in my experience, men very rarely walk out of comfortable lives unless there's someone else to go to.'

Madison blanched. She needed to put a stop to this. She

should get up and walk away, but her feet wouldn't move. There was something in what Savine was saying that was speaking to her – speaking to the part of Madison that was fierce and proud and could make up her own mind, thanks all the same.

'I know you hate the sound of it, but look at it like this. You'll know either way. By Christmas, you'll have found out if your husband is trustworthy or not. But don't sleep on this, Madison. You're better than that.' Savine stretched out her legs and contemplated her perfectly painted toes.

You're better than that. Her words hung in the air. Madison could have pointed out that Savine didn't know her, let alone her husband, but there was a challenge in those words. A challenge to take charge, to find out her own answers.

'I need to get going,' Savine said. 'Got me a hot date.' She pursed her lips and gave a little shoulder-shimmy.

'Sure,' mumbled Madison, her head spinning.

'I'm gonna leave my details at Reception in case you want to reach out. I really do know how you feel.'

Savine got up and stretched luxuriantly, then padded out of the sauna, leaving Madison to her thoughts.

She didn't stay much longer because the heat with no distraction was becoming unbearable. She showered and, getting dressed, she remembered her friends' suspicion that Rich had someone else on the go. The idea had been shut down, but was it a sign that she'd bumped into Savine only the next day? She thought about what Savine had said. That Madison needed to find out what was going on. Maybe that's what she could do. A jolt of anger rippled through her. Rich was content to leave her in the dark while he sorted his head out. Could a bit of low-level investigation be exactly what was required to set her own mind at rest?

As she walked out, she slowed down by Reception. Had Savine left her details, or had she thought better of it?

She stopped by the desk. 'I don't suppose . . .'

'Yeah, Savine left her details for you,' said the receptionist, handing Madison a smart embossed card. Savine ran a well-known PR agency.

Madison tucked the card into her pocket and went out into the cold December air, shivering.

The next morning, Madison was sitting in her car, having dropped off the kids at her dad's, as she often did on a Sunday. She had slept fairly well, despite Rich's absence and the anger still lapping around her heart, but she kept mulling over the conversation she'd had with Savine. She swung to and fro, feeling sometimes indignant that Savine had overstepped the mark with what she'd said, wanting to defend Rich and their marriage to her, then circling back and wondering if Savine had had a point. If Rich had nothing to hide, there'd be nothing to find. And what was her other option? Waiting at home for him to decide to explain what was going on? Meanwhile, she'd be spending the days in an agony of second-guessing.

Finally, she pulled up a number on her phone and stared at it for a long minute, then pressed dial.

'Hello, CRG Management, Amber speaking.'

Madison cleared her throat and put on a bright voice. 'Hey, Amber, how are you? It's Madison!'

'Hey!' Amber replied. 'What can I do for you?'

She was twenty-four, Australian and looked like an advert for the surf lifestyle, even after a few years in grey London.

Madison tried to sound breezy. 'I'm looking to organize a

few Christmas surprises, and I need to make sure I'm up to date on Rich's diary.'

'You guys! That's so cute. And no worries re his diary. He's such a horror for not putting stuff in . . .'

'God, he is,' said Madison. 'Could you just let me know any evening stuff he's blocked out and I'll check it against what I have?'

Amber began to list dates that Rich had booked in for filming. 'Not so many – oh, hang on . . .'

'What is it?' said Madison, as she heard Amber tapping away.

'He's got one or two marked "private",' Amber said.

Madison felt she might be sick. What the hell did 'private' mean?'

'There's one on the thirteenth and another a week later on the twentieth . . .'

'And it doesn't say where he's going or anything?' Madison asked.

'No, I'm sorry – I can ask him?'

'No!' Madison exclaimed, then forced herself to speak calmly. 'Ha, I just want this to be a surprise. I can avoid those days, no problem.'

'He does sometimes block in time as private if it's family stuff,' said Amber. 'I'm just remembering that from a few years ago. I think it was your birthday, actually. I remember him saying the next day.'

'That's so sweet,' said Madison. Her heart leaped in hope. Was Rich simply blocking out time for his family?

She said thank you and goodbye to Amber, and stared at the two dates she'd scribbled down. She pulled out her own calendar. Ah – the thirteenth was the kids' nativity play. How could she have forgotten? The twentieth was blank. Madison was as confused as ever. But at least there was a test. Would he come to the nativity play? Or had he arranged something else for that evening? And what about the mysterious entry on the twentieth? She would find out, one way or another.

9

'Take a note, please, Maddy,' said the red-faced man in front of her, as he ran a hand through his floppy straw-coloured hair, making it even more dishevelled.

Madison gritted her teeth. This was her boss, Jenson. His actual name was Wilfred but some mysterious convention dictated that he was called by his surname. They were in the usual Monday-morning meeting to go over the logistics of the interiors at the Jenson Hotels chain, including the design plans for their new location. Jenson leaned forward and looked at them all. Madison knew what was coming.

'When my father began Jenson's Hotels,' he said, his voice slow and portentous, 'he had a vision. A high-class establishment, where gentlemen visitors to our fair capital could stop and rest their weary heads after a long day doing business.'

Madison tried not to roll her eyes.

'A place of refuge from life's hustle and bustle,' Jenson continued. 'A sanctuary from the chaos of the streets, if you will.' He glanced at Madison. 'Are you getting all this?'

'Absolutely,' murmured Madison. She'd heard this speech so many times before she could have recited it in her sleep.

Jenson got up and paced to the window, staring out of it.

The effect would have been better had two pigeons not been mating on the windowsill opposite.

'And now, with the launch of our newest location, in King's Cross, we have a chance to make my father's vision a reality once more. Jenson's Hotels. The next brick in the wall of our worldwide expansion.'

He was misty-eyed now, clearly dreaming of the day when Jenson's Hotels would be as recognizable a name as Hilton.

'Without further ado, the first action point on the agenda, Maddy, if you will?' Jenson finished, returning to the long table.

'We're going to consider design options for the new hotel, especially looking at a refresh that's more in line with customer expectations. We've got a few Tripadvisor reviews that are less than favourable,' said Madison.

Jenson scowled.

Madison cleared her throat and began to read. 'This one is from FullEnglishBreakfastWasAJoke, of Kidderminster. "Me and the wife stayed in the Central London location for our wedding anniversary and were sorely disappointed. The staff on Reception were absolutely lovely, but the décor of the room gave us both a headache – not what you want on your anniversary. The clashing tartan patterns and creepy deer heads on the wall really put us off."

'Philistines!' said Jenson, slapping his hand on to the table. 'The tartans have been in my family *for centuries*, and as for a deer head on the wall, they aren't even real, more's the pity. Are these people vegans?'

'I don't know,' said Madison.

'Their opinions are to be entirely ignored,' Jenson said, taking out a handkerchief and blowing his nose into it.

Madison's blood boiled. If Jenson had bothered to listen, he would have realized there was a sheaf of customer complaints about the décor, and the outdated bathrooms, which he was too tight to replace properly. If there was anything Madison believed in, it was that good design should be for everyone. She felt *terrible* that this couple's wedding anniversary had been ruined by Jenson's insistence on including every one of his family's tartans to 'honour his ancestors'. He viewed the entire hotel chain as a personal vanity project, ignoring the fact that, after he had taken over from his father, the company had been gathering more and more negative reviews, and was now haemorrhaging money.

Imagining ways to hand in her notice had become a recurrent fantasy. Her current favourite was to spray-paint 'I QUIT' all over the wallpaper in his office, which he'd had specially commissioned at a cost of thousands to showcase all the tartan patterns. She'd been waiting for Rich's show to be confirmed before she did this. It was just one of the ways in which her life was no longer going to plan.

'Sorry I'm late!'

A man Madison didn't recognize had pushed open the boardroom door. He smiled to the rest of the team, the caramel skin around his warm brown eyes creasing. He was tall, with similar shaven hair to Rich and an asymmetrical face that was perfectly framed by stylish wire glasses. *With skin that good he can't be much more than thirty*, thought Madison, followed by *Oh, God, I hope he doesn't start calling me Auntie out of respect*.

'Do sit down,' said Jenson, gesturing to an empty seat beside Madison.

As he walked into the room, she was struck by the easy confidence of his movement, emphasized by his impeccably tailored navy suit. His calm, self-assured energy brought a positive feeling to the room. Madison found it difficult to look away . . . There was just something about him that was hard to ignore.

Despite her irritation with the rest of the meeting, it was her nature to be welcoming to anyone new, so she turned towards him, gave a tiny wave with her fingers and murmured, 'We're still on the first agenda point, here,' gesturing at the sheet of paper in front of her.

'If we could all make our introductions to Nathan,' said Jenson, 'instead of chatting between ourselves . . .'

He was *so* controlling, Madison thought furiously. 'Madison,' she said. 'Design assistant.'

'I'm Nathan,' he said, giving her a warm smile. 'I'm the architect who's been working on the new site.'

The other figures around the table introduced themselves. It wasn't an inspiring selection. Most were friends of Jenson from school, yes-men who agreed with everything he said and had no idea about the lives of their customers. There was also Penny, head of PR, whom Jenson referred to as 'our resident leggy blonde', which caused them both to collapse in giggles. Madison shuddered to think what had gone on between them in the past.

'Shall we continue with the discussion? If you can recap for Nathan, please, Maddy,' said Jenson.

She gritted her teeth: he got her name wrong every time.

Madison felt Nathan stir uncomfortably next to her. 'It's about the décor for the new location,' she said. 'I've been researching a few ideas.' She thought carefully about her next words. She was good with people, she knew, good at knowing how to read them, how to handle them. She was also a good designer, when she got the chance. 'It's about keeping the amazing heritage of Jenson's Hotels, but updating the look to appeal to a modern, fresher audience.'

She saw Jenson wince.

'Now I'm not sure about this updating malarkey . . .'

'I'm really interested to hear what Madison has to say,' said Nathan. 'Please, go on.'

Madison could have hugged him, but she kept her voice confident and professional, sliding across some printouts of mood boards she'd been working on. 'Absolutely. So, research shows that people want a sense of freshness in their hotel rooms, a sense that this is a neutral space, but still a personal one. It's about clean lines, soothing colours, but also the occasional touch to show that we're a family business and we treat our customers like family too.'

Nathan was nodding.

'On this mood board, you can see I've gone with more muted pastel tones, and we could put a different colour in each room. But then we'd look at some accents that are really individual. I was thinking we could use pops of pattern. So, we could have some really nice prints on the walls, showing polka dots, for example, or these geometric shapes that this artist does on Instagram, and then a nod to the tartans, Jenson.'

She looked down at her work and felt confident in it. Yes, these designs weren't groundbreaking or bold, but their clientele didn't want that. She imagined herself, or her friends, getting ready in one of the rooms – soft lighting, gentle colours that were still warm, and little finishing touches that would make their guests feel time and attention had gone into preparing the design for them.

Nathan had pulled over one of the sheets of paper and was studying it closely.

'I'd love to hear thoughts from around the table,' Madison said.

There was a deafening silence. As usual, everyone was waiting for Jenson to speak.

'I love these,' said Nathan, glancing around. 'They're confident, but accessible too. It's for everyone. It's a nice unique look and it'll work well in both natural and artificial light. Very cool.'

Jenson snorted. 'Nathan, my dear chap, perhaps stick to making sure the building stays upright!'

He guffawed at his own joke, and Madison recoiled at the rudeness of his comment. Nathan was sitting bolt upright, his face inscrutable.

'You really need to understand the heritage of our brand,' said Jenson. 'This looks . . . I don't know, sort of Scandinavian?'

'That's the point,' said Madison, evenly. 'It's an enormous design trend. People like it. Clean lines, neutral spaces. This offers that, but with an individual touch so it's not cold.'

'Other thoughts?' said Jenson.

'Where's the tartan?' said Penny, and Jenson clapped his hands in glee.

'Exactly,' he breathed. 'Exactly, Penny. Thank you. Someone who understands.'

Madison resisted the urge to put her head into her hands and scream. Her heart was beating loudly, and if she let herself, she might cry, but she channelled her dignity and remained poised. 'We've had a lot of feedback from customers who were . . . unsure about the tartan,' said Madison. That was putting it mildly. People thought the rooms were shabby, old-fashioned, said they were unclean. Madison knew how hard the cleaners worked, but it was difficult to make those rooms look fresh.

'What's the deal with the tartan?' said Nathan.

'Oh, God,' Madison breathed.

Twenty minutes later, they emerged from the boardroom.

'Do you wish you hadn't asked?' said Madison.

Nathan glanced around. 'Honestly, is that guy for real?'

'Sadly, yes,' said Madison.

Nathan whistled through his teeth. 'Glad I'm only on this contract for a few months.'

'I'm so jealous.' She felt deflated at her lack of an escape plan.

Nathan glanced at his watch. 'Fancy grabbing lunch together?'

'As long as you promise we don't have to look at *anything* remotely resembling a certain checked pattern.'

He raised an eyebrow. 'Sorry, Madison, I think you'll find you're talking about the very distinguished heritage of Jenson there.'

She chuckled, and they headed out to a nearby café.

Settled with sandwiches, they kept chatting.

'Honestly, I hope you don't think this is patronizing, but I really liked your designs,' said Nathan. 'I thought they were great for a hotel chain. Recognizable, but not too out there.'

'Oh, thanks,' said Madison. 'I always try to think of what the customer would like.'

Nathan was nodding. 'I do the same, to be honest. So many architects seem to let their egos take over and it's all about doing the wildest, craziest building, but I want to do something that feels . . .'

'A bit more like home?' Madison heard herself say.

Nathan's face broke into a smile. 'Yeah. You know what?

I think that's it. At least with something like this. So what's gonna happen with your designs?'

She sighed. 'Jenson will ignore them. He'll be putting the tartan back as we speak. And I promise you, we'll end up doing the same as we've always done in your lovely new building.' She felt despondent. What a waste of her time and energy. 'Sometimes I think maybe I should just play the game and tell Jenson I love the existing look,' she said. 'It's what everyone else does. Then they just get to go home and not think about work.'

'I would personally love to see you pretending to think a stuffed deer-head on the wall is a good idea,' said Nathan. 'But I somehow get the impression that's not how you operate.'

Madison took another bite of her sandwich. When she'd swallowed it, she said, 'Yeah, you're right. I just can't back an idea I don't think is good.'

'Honest to a fault?'

'Something like that. I took that job to get back into work after having my kids, and hoped it would contain a teeny possibility of doing some design work. Some hope that was. But you know how tough it is out there. I just have to stick with it and forget that it's not exactly my dream job.' She felt miserable as she uttered the words, and realized the truth of them.

'So what is it you dream of, then?'

She paused. It had been ages since she'd thought like that. 'I guess I dream of being in a job where I can design stuff that people really, really like. That shows them you don't have to have loads of money to create a beautiful room that feels like you. That design isn't intimidating, but for everyone.' She felt herself flush again. 'Sorry, that was quite the speech.'

'No, no, it's great,' said Nathan. 'I'm just thinking how on earth that's going to happen when you're working for the likes of him.'

'Short answer, it isn't,' said Madison, grimly.

Nathan was chewing slowly. He swallowed and dabbed his mouth with a napkin. 'Listen, I might have an idea. I've got a friend, she's kind of . . . semi-famous now?'

'Check you out,' said Madison. There was something about bantering with Nathan that was so easy.

He rolled his eyes. 'Sorry. There's no way to say that without sounding like a prick. But, yeah, she did really well with modelling, and she's been doing some fashion design of her own. She's just bought this gorgeous house in Dulwich.'

'Nice,' said Madison.

'I know she's keen to work with a designer to do it up,' he continued. 'She's got a real flair for fashion but not so much with interiors. She was asking me if I knew anyone.' He shrugged. 'I could mention you?'

'You're gonna need to give me a name,' said Madison.

'It's Mellow Stephenson,' said Nathan.

Madison's cheeks creased in amusement. She knew who Mellow Stephenson was: she'd graced the cover of *Vogue* at least twice, and fronted a campaign for Rihanna's new hair-care line, a first for a model with dreadlocks. 'Nathan, she's seriously cool. And she's, what, twenty-five?'

'Twenty-eight,' said Nathan.

Madison was suddenly self-conscious, sitting next to this young man, talking about her design ambitions. How must he see her? He was probably just being kind, indulgent and polite. 'She must have a bag of influential people she could speed-dial. She's not going to want the likes of me, a nobody, mother of two, doing her bathroom,' said Madison.

'You don't know that!' Nathan said. 'And what have you got to lose? It's a free rein. You could work on a few designs, and I can show them to her. If she doesn't like them, nothing changes. If she does like them, boom! You're working with someone who will absolutely get your name out there and give you the credit you deserve.'

He was right. Madison knew it. She fiddled with the crumbs on her plate, buying time. Here was the kind of golden opportunity she'd dreamed of, and that had been granted to her once, by Astrid. She could still remember the moment when Astrid had rung her to say she'd got the job on the show. Her first day on set was still one of the best she'd ever had. It had been so much fun, even though the hours were long and the pay terrible. And while she wouldn't change the kids for anything, sometimes she wondered what would have happened if she'd been able to work for just a *little bit longer* before taking time out. She'd only just been getting started, really.

So why wasn't she seizing this opportunity with both hands? She could practically hear her twenty-something self screaming at her to go for it! But her forty-year-old self felt as if she was clinging to the walls of the ice rink, her feet slipping from under her. What would she even design? Before, she'd always been brimming with inspiration. Now she was completely devoid of ideas.

Nathan was still looking at her, hopefully.

'I'll think about it,' she said.

'We could go over any ideas you've got,' he said. 'Sometimes helps to have another head on a project.'

She knew he meant to be nice and that he was trying to support her, but the fact was that her mind had gone blank. That made her feel even worse. She might be able to knock together

103

a few basic concepts for a hotel chain, but there was no way she could cope with anything more demanding. She crumpled up her napkin and forced a smile. 'Best get back to the office. It was lovely meeting you.'

10

The next couple of days passed in a blur. It was amazing how she seemed to adjust to a new normal, even if sometimes she was still engulfed by waves of disbelief and sadness. Rich was in contact to make arrangements, but was quick to leave when she arrived home if he'd been with the kids. He avoided any conversation with her, and Madison wasn't about to talk to him: she had resolved she would find out exactly what was going on before she made her next move.

Since her conversation with Savine, something in her had toughened up. Another conversation was also playing in her mind: the one with Nathan. She kept rerunning an alternative version of it in her head, one that came after her panic at not having any instant bright ideas had settled. In the first version she had said, 'Yeah, I'll think about it.' In the alternative one she said, 'Here are my designs,' and produced a portfolio she was proud of. It was a version in which she also said, 'Call her right now and tell her I'm the best designer in London.' OK, that was definitely over the top, but *if* her career had had some attention for the past few years, maybe she'd have been able to explore the opportunity instead of dismissing it outright.

And then there were moments when she just wanted to give up.

Madison was always cooking extra food and taking it round to her dad, especially his favourites from her mother's recipes.

'Not long till Christmas now,' he said to her one evening, as she loaded Tupperware boxes into his fridge. 'You'll need to let me know what those little ones want.' He gave her a soft look. 'And my girl, who'll always be a little one to me.'

Tears pricked. It had been a long day, with no word from Rich, and the kids had been asking when he was coming home. She hated lying to them so, so much, and she felt briefly furious with Rich for putting her in that position. Just then all she wanted was to collapse into her dad's arms and cry, and for him to make everything OK, just like when she was little and had grazed her knee. He never used to be so emotional in his words, but old age was softening him.

'I hope you know how proud I am of you,' he said, smiling. 'All you've achieved. A beautiful family, all of your own.'

At his words, Madison bit the inside of her cheek. There was no way she could shatter her dad's image of her. He'd suffered so much since her mother's death, and she just couldn't tell him about her troubles. It was kinder to let him believe she still had the perfect family life. 'You're family too, Dad,' she said, her voice choked. 'The kids are already excited about you coming for Christmas.' She patted his arm and moved her attention to stacking the fridge, breathing deeply. In her mind, she was focused on one day: 13 December. She purposely hadn't told Rich that it was the nativity play. Normally she double-checked he had remembered key events, but this time she wouldn't. She'd see just where his head was at.

The night before the nativity, she slept badly. It had become a real test in her mind. If his family truly was his priority, he'd be there, without her reminding him. But she also hated using her kids as part of this test. She'd wavered about sending him a text message, asking what time he'd be free for the play, but every time she'd typed it, something had stopped her pressing send.

When she dropped off the kids on the morning of the play, promising she'd see them later, Chloë's teacher, Miss Mayhew, pulled her to one side. 'Hi, Madison. Any chance you and Chloë's dad could pop in earlier this afternoon for a bit of a chat?'

Madison frowned. The phrase 'bit of a chat' was surely anxiety-provoking to any parent. 'Sure,' she said carefully. 'Everything OK?'

The bell rang.

'I've got to go,' said Miss Mayhew. 'Let's discuss it later, when we've got time.'

Madison climbed into the car and rested her head on the steering wheel. There was a tap at the window. She glanced up to see Jess smiling at her, and put the window down.

'Hey, babe, how was the massage?'

'It was amazing,' said Madison, mortified. 'Jess, I'm so sorry – it was clearly so relaxing that I forgot to text you about it.'

Jess waved a hand. 'Don't worry. Just as long as you're feeling a bit better about things.'

Madison thought back to the conversation she'd had with Savine. Since then, she'd begun to take action. She could feel a shift in her mentality. Yes, she wanted to fix her marriage, but she was also waiting for *him* to prove he wanted family life too. She wasn't about to beg him to see how good it was. 'Things are definitely clearer,' she said.

'That's great.' Jess beamed. Then her face became a little more clouded and hesitant. 'Are we seeing you *and* Rich later?'

Madison nodded. 'For sure.'

'Fancy a coffee?'

She knew that Jess wanted an update on the situation, but she didn't feel like going into it right now. She loved that Jess backed their marriage, but she needed to navigate this in her own way. 'Sorry, babe. Busy day,' she said, putting her car into drive mode.

Jess stepped back. 'No problem. See you guys later.'

At home, Madison stared at her phone. She could feel a tension headache coming on. She was now worrying about Chloë, and what her teacher was going to say. She had to contact Rich. He should be there, too.

She rang his number, and it clicked instantly to voicemail, so she hung up. Since when did she feel nervous phoning her husband, the father of her kids? She reached for WhatsApp instead – if he was filming, it was easier for him to check a message than listen to a voicemail.

Hey – Chloë's teacher wants a meeting with us at school, before the play. Are you OK to meet me there at 3.30 or come via here, and we can go together? Let me know. This was where she'd usually add a kiss, but was it OK to do that now? Her hands hovered over the button before pressing send.

Only one tick appeared. She frowned. Ordinarily, she'd think nothing of that, but she found herself staring at that single tick and her heart rate rocketed. What if he had his phone off because he was with someone else? What if he was, right now, in a hotel room with some other woman?

Deep breaths, Madison told herself. It's most likely he's filming.

But what if he isn't? the voice in her head said. It was Savine's voice, she realized. *Or what if he's cheating on you with someone at work? Or someone from the agency?* Could he even be seeing Amber? It would be the perfect ruse. Amber would know just how to cover for him. Panic rose in her chest. *Stop it, Madison.*

What could she do? She toyed with ringing his agency and asking for his agenda, but to do so again might look weird.

She scrolled through her list of contacts. OK, there was Marvin, the cousin he was staying with. *If* he'd told the truth. Madison's heart was racing. That was the thing with trust. If you started doubting one thing, it wasn't long before the rest came tumbling down.

She called Marvin's number.

'Hey, Madison!' came his relaxed, baritone voice.

She was relieved it was Marvin she was dealing with. She always felt uncomfortable around Rich's brother, like she didn't quite measure up. 'Hey, Marv,' she said.

'What can I do for you?'

She hesitated. What was she meant to say? *Just wondering if you could shed any light on my husband's state of mind and if he might be seeing another woman?*

'Just trying to track down Rich. Is he with you?'

'Nah, sorry,' said Marvin. 'I've not seen him since last night but he had an early start filming so I guess that's where he is.'

'OK, cool. If you see him, could you ask him to call me?'

'Yeah, of course.' There was a pause. Madison could tell Marvin kind of wanted to say something. 'Listen, Madison, I hope you're OK.'

'Thanks, Marv,' she said, voice wobbling.

'You guys will work it out,' he said.

She shut her eyes and forced herself to say the next words. 'Do you know what's going on with him?'

She held her breath. She felt Marvin lapse into another silence on the end of the phone. She'd overstepped the mark. At the end of the day, he and Rich were family, had grown up together.

'Can't say I do,' he finally answered. 'And that's the truth. He doesn't want to talk to me, besides saying he needs to stay for a bit.'

'And how long's a bit?' said Madison, her voice pleading.

'I honestly don't know,' said Marvin. 'Listen, I've got to go. But look after yourself, yeah?'

She sniffed, trying to hide the wobble in her voice. 'Will do.'

Immediately after the call, she returned to WhatsApp. Still a single tick.

'Get a hold of yourself,' she murmured, as she blew into a tissue. 'At least he's staying where he said he was.'

She did the washing-up from the kids' breakfast, made a shopping list and opened her work emails. The usual list of tedious tasks that Jenson insisted on. She replied to a few from him, then noticed one from Nathan, entitled *Did you . . .* She clicked open. The rest of the text said . . . *have a chance to think yet?*

Madison exhaled. Truth was, she had zero mental capacity to think of anything beyond what her home life had become.

She flipped on to Mellow's Instagram. God, she was stunning. There were photos from previous modelling campaigns she had done with Gucci, Versace and Nike, and pictures of her travels, most recently to Morocco. Madison clicked through the pictures. *Wow, she's definitely got an eye for design,* she thought. There were photos of colourful fruit and veg in the market, some close up, so that colour and texture filled the images. There was a gorgeous photo of Mellow posing with a rug-seller, both grinning, and captioned 'Finally agreed on a price', then a picture of a beautiful handwoven rug, the colours earthy yet vibrant. Finally, there were several ceramics she'd bought, thrown in turquoise, navy and the traditional clay tone, each one glossy and gleaming.

Madison felt the cogs in her head turning. Could she base a kitchen around the colours of those beautiful ceramics? She closed her eyes. She was imagining tiles fired in the same colours, arranged in a haphazard pattern to give that individual feel. A big kitchen table, set with textiles in the same colour as the rug, and with a statement fruit bowl, filled with glossy red apples or bright oranges, to act as a focal point. This was how design should feel. Individual. Personal. Something that could remind you of the very best life had to offer, where you could make good memories.

She grabbed a pencil, then—

Ping.

It was an email from Jenson.

Hi, Maddy,

I have reviewed the suggestions you made for the toothbrush holders in the bathrooms.

They seem expensive and frivolous.

In fact, I think the existing ones are more than adequate, and it's part of our sustainability commitment to avoid unnecessary purchasing.

Please be mindful of this going forward.

Madison wanted to scream. As if this was about sustainability! She had encouraged Jenson to use more recycled and reused materials, leading to him pooh-poohing the idea of 'second-hand goods'. What she had suggested were some toothbrush holders in cream ceramic, with a slightly more contemporary square shape than the ones that had been in place for the best part of a decade. They were about as innocuous as you could find.

She began to type a reply.

Dear Jenson,
I QUIT.
And here's an idea – why don't you shove your toothbrush

She broke off as fear took hold of her. She wanted nothing more than to quit her job. But the idea was that she would work on Rich's new show. The show she didn't even know was going to happen – Rich had said he wasn't meant to be discussing it until everything was official. Over the years, they'd often talked about how amazing it would be for him to have his own show, and shared in the anticipation of that ever happening. But as Madison thought about it now, she realized he hadn't included her in proper discussions. It was one thing to imagine it as a fantasy of what might happen in the future, quite another to share with her the specific discussions he'd been having and the timescales they were looking at. Her frustration built, as she realized the implications. Such a change would be really significant for their family, she'd always known that, but that was precisely why she *should* have been included in the discussions. And now, even if the show *did* happen, would he offer her a role on it? She imagined the producers discussing her in one of those five-minute chats over coffee.

Rich has been asking about his wife working for us, one would say.

Who is she again?

Not sure . . .

She's been out of the game so long. I just think we want someone a bit . . . fresher?

The imagined conversation sent a shudder of horror through her and she began to spiral in waves of self-doubt. Who was she kidding, thinking that Mellow would be interested in her designs? She deleted the email from Nathan and replied to Jenson, saying that, on reflection, she agreed with him.

It was a horrible day. The hours rolled past, her mind veering between worrying about Chloë to fending off work emails to trying to work out the logistics of Christmas presents, accompanied by the ever-changing emotions around Rich. She felt tight with anxiety, her stomach churning so that she could barely eat anything for lunch. She kept checking her phone to see if Rich had replied, her heart sinking every time she saw the single tick. She really needed him to come through, to be there as a parent to their daughter.

In the afternoon, she rang him again. It clicked to voicemail.

OK, should she be worried? She told herself no. If anything had happened, she would have heard.

She checked his Instagram, and saw a story had appeared. It was a video of Rich sanding some shelves, his T-shirt sleeves rolled up. He looked to camera and said, 'Best way to keep warm in cold weather!'

What the hell? Madison thought. She was worrying about their daughter, worrying about their *marriage*, and Rich was posting videos that showcased his biceps to best effect!

She left him a voicemail this time.

'Hey – so we need to be at the school for three thirty to have the meeting about Chloë. It's now three. I've not heard from you. Rich, you need to be there. This is our daughter. Whatever's going on between us, we need to be there for her.'

She took a last glance at her phone, her heart sinking when she saw no reply from him, got up from the kitchen table and went upstairs to apply her makeup properly. *Fake it till you make it,* she told herself, practising a confident smile in the mirror. Then she got into the car and drove to the school.

Miss Mayhew welcomed her at Reception. 'My husband's been held up,' Madison said. 'But he'll join us as soon as he can.'

'It would be great if you could both be here,' said Miss Mayhew.

'Let me call him again,' said Madison. She stepped outside briefly and rang Rich's number. *Please please please pick up,* she begged. Voicemail again. There was no point in leaving another message.

'Any luck?' said Miss Mayhew.

Madison smiled tightly. 'He's travelling right now.' As far as she knew, that might be true. 'If he can join, great, but if he misses it, I can tell him what's going on.'

Miss Mayhew showed her into one of the classrooms, filled with tiny chairs and hand-made Christmas decorations, and they sat down.

'I just wanted to have a chat about Chloë,' said the teacher. 'She's normally so bright and confident, but recently she's just seemed . . . a bit out of sorts, somehow.'

'How do you mean?' Madison's heart sank. More than anything, she wanted her kids to be happy.

'She's a bit distracted,' said Miss Mayhew. 'Normally, she's able to focus on what she's doing, but now I'm having to call her to attention, and she just seems a bit disengaged.'

The temptation was to get on the defensive, to say that Chloë was allowed to be off her game every once in a while. That it was only human sometimes to be distracted. But she knew she was lucky to have a teacher who was so aware of her daughter's moods. She swallowed her pride. 'Thanks for letting me know,' she said. 'I appreciate it.'

Miss Mayhew nodded, evidently relieved that the conversation was clearly going to be constructive. 'She's normally so confident, and I just wanted to make sure that things are OK. You know, if there's anything else going on, or if we need to look at any extra support?'

Madison felt a flash of anger at Rich. Where the hell was he? Why wasn't he hearing the effect that his actions were clearly having on the kids?

'Things are really busy at home,' Madison admitted. 'And her dad's been away working loads.' That was the line they were still telling the kids. They'd gone through periods of Rich being away a lot when they were younger, but maybe now they were picking up on the strange atmosphere in the house. She'd thought she was doing a good job of pretending things were normal but you couldn't fool kids: they were more perceptive than many adults.

Miss Mayhew was nodding. 'Even something like that can be disruptive. Is she still spending time with Sienna out of school?'

Madison frowned. Come to think of it, Chloë hadn't been round to Jess's in a while. Normally Jess was constantly inviting her round, organizing amazing sleepovers and insisting she'd look after the girls after school. 'That seems to have dropped off a bit, actually.' Probably because it was very much

Madison's turn to have the girls round. Chloë and Sienna were officially 'best friends' and loved spending time together. She couldn't remember the last time she'd hosted, and another rush of guilt flooded her. Maybe Jess was waiting for her to return the invitation. Madison was always *meaning* to host them, but Jess would ask first, offering a trip to the cinema, to the playground, or to a film night at theirs, with separate films for the mums and the kids, and different refreshments too. Madison smiled internally at the memory of Jess talking about 'adults' lemonade' and winking at the gin and tonic her husband was mixing. That was back when life felt simple.

'Sometimes they have little fallings-out, and it's perfectly natural,' said Miss Mayhew, snapping Madison back to the here and now. 'Christmas might be a good break for everyone. You'd be amazed how things can change with a few days off.'

'So what should I – we – be doing?' said Madison. Now, as well as anger, she simply wanted Rich there. He had always been good at talking to both of their kids. He'd made a special effort to carve out a good relationship with Chloë. He knew he'd always have football and gaming time with Jordan, plus their regular visits to the barber, a bonding ritual between father and son, and he didn't want Chloë to feel left out compared to her brother.

'Keep things as normal as possible, don't go over the top, but maybe make time to talk to her. Find out what's going on, listen to her day,' Miss Mayhew said. 'I mean, I'm sure you do all that already, but sometimes an extra check-in can really help. Or structuring the questions a bit more, like what was the best thing about her day or the worst.'

Madison nodded. 'Thanks. That's super-helpful.'

Miss Mayhew put her head to one side and regarded her. 'Look after yourself too. You're doing an awesome job. Don't forget that.'

What was it with people showing her these little kindnesses that was seriously getting to her today?

The sound of kids chattering and cheering in the hallway signalled that the conversation was coming to an end.

'Are you ready for the chaos of the nativity play?' said Miss Mayhew, smiling broadly.

'Oh, I can't wait!' said Madison. 'Highlight of the year.' She wasn't lying. The nativity play was fun, full of noise and laughter, and featured quite a few characters who *definitely* weren't part of the traditional story, but the inclusive vibe made Madison love it all the more.

She made her way into the 'backstage' area, smiling to see that someone had stuck up Hollywood-style stars, as well as copious amounts of tinsel. The littlest kids were practising their songs again, their voices piping up as the teacher implored them to please sing the words at the same time as each other. Good luck with that, thought Madison, wryly. It didn't seem a minute since her kids had been that age.

She spotted Chloë perched on a chair, swinging her legs to and fro, with a worried expression on her face. Madison's heart sank. That wasn't Chloë. She was normally a chatterbox and a fledgling drama queen, keen to be around her friends.

'Hey, baby,' she said, kneeling beside her daughter. 'How are you feeling? Ready for the show?'

Chloë didn't reply, just scuffed her shoe along the floor.

'You feeling OK?' Madison tried again.

Chloë kept her gaze down. 'Where's Dad?' she mumbled.

Madison was jolted. She had no idea, was the answer. 'I'm

sure he's on his way,' she said, keeping her voice even and light. 'You know how busy his work is.'

Silence from her daughter. It was such a contrast to the excited burbling of the other kids around her.

'And he'll definitely be here to watch you in the play,' Madison said. Normally talk of performing got Chloë enthused: she had inherited her dad's love of the spotlight. Now she just scowled.

'I don't want to do the play,' Chloë mumbled.

'Chlo, what do you mean? You've been loving it during rehearsals. Remember all the stuff you told me about the Christmas Worm?'

Even in the midst of feeling so worried, Madison had had to work hard not to laugh at the concept of a Christmas Worm at the nativity. She definitely didn't remember *that* from Sunday School as a kid.

Then Chloë uttered the words that were guaranteed to strike fear into the heart of any parent: 'Where's my costume?'

Madison frowned. 'What do you mean?'

'My costume,' repeated Chloë. 'I gave the letter to Dad. Is he bringing it?'

Madison forced herself to breathe slowly in a bid to control her building panic. 'Wait here, baby,' Madison said. 'Be back in a second.'

She stepped outside once again, shivering in the cold. Her message still wasn't delivered. Where the hell was Rich? And why hadn't he passed on the letter so they could both be on the same page? In the turmoil of the last few weeks, she'd some-how presumed that the school would be sorting out costumes for the kids as she hadn't heard anything otherwise. And now Chloë was paying the price for the lack of communication between them. She had to fix this, and fast.

She called Finn's number and crossed her fingers he'd pick up.

'What can I do for you, Madison?' he said. 'Please say it's an emergency cocktail, the day I've had, and Andrew won't even *listen*—'

'Babe, not tonight, I'm so sorry,' said Madison. 'We've got a situation to deal with.'

'Everything OK?' said Finn, his voice serious now.

'Yeah, broadly speaking,' said Madison. 'But I'm at Chloë's nativity, and she doesn't have a costume. Turns out I was meant to be sorting that. Not that anyone told me.' Her tone was sharp but she was fuming. She would have remembered if she'd been asked to do it – she loved making costumes for the kids.

Madison shut her eyes and hoped Finn would come to the rescue. She'd wondered about asking Jess for help, but she knew that Jess would have been preparing Sienna's costume for ages and couldn't face her friend's wide-eyed stare of disbelief if she admitted she hadn't been doing the same. At least she didn't have to sort a costume for Jordan as well, she thought, thanking God that his contribution to the play this year was helping with the design and setting the stage with props.

'Goodness, Madison, what else do they want you to do – hand-stitch their uniforms for next term?' said Finn. 'The amount they expect of you!'

Madison could have hugged him. 'Thanks, Finn,' she said.

'So listen – what are we talking? If it's a shepherd, tea towel over the head. Get a stick from the park and that's her staff. If she's got Mary – star material! – it's just a load of blue material and a bit of tinsel. That shop near the station sells literally everything, including fabric.'

'Babe, you're clearly used to simpler school-play times –

production values have gone up.' She sighed. 'And there are new roles.'

'Three wise women? Love that!'

Madison snorted. 'No. But if you find them, send them my way.'

'What are we talking, then?'

She hesitated. 'The Christmas Worm.'

'Sorry, the line's breaking up? Thought you said—'

'The Christmas Worm.'

There was a pause, then the sound of Finn laughing into the phone, which made Madison start spluttering too.

'Madison, what the . . .' Finn was still laughing '. . . I'm sorry, I just cannot . . . It's the fact it's *the* Christmas Worm . . .'

'Not any old Christmas worm,' Madison choked out, through her giggles.

'Oh, no,' said Finn. 'The one and only Christmas Worm!'

'The one we've all heard so much about?' said Madison, sending them off again.

'I mean, in Ireland, Christmas wasn't Christmas until the Christmas Worm made an appearance,' said Finn.

'Highly traditional,' said Madison.

'I hear that, actually, the Christmas Worm was first at the manger . . .'

'Technically that could have been true,' said Madison.

'Just minding its own business on the stable floor,' said Finn, and they were off again, Madison getting strange looks from the parents making their way into the school.

'Finn, focus,' said Madison. 'I need to find a costume for it in the next half-hour or Chloë is screwed.'

Finn exhaled. 'Let me think. Ah! Heidi Klum went as a worm to her Halloween party. Looked incredible.'

'Did she?' said Madison, putting her phone on speaker as she googled the image. 'I mean, that's an insane costume. But, Finn, it's made of fibreglass and it took months to make.' Her heart sank.

'I'm thinking,' said Finn. 'Oh! Madison! I might have it. I'll be there as soon as I can.'

'Thank you so, so much,' said Madison. 'You are literally a life-saver.'

'Just promise to sneak me in at the back to watch our girl in action,' said Finn.

An hour later, Madison took her place in the seats Jess had saved, and felt she'd aged a hundred years. Finn was standing at the back – he said he might have to dash off before the play had ended – so there was still an empty chair beside Madison. An empty chair, and no word from Rich.

Madison glanced at Jess, who was sitting to her right. But Jess was turned towards her husband, Michael, their hands intertwined, his thumb running reassuringly over hers. Madison couldn't help feeling jealous, and sad. Michael was here, on time, and was looking at Jess with an expression of pure love. She had a husband who still hadn't switched his phone on.

She released a deep, controlled sigh and searched the seating area at the front of the stage, where she saw Jordan chatting animatedly to his mates. She smiled. Her little boy was grow-ing up fast. He'd be in secondary school next year. *Where had the time gone?*

'Is Rich nearly here?' said Jess, turning to her.

'Jess, I'm not even sure he's coming,' said Madison, her voice low. She was sick of pretending right now.

Jess's face creased into concern. 'Oh, hon, of course he's coming. He'll just be held up.'

'I've not heard from him all day.'

'There could be a million different explanations for that,' said Jess. 'He's probably just gone into work mode.' She turned to Michael. 'You do that, don't you, babe? When you're super-busy? You just go into shut-down mode.'

'Yeah, I can do,' said Michael. 'But I wouldn't dare let you be anywhere except the centre of my attention for too long.'

Jess leaned over and kissed his cheek, and Madison felt even more alienated. She wondered how much Jess had told her husband about her issues, and felt uncomfortable.

'We're meant to be taking the kids for dinner after,' she said.

'Well, if for any reason he can't make it, you can come with us,' said Jess. 'The girls would love it.'

The last of the latecomers were shuffling in, and Madison turned to see the teachers shutting the doors to the hall. Finn gave her a thumbs-up, and she smiled back. She glanced down at her phone. They were already five minutes late starting, and nothing from Rich. She turned to the stage. She took some deep breaths to steady herself and focus on the present moment.

Jess nudged her thigh. 'There he is.'

She turned to see Rich moving down the hall, then squeezing past the row of people to take his seat in the empty chair next to Madison. She was struck with two contradicting impulses: first, to rage at him for leaving her without communication to handle a meeting with the teacher, and a potential costume disaster; second, relief. So this *was* what the private appointment on his calendar had been. Maybe she'd been worrying needlessly. The contradiction in her feelings resulted in her hissing

'Where the hell have you been?' at Rich, while reaching out a hand to squeeze his knee.

'Awful day,' he muttered. 'Have you got a phone charger?'

'Yeah,' she muttered back, handing him her portable charger. 'But where were you? I got called in for a meeting about Chloë.'

'Chloë?' he said. 'Is she OK? What's going on?'

'She's fine,' Madison said, dropping her voice as the lights went down. 'Her teacher thinks she's a bit off.'

They were shushed by someone in the row in front of them, and any further conversation was curtailed as the curtain went back to reveal the children standing in the traditional nativity scene. Despite the stress of the day Madison's heart lifted.

The old favourites were there – Mary, Joseph, the shepherds off to the left – but there were definitely some new arrivals at the manger.

'Is the narrator . . .' murmured Jess.

'Yeah, I think they're meant to be Bruno Tonioli from *Strictly*,' whispered Madison, as the child introduced themselves in an attempt at an Italian accent and pirouetted, before announcing the imminent arrival of the Son of God.

There was a packet of nappies, given by one of the wise men, and Jesus's nan, who kept jumping in at the wrong time to give advice on how Baby Jesus should be raised and offer cups of tea.

And then – silence. Murmurings from the audience. Madison craned her neck to see what was going on. The play seemed to have to come to a standstill.

'Behold the arrival of ze Christmas Worm,' said Bruno Tonioli.

Madison craned her neck a bit further, and saw Chloë, wrapped tightly in the single leg of one of Finn's glittery disco leggings, on the floor, slowly scrunching her body to and fro, making her way across the stage.

'Oh. My. God,' said Madison, a ripple of laughter rising in her, mingling with pride.

Rich glanced at her, their eyes caught, and he leaned in to whisper, 'Full method for our girl.'

'She'd give Daniel Day-Lewis a run for his money,' Madison whispered back, and they smiled at each other in a way that made her heart thump.

The rest of the audience had caught on to the arrival of the Christmas Worm, and were craning their necks to see, laughter echoing round the hall.

Finally, Chloë stood upright, with the help of Jesus's nan and a sheep, and gave a beaming grin at the hall.

Rich stood up and whooped. Chloë saw him and smiled even more brightly.

'I am the Christmas Worm,' she announced, every word clear and loud. 'I am here to welcome Baby Jesus and talk about the importance of recycling.' She paused. 'Reduce, reuse, recycle – that's my motto! Even scraps of food can go in the compost to help feed me and my fellow creatures.'

The recycling message was *slightly* off piste, Madison had to admit, but Chloë's charm as the Christmas Worm carried it off, and the audience began to clap when she finished her speech.

There was another ensemble number by the kids, and then it was time for Bruno to bid them all a very merry Christmas and a safe journey home. Everyone in the hall got to their feet and the applause was thunderous. Madison felt a certain warmth in the pit of her stomach that she hadn't even realized was missing – yes, she was feeling Christmassy. She looked at the back of the hall and quickly waved to Finn as he ran out.

'You guys still going to dinner?' Jess asked Madison. Although unsure, Madison nodded.

'No problem. Family time with Rich will be good and we can all catch up soon,' Jess said discreetly.

Madison hugged Jess, waved goodbye to Michael and turned to Rich, who was checking messages. 'So what happened?'

'Total nightmare,' said Rich. 'So many problems with the filming, went to the wrong location twice – not my fault, Amber messed it up – then realized my phone hadn't charged overnight and didn't have a second to find a charger.'

Madison couldn't help raising an eyebrow. 'No one on set had one?' She hated how it sounded, playing detective with what Rich had said. Once trust was broken, it really was broken, she reflected sadly. Now she was examining everything he said for lies.

Rich kissed his teeth.

'How did you manage to post on Instagram if your phone was dead?' she asked. He let out a deep sigh. 'I gave the production assistant my log-in, if you must know. And, yeah, of course someone must've had a charger, but you don't understand what it's like on set these days – everyone is just so busy, flying around, Astrid stressed, and I didn't want to look incompetent.'

Actually, she knew perfectly well what those days were like back from when she'd worked in TV, and also in her present-day life. She was often racing from work to pick up the kids, look after her dad, make dinner, tidy the house. Did he have *no* idea?

Rich was continuing to talk: 'Then I lost track of time, and I managed to charge it for a bit, but the battery just kept dropping off – look, even now when I take it off the portable charger, it drops really fast.'

Madison rubbed her temples. Rich was reminding her of Jordan making excuses as to why he couldn't do his home-work. She faced a choice: she could press the issue, or she could let it go and continue with the good vibes. She chose the latter. 'Sounds really stressful,' she said soothingly. 'Let's forget about it for now, and take the kids out for pizza.'

Rich was staring at his phone. 'Babe, I can't, I'm sorry,' he said.

She hated the way part of her still melted when he called her 'babe', while another part couldn't believe he was heading off. 'What do you mean, you can't? This is their nativity play. They've done amazingly. And I've just had a meeting about Chloë. We need to be there for her. Did you not hear what I said?'

'But she's OK, isn't she?'

'As far as we know,' Madison said. 'But we need to spend time with her.'

'I'll talk to her,' Rich said. 'I promise.'

'But what is *so* important you have to leave now? This is a moment where we need to stick together.'

'I've got a work thing. A meeting.'

Madison couldn't help pulling a face. 'What, at eight o'clock in the evening?'

He sighed.'Don't be like this. You know how it is. All about making contacts, isn't it?'

So now she was expected to understand, was she? And, yeah, she got it – the TV industry *was* about those snatched moments of connection that could make or break your career. But this was something they'd previously have talked about together.

'So who is it?'

'I can't say,' said Rich. He bashed at his phone a bit more. 'This thing isn't working. I need to ring Amber.'

Madison saw Chloë and Jordan making their way towards them, Chloë's face radiant. She switched modes. 'Baby!' she cried. 'You were magnificent!'

'I know, Mum,' said Chloë, now every inch the diva.

Rich reached down and picked her up. 'A shining star,' he said. 'We're so proud of you, Chlo.'

Madison hugged Jordan and watched as her daughter rested her forehead briefly against Rich's. The love between them was beautiful to behold.

'What was your favourite bit?' Chloë was saying.

'Definitely when you came in,' Rich replied. 'It's all about capturing the crowd right from the off and you did it perfectly. And we could hear every word, too. Speak up, get your voice heard. Isn't that right?'

'Yeah, that's right,' said Chloë. 'And do the recycling.'

'Every week,' said Rich.

'Jordan, you made the North Star really shine. I bet you used all the glitter you could find in the school?' Madison said, not wanting him to feel left out. Jordan nodded vigorously. She chuckled, and Rich stretched out his hand towards Jordan for a well-done fist-bump.

'Where we going now?' said Chloë.

Rich looked at Madison, his eyes darting to and fro.

Madison stayed quiet. If Rich was going to head off again, he could explain why for a change.

'Mum's going to take you two little stars for pizza,' he said. 'I've got to—'

'Work?' Chloë interrupted, her face falling.

He nodded as he put her down. 'Sorry, Chlo. But you know

how it is. We have to be professional and work hard. Just like you did up on that stage there.'

Madison watched as a range of emotions flickered across her daughter's face. Disappointment, but also respect for what her dad was saying. They'd instilled the importance of working hard into their kids. But Madison wanted to instil the importance of family, too.

'How about you and me go out for pizza, just the two of us?' said Rich. 'At the weekend?'

Chloë smiled. 'Yeah. I get to choose the toppings? For both pizzas?'

Rich inhaled through his teeth and made a show of considering the questions. 'You drive a hard bargain. But OK.' He offered her his hand, and she shook it.

His phone buzzed. 'Ah, great. Uber's here,' he said. 'Amber's sorted something out today, at least.'

Madison folded her arms across her chest. She felt numb. Her mind was whirring. Was Rich taking her for a fool?

'Jordan, we'll do something too, OK?' Rich said. 'Your choice.' Jordan threw him a brief smile.

Madison bundled the kids out of the hall and into the car, heading for home. She couldn't face a restaurant. She was going to let them order whatever pizza they wanted, and watch whatever they chose on TV.

There was only one person she wanted to talk to.

11

Back at home, with the kids settled in front of a Christmas film, Madison pulled out Savine's business card, turning it over. She felt as if she was going out of her mind. One moment, she imagined Rich lying to her, so smoothly, heading off to meet another woman, explaining how he'd had some family stuff to attend to but was all hers now. Or did she believe what he was telling her – that he was heading off to some business meeting? But, if so, why not be upfront about it? Why not let her in?

She put Savine's number into her phone, her finger hovering over the call button. This felt like a point of no return.

Jordan bounced into the kitchen, making her jump. 'Is there more pizza, Mum?'

'No, baby.'

He groaned. 'I'm starving.'

'I can put some garlic bread into the oven, from the freezer?'

'Yeah!'

She drew herself up and looked at him. 'Yeah? I think you mean . . .?'

'Yes, please, Mum,' Jordan said.

'That's better.'

He bounded out of the room. Madison opened the freezer,

took out the garlic bread and put it into the oven. What would she even say to Savine? What was Savine going to do, exactly? All Madison knew, though, was that Savine had seemed to understand how to handle what she was going through. Savine had told her what to do, and the prospect of her doing so again was appealing when Madison felt so lost. She was almost embarrassed to look to a stranger for answers, though.

A message pinged up on her phone. The restaurant she'd booked, for the four of them. Saying her card would be charged, as they hadn't turned up for the booking. 'Well, thank you very much,' said Madison, anger coursing through her again. It wasn't *her* fault that dinner wasn't on but she was the one paying for it – literally. She jammed her finger on the call button, half hoping, half fearing that Savine would answer.

A few rings, and Madison was about to hang up when she heard, 'Hello, Savine speaking.'

Madison swallowed, unable to form words. 'Uh . . .' she said.

'Who is this?'

'It's . . . From the sauna?'

'Madison!' Savine's voice was now warm and reassuring. 'I wondered if I'd hear from you.'

'Yeah,' squeaked Madison.

'Just speak,' said Savine. 'I'm listening.'

Madison got up and shut the kitchen door, then let the words tumble out: Rich's phone being off all day, him heading off to some mysterious event, without explanation.

'I don't even know where he is,' said Madison. 'And all I really want is . . . like, a spy camera on him. So I can just see. With my own eyes. And that's a horrible thing to think about your husband.'

'I thought it plenty of times,' said Savine, evenly. 'I get it.'

'Look, Savine, this feels crazy. I met you once. And here I am, looking to you for help. For answers.'

'I can't give you answers,' said Savine, her voice full of compassion. 'But I do understand how you feel.'

'What if tonight's the night when I could actually catch him out? Find out what he's doing, who he's meeting? But I can't. Instead I'm stuck at home, looking after the kids – which, by the way, he completely presumed I'd do.' Madison chewed a corner of her nail in frustration.

There was a silence. An idea had begun to form in Madison's head. A terrible idea, she told herself.

Savine cleared her throat. 'Do you know where he's gone?'

'No idea,' said Madison. She imagined the whole of London, how enormous it was, and her husband a little speck somewhere within it.

'Is there any way you can find out?'

Madison sighed. 'His agency organized the transport.'

As soon as the words were out of her mouth, she regretted it. She'd now let slip that Rich was some kind of public figure. 'Savine, shit, I didn't mean to . . . I mean, it's not like he's super-famous, but . . .' She was tongue-tied now.

'It's OK,' said Savine. 'Believe it or not, I'm good at keeping secrets. It doesn't matter who he is.' Madison heard her take a deep breath. 'Look. This is a huge overstep, I know. But if we could find out where he's gone, if it's somewhere accessible, I could go along. Turn up for a bit, see if he's there, who he's with.'

The words hung in the air between them. That had been what Madison had been thinking but hadn't dared to say. Asking a stranger to follow her husband? It was extreme.

'Sorry,' said Savine. 'Ignore that. We can just leave this as a chat between us. In fact, I should probably go—'

'Wait,' said Madison. Her blood was rushing in her ears. 'I had the same thought. It's just it seems so . . .' She couldn't find the right words.

'It crosses a line,' said Savine.

'And I don't know if we can come back from that line,' whispered Madison. 'What if he's completely innocent, and I've got someone to spy on him?'

'I do understand,' said Savine. 'Listen, you're in control of this, OK?'

But the thought was like a genie that had escaped from the bottle. Madison's mind was churning rapidly. Yes, it crossed a line – but Rich had blindsided her, left her second-guessing since he'd gone to his cousin's place. She had no idea when he was coming back. He'd been unavailable when she – and her daughter – needed him. He'd left them in the lurch tonight, with no warning, on what was meant to be a celebratory family dinner out. She would *never* have done that.

'We're doing this,' said Madison, surprised at how firm her voice was.

'You sure?'

'Yes,' said Madison. 'But how do we find out where he's gone? I can't ring up his agent's assistant – there's no way it wouldn't look suspicious.'

'Look, are you OK to tell me his name and agency? Let me do the talking?'

Madison hesitated again. Telling Savine Rich's name made it all real. It also made them potentially exposed. What if Savine *did* see something? What would stop her going public with the story? Madison felt waves of anxiety. But she'd come this far. Maybe Savine wouldn't be able to get any information about where he'd gone.

Her voice quivering, she told Savine Rich's name and his agency.

'I promise you, this goes no further,' said Savine, before ringing off.

Staring around her kitchen, Madison felt as if she was in a parallel universe. Everything looked the same, but something fundamental had shifted. She felt dazed. After what felt like a millisecond but also an eternity, her phone rang.

'OK, I've got the address,' Savine said smoothly. 'It's No Gloss Gallery, out east. Which is quite convenient for me to get to. If that's what you want.'

Madison gave an incredulous laugh. 'But how did you . . .?'

'I'm quite a big deal in PR,' said Savine. 'A little gentle pressure on the receptionist that we needed to courier something to Rich urgently and voila. But listen, we can back out now.'

'No,' said Madison. Her whole body had begun to tremble with adrenaline. 'I'm going to spend the night torturing myself about what Rich is up to, so if there's any way of knowing for sure I'll take it.'

'OK,' said Savine. 'I'll call you when I'm there.'

She rang off. Madison went upstairs, splashed water on her face, then forced herself to look in on the kids, who were just finishing a film. They were slumped together on the sofa, Chloë tucked up against Jordan, clearly delighted to be spending time with her big brother. The scene was so sweet and wholesome that Madison almost wanted to switch off her phone and dive on to the sofa with them, pretending that nothing was happening. Instead she discreetly took a picture, knowing these moments would become rare once Jordan entered secondary school and the stroppy teen years.

'Do you want another film?' she said, trying to sound normal.

'Yeah!' said Chloë.

'You never let us watch two!' said Jordan, delighted at this turn of events.

'It's a special day,' said Madison. 'Don't get used to it.' She returned to the kitchen and poured herself a large glass of wine, nearly spilling it when her phone rang again.

'I'm just heading in,' said Savine's voice. 'I've got my airpods on. So you should be able to hear some of what's going on. I'll keep you updated as much as I can.'

Madison googled the gallery so she could visualize it. It was an ultra-trendy modern building, a squat block of concrete with the name picked out in fluorescent block capitals.

Through her phone, she heard excited chattering, laughter, and she could imagine the scene: everyone queuing to get in, gossip being swapped, the odd cigarette being lit, friends waving to one another. She missed that buzz, she realized. It just added to the pain. Why would Rich go to something like this without telling her – without inviting her? She'd love to go to a gallery launch.

'Just joining the queue,' murmured Savine. 'No sign of him. But he may well be inside already.'

'Name, please?' a deep voice said. Must be a doorman.

Savine gave it confidently.

'Sorry . . . I'm not seeing you on the list . . .'

Savine sighed. 'There's been a mistake, clearly.'

'Rules are, if your name isn't down I can't let you in,' said the bouncer.

'Listen,' said Savine, calmly. 'I don't want to pull a don't-you-know-who-I-am routine but I do run Knight and Day PR. Which represents some pretty big names. So . . .'

'Sorry. No can do.'

Madison held her breath. Surely they weren't about to fall at the first hurdle.

'I'm here to meet Rich Sykers,' Savine said smoothly, 'who will be most disappointed if I'm not there. I presume he *is* on the list?'

'Yeah, he's arrived,' said the bouncer. 'Listen, the queue . . .'

'What's going on?' came a female voice.

'This lady isn't on the list, but wants to come in.'

'Savine Knight, of Knight and Day PR?'

The owner of the female voice gasped. 'Of course. I'm so sorry. Please do go right ahead.'

'Thank you,' purred Savine, and Madison heard gentle background music rise as Savine entered the gallery.

Just who *was* she? Madison typed her surname into Google, and gasped as a raft of awards Savine had won and campaigns she had worked on came up. 'I can't believe you blagged your way in,' said Madison, into the phone.

Savine chuckled. 'It's hardly a royal wedding – hello, I'll take a glass of that, please.'

The sound of Savine swallowing. 'Mmm, real champagne. The good stuff.'

'What's it like in there?'

Madison's phone pinged with a picture message from Savine. She had taken a selfie, posing next to the 'No Gloss Gallery Presents Ebb and Flow' sign. She looked stunning. The forest green velvet suit and layered gold necklace really suited her. Madison instantly zoomed in on the image, barely able to make anyone out, but even she could tell that the room was filled with people in beautiful, vibrant clothes. She zoomed in even more, wondering if one of the pixels was Rich, if one was the other woman. She felt sick to her stomach.

'OK, you've gone quiet,' said Savine calmly. 'Breathe. I know this is bad. But I'm on the case – hel-*lo*. Now, excuse me one moment, a very attractive man has just very deliberately caught my eye . . . '

'What are you doing now?' hissed Madison.

'Moving further into the room, trying not to look like a madwoman by talking to myself. All I need you to do is keep breathing for a bit, OK? And let me handle this.'

Madison tried to focus.

'So,' she heard Savine purr, 'what do you think? Apparently this crashing wave represents the artist's emotions.'

'It's a slight contradiction to the overall theme, actually,' she heard the man reply, his voice playful.

'I'm not so sure,' Savine replied. 'It's the ebbs and flows, right? The ups and downs of life.'

'Well, I guess all art is open to interpretation . . .'

'Another way of saying you can't possibly be wrong?' Savine said, with a chuckle.

'*Touché*,' said the man, and she heard champagne flutes clink. 'So can I put a name to the particular piece of art in front of me?'

'You're lucky you're cute enough to get away with a line like that. I'm Savine.'

'Fair enough! I'm Nick.'

Madison gritted her teeth. Savine seemed to be getting somewhat distracted from the task in hand. She coughed discreetly down the line.

'Nick, I need to circulate a little but maybe we can catch up later,' Savine said.

'I'd like that,' said Nick.

'Madison, I'm on it,' said Savine. 'You can't begrudge me a little fun along the way.'

'I'm dying over here,' said Madison, swigging her wine.

'I know, I know,' said Savine. 'But I'm looking out for him all the time. And trying to get a sense of what kind of event this is.'

'Well?'

'Trendy crowd, very cool. Lots of model types.'

Madison's heart plunged.

'Which means absolutely nothing,' said Savine, quickly. 'Oh. I think I've seen him. Hold on.'

Madison's heart was thumping now. Was Rich's arm round some gorgeous twenty-something?

'Give me a few minutes to scope this out,' murmured Savine. 'I'm going to hang up, but I'll call you back. I'm not going anywhere. I just need to be natural and that's a little hard with you in my ear, no offence.'

She ended the call, and Madison was back in her kitchen, the kids chattering in the living room. It was so surreal. She looked at the walls she'd painted so carefully, the mix of prints she'd bought from a variety of artists – she could never resist – mingled with family photos and drawings the kids had done. Normally this was where she felt safest in the world. But now anxiety coursed through her.

Ten minutes passed, then fifteen.

Madison stared at her phone, willing Savine to call her back.

What was she seeing? Maybe she'd confronted Rich, outing him in front of everyone. Her palms were sweaty at the thought. Had she been right to trust Savine, whom she had met once, in a sauna. She could have trusted Rich, and carried on. Now maybe she'd made everything worse—

The phone rang and she snatched it up.

'OK, I'm in some random corridor, through the fire escape, but I can speak properly here,' said Savine. 'So – he's here.

137

The artist is Cassandra Delaney. Very hip, very trendy. Early twenties.'

Madison felt sick. 'Is he talking to her?'

'He said hello, but it looks like they don't know each other.'

'Really?'

'Yeah. It looked like polite chit-chat and congratulations. Madison, if I'm honest, he just looks a bit . . . lost? He's not really speaking to anyone.'

Madison could imagine him so clearly. He'd have one arm folded around his torso, unconsciously defensive. She knew that Rich came across as self-assured, but there was another side to him: he felt he wasn't good enough. Before kids, when they'd gone out together, she'd often been the one to give him confidence. They'd been a team. She could remember more than one occasion when they'd both been a little daunted at attending some event, but striding in there together, hand in hand, all the nerves had vanished. And they'd had *fun*. So why was he now not wanting to go with her to this kind of thing?

'Hang on, I can see him through these doors . . .' said Savine. 'He's looking round – I don't know, looks like he's trying to find someone to talk to.'

'Or looking for someone?' said Madison, her heart sinking.

'Maybe . . .' said Savine.

There was a pinging sound.

'Battery's low,' said Savine.

What was it with today and technology? Madison thought grimly.

'Hang on, it looks like he's going.' She heard Savine push her way through the doors, the sound of the crowd rising again. It seemed the night was only now getting going.

'Yeah, he's heading out the front,' said Savine, then, 'Oh, hello, you!'

At that point, the line cut out completely, and Madison was left holding her phone and staring blankly at the screen.

Even though she knew she was torturing herself, she went to Cassandra's Instagram and began flicking through the images. They were mostly of her artworks, which were principally collage pieces, composed of photos, stencilled with different designs and slogans. There were a few shots of the artist, her arms covered with random tattoos, although she mostly kept her face partly concealed. She had an attractive, clean look, her bright auburn hair scraped back, which accentuated her green eyes.

'She's not really Rich's type,' she murmured. Still, she couldn't stop herself scrolling further back through Cassandra's Instagram. She googled her, and found a brief interview with her, which heralded her as a new talent of a generation. She scanned it, not even knowing what she was looking for – did she expect Cassandra to state she was having an affair with a married man? But *why* was Rich there? And why hadn't he been upfront about it?

Then she looked at the gallery Instagram page. The exhibition opened properly at the weekend, but there was an invitation to come for private viewings, by appointment only. Madison hesitated briefly, then typed a message: *Big fan of Cassandra's work and represent a collector. Wonder if I could come by tomorrow?*

She couldn't believe her audacity. She doubted they'd reply, but a message popped up almost instantly: *Absolutely – 11 a.m.?*

Holding her breath, she messaged back to confirm the appointment. She wasn't sure what she expected to find, but if there was any chance to find out more about what was going on, she'd take it. Yes, Savine had helped her tonight, but the more she could take matters into her own hands, the better.

She looked up at the clock in the kitchen. It was late, way past the kids' bedtime. She told herself to switch back into Mum mode, but she needed five minutes to reflect on everything that had happened. She'd asked Savine – a stranger – to follow Rich. She still wasn't sure what he was doing there, or who he'd been expecting to meet at the gallery, or why it had been so important to go there. She felt the emotional distance between them widen even further – or had she always experienced these blank spaces with him, just not noticed them before? She thought of Savine, her successful career, how confident she'd been blagging her way into the gallery and enjoying flirting with that guy. Madison felt as if she was lost in a dark wood, with different paths before her. There was the route that led to a return to normal. That was the only one she'd been able to see before. But now, somehow, she could see a path that looked more like Savine's.

Questions flashed across her mind: what *would* Madison be like if she was single? Or if she could devote time and effort to her career? What would her life be like if she had Savine's confidence? The uncertainty was killing her. She just hoped she could find her way through the forest soon.

She steadied herself, and went into the living room, where the kids were sprawled on the sofa, watching the film, Chloë half nodding off, her Christmas Worm costume lying crumpled beside her.

Now it was Madison's turn to switch off her phone. She was going to be with her kids, in this room. Whatever else was happening in her life didn't matter as long as she was with them. 'Room for your mum?' she said.

The kids moved apart and she sat between them. Chloë put her head into her lap and Jordan nestled against her other arm.

'You know I love you, guys?' Madison said.

They tore their eyes from the screen to look at her. 'Yeah, Mum,' said Jordan. 'We love you too.'

12

Madison shivered as she stood outside the art gallery in the cold December air. She'd dropped the kids at school, then headed home to change into a trendy outfit that screamed, 'I buy artwork for important clients and definitely belong in this gallery'. She'd settled on a black polo neck, baggy black trousers and colourful trainers, topped with a faux-fur dark pink coat. After a little more faffing while she chose her jewellery, she'd caught the Overground to East London, then threaded through the streets to get there.

Despite her nerves, she wondered when she'd last been somewhere new. Smiling, she texted Ladene. *Remember our random neighbourhood adventures?*

Ummm, YES, replied Ladene.

When they were teenagers, and on into their twenties, they'd played a game of shutting their eyes and whirling their fingers round a tube map until one of them shouted, 'Stop!' Then they had to go to that neighbourhood and explore it for a day. That was well before smartphones, Madison thought wryly. They'd just turned up and begun walking around, often having to ask strangers for directions as to how to get back to the tube. Occasionally, it had been a total washout – Acton in pouring rain hadn't been much fun – no offence, Acton – but more often, they'd had amazing adventures in their own home city, stumbling across interesting cafés and shops, random museums and quirky streets.

I miss those days, Madison typed back, feeling wistful. Life was simpler then.

Lol, babe, those days can literally be here again tomorrow, Ladene wrote back. *Next time you've got a kid-free few hours, message me and we'll switch our phones off and have an old-school adventure.*

If only it was that simple, Madison thought.

Another voice piped up in her head. Why *couldn't* it be that simple? Yes, they might have to end the adventure after a few hours rather than allowing it to move on into the evening, or even, as it had on one memorable occasion, end at dawn on Primrose Hill, but what was stopping her? The idea was exciting, but made her feel anxious and, anyway, she was by the art gallery now.

It looked shut. She peered through the door and spotted a glum-looking guy on Reception. *Very much* not *Cassandra*, thought Madison. What had she been hoping for? To look into the woman's eyes and see the answer to the mystery of why her husband had walked out? This was daft. She was about to turn and go when the guy on Reception noticed her. He rose slowly to his feet and came to unlock the door.

'Hey,' he said, his voice slow and dull. He was very pale, with a kind of vampire air, thought Madison. 'Here to see the exhibition, right?'

'Yeah,' said Madison.

He ushered her in and stared at her in silence. Was he always like this or had he just had a massive night previously?

'Good time last night?' ventured Madison.

He shuddered. 'Not my thing. I don't really like people.' He picked up a book and waved her into the main room of the gallery. 'Exhibition is through there.'

Madison walked into the middle of the empty room. It was almost eerily quiet, the walls painted pure white, the floor polished concrete. How different from last night, she thought. She'd not heard from Savine that morning and felt uneasy: had she been wrong to trust her? Had Savine seen Rich do something she couldn't bear to tell Madison? Or was there simply nothing to report? More than anything, she realized what uncharted territory she was in: a stranger knowing the most intimate, fearful details of what she was presently going through. It was lonely.

Madison stared at the art on the walls. She recognized a few images from Instagram. They left her cold. She stood in front of one collage, a composite of Minnie Mouse and *Mona Lisa*, with squares of neon scattered across it. Each to their own, but the pictures seemed to have been made to provoke, as opposed to saying something with emotion behind them.

Madison heard footsteps and turned to see Cassandra making her way across the gallery. 'Hey,' she said.

Madison felt adrenaline go through her. Cassandra was tiny in real life, with auburn hair that fell all the way down her back. Her eyes stood out against her hair colour, and there were marked shadows beneath them. Madison wondered if she'd literally just got Cassandra up after her big night. In the photos of her online, she'd been dressed in the edgiest fashion – Madison had felt old when she contemplated the photos in which Cassandra looked as if she'd been dragged through a hedge backwards, then wrapped in mesh – but today she was dressed simply in black cargo pants and a black hoodie. Feeling judgy, she reminded herself that she herself hadn't looked like she did now two hours ago.

'Thanks for letting me come by,' said Madison.

'No worries,' said Cassandra, pulling her phone out of her pocket. 'Shit – one moment. My dad.' She answered the phone in Spanish, and began to talk fluently, turning away from Madison.

Madison stared again at the works on the walls and tried to dredge up a positive opinion that would sound sincere.

Cassandra hung up.

'You speak Spanish?' said Madison, opting to state the obvious and hopefully buy some more time.

'My dad's from Spain,' said Cassandra. She shifted her weight to one side and wrapped her arms around herself. 'So what do you think of the art?'

'It's really . . . bold,' said Madison. 'Colourful. What would you say the inspiration is behind this one?' *If in doubt, ask a question.* She gestured to the image of Minnie and the *Mona Lisa.*

Cassandra shrugged. 'It's a statement on icons. Modern and classic. Is there a difference?' Her voice was flat.

'Great to know,' said Madison, evenly. She pointed at an image of lips made up of tiny photographs of other lips. 'And this one?'

Cassandra blew out air. 'I guess it's about modern beauty standards. Everyone having to look the same.'

Madison couldn't resist. 'Did it take absolutely ages to find all the images of lips?'

Cassandra smiled – a real smile. 'Yeah, and even longer to arrange them all. I was seeing lips every time I closed my eyes.'

Madison laughed.

'You know, in Spain we're a lot more direct,' said Cassandra. 'Tell me. What do you really think?'

Madison took a deep breath. She'd got used to telling people what they wanted to hear, particularly at work with Jenson, but maybe also with Rich. She poured so much energy into supporting him, into cheerleading him. When he was at home, they tended to watch his choice – he said his downtime was so rare that he really wanted to make use of it to see the films he loved, which often meant repeats of classic action films. She'd always gone along with it, thinking that a repeat viewing could be cosy, but now she was starting to see it differently. Why wasn't he putting some effort into them watching something new together? Why couldn't he watch something that might be more to her taste? When had he last asked her what she really thought? Now Cassandra was standing in front of her, eyebrow raised, expecting an honest opinion.

Madison cleared her throat. 'You know, everyone has their own individual taste. But I just don't think these are my cup of tea. They're very cool, I can see that, but I'm not sure I see much . . . personality in them, or something.' Had she really said that? She shut her eyes in mortification.

'Bravo,' said Cassandra, softly. 'Finally, someone who is going to tell me the truth.'

Madison opened her eyes and stared at her. 'Excuse me?'

'I don't like these much either.' Cassandra sighed. 'But I was advised to make this kind of stuff. As you say, it's cool.' She shrugged. 'It sells. Bankers like to have it in their apartments, apparently. So the gallery likes that as they make a sale. And people keep telling me it's amazing, that I should do more like this. Even my partner! Who is really old enough to know better.'

Older. Partner.

Madison's thoughts raced. Could she be talking about Rich? 'So your partner likes this kind of stuff?'

She sighed. 'My partner likes to feel cool. Maybe it's the age gap. For me, I don't give a shit.'

Likes to feel cool – well, that was Rich, wasn't it? Image-conscious, sometimes to a fault.

'How long have you been together?'

Madison thought that Cassandra looked taken aback by the blunt question. She had to be more careful.

'Only a few months,' said Cassandra. 'But I like to keep my personal life personal. I'm sure you understand.'

Madison knew she had to back off, but it was hard to ignore the small voice in her head saying, *She's beautiful, intelligent and influential. Rich would like her.*

'I was enjoying hearing your opinion about the collection,' said Cassandra. 'Tell me, what kind of thing do you like? What was the last exhibition you went to that was really amazing?'

To her mortification, she could barely remember an exhibition she had been to recently. 'I've not been to anything much for ages,' she said slowly. 'Kids. Family life.'

Cassandra looked perturbed. 'But surely you must see loads of art in your line of work?'

Madison scrambled to recover her back story. 'Oh, yes, of course – but it's so hard seeing *all* the things you want to. I loved Alvaro Barrington's exhibition at Tate Britain, which pays homage to the women who shaped him. His use of colours, paint and mixed media just provides so much depth and emits so much emotion that . . .' Madison trailed off, feeling guilty for talking so passionately about someone else's work.

'I totally know what you mean,' said Cassandra, her eyes

flashing. 'I love that! You really feel so alive, don't you, so many emotions?'

'Yeah, that's it,' said Madison. 'And I love the feeling that someone else knows just how you feel.'

'Totally,' said Cassandra. 'I always liked that in the art galleries in Spain. My dad took me a lot when I was little. I'd look at all the old paintings, and think, *Those people aren't so different from me.*'

The two women stopped talking, and smiled at each other.

'I have to say, you're a lot more fun to talk to than the usual art people who come here,' said Cassandra. 'They look for five minutes and want to know if I think the value will increase. Tell me, who is it you work for again?'

Shit.

The moment she'd been dreading. She couldn't lie. Cassandra had almost detected her once before and now her luck had run out. 'I have to confess. I don't work in art. I work as a design assistant for a terrible hotel chain.' Madison twisted her hands awkwardly. 'But I'd love to get out of that and back doing something more creative.'

She winced as she waited for Cassandra's response. The artist was giving nothing away, bar a raised eyebrow.

'So you came here for . . . inspiration?'

Madison considered the question. She wasn't going to tell the truth: that she came because she suspected her husband was cheating on her, and she'd not heard from the friend she sent to spy on him since the night before. She could almost laugh at how crazy that sounded – almost. But she *had* been inspired. When she and Cassandra had been talking about Alvaro Barrington, she had felt a spark that had been missing for ages. Was that inspiration?

'Yeah. Yeah, I guess so,' Madison said. 'When I said about not seeing much art, because of kids, that was true. So I suppose I just wanted to pretend I was part of this world.'

'Well, I'm pretty flattered,' said Cassandra. 'And if these don't inspire you, maybe I could show you some of what I really want to be working on.' Madison could tell from her expression that this was what really mattered to her. 'No one knows,' Cassandra added.

'I'd be honoured.'

Biting her lip nervously, Cassandra pulled out her phone. 'OK, so I've just got a few photos, but I've been painting these.'

Madison peered at the phone. They were the most beautiful paintings of women of all shapes and sizes, dissolving into water. Some were in seascapes, some in rivers, one in a swimming pool. Some were melancholy and still; in others the water was clearly moving in waves and currents. The swimming-pool painting popped with bright colours, making it slightly otherworldly.

'I *love* these,' gasped Madison. 'They're amazing!'

Cassandra beamed. 'Really?'

'Really,' said Madison. 'Tell me about them.'

'I wanted to celebrate women in all our complexity,' said Cassandra. 'The ways that we flow and change. The way we move in currents all of our own.'

Madison felt tingles go up her spine. 'That's beautiful.'

'But I worry that no one will be interested,' she said. 'And they're so different from this' – she indicated the gallery – 'just when I'm starting to make a name for myself. To make some money, too,' she added.

Madison nodded. She knew how important that side of things was. It took her a moment to realize that the younger woman was really looking for her advice. She considered her answer. 'The thing is, life always involves compromise. But you should do something where you feel that you *don't* make any compromise. Something that's just for you. So keep doing these. It doesn't matter if everyone hates them. Or if you never show them to anyone else. But make sure you have something that's just yours.'

Cassandra's eyes lit up. 'Ah! She's here!'

Madison turned to see a woman with short pink hair and round spectacles making her way across the gallery towards them. Cassandra took the other woman's hand, drawing her close. 'Let me introduce Alice, my partner.'

'Very pleased indeed to meet you,' said Madison. *Very, very pleased indeed.*

She turned to Cassandra, conscious that she didn't want to take up any more of her time. 'It was lovely meeting you, and thank you so much for showing me your real work. I'm following you now, so let's stay in touch.' She smiled and waved goodbye to both women.

Outside she inhaled deeply. So Cassandra's partner was a woman. There was no way Rich was having an affair with her, then. Relief coursed through her. Maybe he *had* been there for work reasons, scoping out something new and trendy. That would be just like Rich. Or maybe he had been expecting to meet someone there, a producer perhaps, who hadn't shown up, and that was why he'd headed off without seeming to know anyone.

She glanced at her watch. It was only about lunchtime. The advice she'd given to Cassandra was swirling in her head. That you should have *something* in your life that was yours. Something you could do exactly as you wanted. It didn't matter how small it was – Madison remembered her mum getting back in on Sunday after church and insisting she was going to have exactly one hour to herself, not wishing to be disturbed, listening to reggae, reading a book, applying a fresh coat of nail polish before she finished off dinner. As much as she loved the rest of her life with the family, she needed that hour to be just hers. Madison understood, perhaps more than she ever had before. 'So start now,' she muttered.

She walked away from the gallery, then found herself wandering down Brick Lane. She remembered days out there with Ladene, trying on vintage clothes, giggling at the wild outfits they'd put on, scoffing a bagel, heading into the record shop where Ladene would flick through all the new releases and insist on in-depth chats with whoever was working there.

Hungry, she bought a salmon and cream-cheese bagel, like old times, from the 24/7 bakery, and strolled along the street, peering in at the windows of clothes shops, noticing what looked the same and some very striking differences – a trendy prison-themed cocktail bar, an independent bookshop, an old brewery that now held a variety of pop-up stalls and food trucks.

She took a turn down the side streets and found herself in front of the most beautiful mural – a Black woman, hair cut in a soft bob, loose curls flowing, chin raised, gazing with hope and dignity into the distance. Madison stared at it for a long time. She took a photo of it and sent it to Ladene. *Prize if you can guess where I am.*

Babe, that is too easy! Ladene typed back. *Somewhere in Brick Lane.*

You know that just from this mural?

That's by Dreph, Ladene typed back. *You're only in one of the most famous places for street art in the world* 😊 *Take a look around you – so much amazing stuff!*

Trust Ladene to be all over it, thought Madison, but she felt a buzz of excitement as she walked around and took in the different murals – some stunning, realistic portraits like the one by Dreph, others more stylized and abstract. She pulled out her phone and began taking photos, sometimes of the whole piece, sometimes of close-up details she liked: a particular texture or colour combo that spoke to her, sometimes not even of the image itself, but of an interesting other detail – a crack in a wall that created a dramatic shape, the overlay of different posters, some half scraped off, new ones pasted on top, forming a kind of history of what had been going on.

Madison lost track of time. For the first time in ages, she wasn't thinking of anyone else. She was completely absorbed in what she was looking at.

Her phone rang.

Jess.

'Hey, babe,' she answered. 'Everything OK?'

'Hon, I'm here with the kids,' Jess said. 'I was going to ask *you* if everything's OK.'

'The kids?' said Madison. She glanced at her watch. 'But it's after-school club today.'

'It finished last week,' said Jess. 'But it's OK, I'm in the playground with them, won't take you too long to get here, will it?'

Madison swore under her breath. 'It will. I'm in East London.'

'Way over there?' Jess said, and Madison wondered if she heard disapproval in her voice.

'Look, I know it's a massive favour, but could you possibly take them back to yours? I'll be there within the hour.'

'Uh . . .' said Jess, hesitating.

'Or I can ring Rich,' said Madison, a little surprised by Jess's hesitation. 'He might be able to get there quicker.'

'No, don't worry, it's fine. I'll take them back to mine.'

Just like that, it began to rain, dampening her spirits further. Madison dashed for the Overground and managed to catch the next train. What was she playing at? If you'd told her a month ago that she would have sent a woman she'd met in a sauna to spy on her husband at an art gallery, then gone along to meet the artist herself, and had ended up wandering in Brick Lane instead of getting to her kids on time, she would have been appalled. So why didn't she feel worse? She felt guilty about leaving the kids and making the mistake about after-school club. But wandering in those streets, looking at the art, she'd felt like herself. And was she meant to feel guilty about that?

13

Arriving at the nearest station to Jess about forty minutes later, Madison walked briskly to her door. She rang the bell, and Jess answered.

'I'm so sorry,' said Madison. She felt more flustered now that she was faced with Jess looking so calm and perfect. She stepped inside, kicking off her shoes, and noticed Jess's immaculate décor had been upgraded again since she'd last been here – the new herringbone polished floorboards in the hallway, the living room a beautiful symphony of cream and taupe. The large, close-up black-and-white photo of Jess and her husband on their wedding day, their faces pressed together, looking like film stars, had always been there, but now it felt like a stark reminder that Madison was no longer in a loved-up state. She looked at Jess's Christmas tree, which was entirely done in white lights with pretty snowflakes, and an angel at the top.

'They're just finishing off a film,' said Jess. 'Come into the kitchen for a second?'

Madison followed her through.

Jess shut the door. 'What's going on, hon?' said Jess. 'It's not like you to leave the kids stranded.'

Madison pressed her lips together. She was already on the defensive. Yes, it had been a slip-up. But she could do without Jess's saintly vibe right now. 'Thank you so much for stepping in,' she said, and meant every word. 'You know how much I appreciate your support.'

'I feel like something's off,' said Jess. 'I thought it was all OK with Rich again. When he turned up at the nativity play, everything seemed good.'

Madison looked at her best friend, whose eyes were wide and imploring. She could feel how much Jess wanted things to be OK, wanted things to be back to normal – the two couples arranging hang-outs, the kids playing together. Frustration rose in her. It was as if Jess didn't want to know what a massive effect Rich leaving had had on her, how much she'd had to bottle up and endure just to keep functioning. And it still wasn't over. The longer Rich was away, the more it would take to repair their relationship. What he had done couldn't just be brushed under the carpet. It couldn't be neatly erased under the guise of Rich being a man who was stressed. That simply wasn't going to be enough for Madison, not now. She'd been so eager in the past to make excuses for him, but now she was starting to see things from her own side. Why couldn't Jess do the same?

'I don't know,' said Madison. 'Yeah, it was nice at the play, after he hadn't been in touch with me all day. Then he headed off instead of coming for pizza with us, to some random work event that he'd told me nothing about. And . . .' Madison wondered whether to confide in Jess or not. She hated the amount of secrecy that the situation was generating. It wasn't like her to keep things from the people she loved. 'Look, I know this sounds mad, but I met this woman the other week, and she's been in the same situation. Last night I got her to follow Rich to this art gallery he was going to, some fancy exhibition, but she thought there wasn't anything dodgy going on—'

Jess raised a hand to her mouth in shock. 'Madison, *stop*. What are you telling me? You had Rich *followed*?' She was staring at Madison as if she didn't know her.

'I know how it sounds—'

'Do you, Madison?' Jess rubbed her temples. She'd always done that when she was upset. 'Because it sounds pretty . . .'

'Do not say crazy,' said Madison, her voice wobbling. 'You don't know how this feels.' She had to bite her tongue not to say more. It was OK for Jess, who had the perfect husband, the perfect relationship, but Madison was watching her life crumble.

'But you need to *trust* him, not make things worse by doing stuff like having him followed,' said Jess, her voice insistent.

'What would you do?' Madison retorted. 'Literally, think about it. Wouldn't you want to find out, for sure?'

'I'd try to talk to him,' said Jess.

'Like I haven't? Like he hasn't just cut me off? If Michael started acting *so* weirdly, what would you do? Just sit back and take it, like you seem to be expecting me to do? Wait around till he decides he can be bothered to come home?'

'Don't deflect—'

The kitchen door was pushed open and they jumped.

'Mum, Sienna won't let me have a go,' said Chloë, her voice wobbly.

'A go at what?' said Madison, forcing herself to keep her tone soft.

She and Jess glanced at each other. One thing was agreed between them in that glance: they kept this away from the kids.

'On the Switch,' moaned Chloë.

Jess frowned and got up. 'The rule is one turn each. Sienna knows that.' She glanced at Madison. 'I'll have a word.'

'Come on, Chlo, let's get rounded up and go home.' Madison was feeling wrung out by the conversation with Jess. They'd nearly stepped into a major argument, when all she wanted was understanding.

Madison shooed Chloë back into the hallway and instructed her to put her shoes on. Jordan emerged from the living room and got into his coat.

'Come and say goodbye,' Jess said to her daughter, and Madison heard a sulky 'No' from the living room.

'It's OK, Jess,' she said wearily. 'You helped me out by having them.'

Jess nodded and pressed her lips together. 'I'm sorry,' she said. 'For not getting it. It's just hard knowing the right thing to say.'

'Yeah,' said Madison.

'Just . . . focus on what else is going on for you, OK? I still believe this is going to come right.' Jess opened her arms. 'Come here.'

Madison hugged her. She felt exhausted. Life had been so safe and stable, and suddenly she was being blown this way and that.

'You OK, Chloë?' said Jordan, as they walked home. It was unusual that he'd show brotherly support so overtly. Her kids loved one another but, like any siblings, they also squabbled and competed with each other, each day a tumultuous mix of love and rivalry.

Her daughter sniffed.

'Why do you ask?' said Madison.

'Sienna was being a cow to her,' said Jordan.

'Don't use that language,' said Madison, as a reflex. Then, 'Really?'

Chloë nodded. 'It's OK, though. I don't want to make a fuss.'

'It's not a fuss to speak up if someone's being like that to you,' said Madison. She'd have to talk to Jess if things continued like this after Christmas.

To her surprise, as they arrived at home, the lights were already on. She opened the door. Rich was sitting in the kitchen. Her stomach plunged. She had not been expecting him. And she wasn't particularly sure she wanted to see him, especially as he'd given her no notice that he was going to drop in.

'Hey,' he said, the kids running to greet him. 'Thought I'd come round and we could order that pizza we didn't get last night.'

Madison stayed silent. This was all she'd wanted yesterday: a family treat. And now he wanted to drop by and be the fun dad for the kids when it suited him? 'They had pizza last night,' she said, her voice cold.

'I know, but I wasn't there,' Rich said.

Your decision, thought Madison, but she didn't voice it.

'I want pizza again,' announced Chloë, confidently.

Now she was in an impossible position. Refuse, and undermine Rich in front of the kids, plus look like a spoilsport. Agree, and it was like nothing had happened.

'Same as always?' he asked her, pulling out his phone.

She was hungry, and she was tired, and she was confused. The kids were looking at her expectantly. 'Sure,' she said.

He finished tapping into his phone and leaned towards her. 'Sorry about last night. I had to go to a work thing.'

'Where was it?'

'This gallery out in East London.'

So, he was telling her the truth about that. She felt tired to her bones, too exhausted to ask any more questions. She felt caught between two voices in her head: the one that Savine encouraged, to take action, trust no one and find out everything. And Jess's voice, which urged her to trust in her marriage. She was losing her own voice. 'Cool,' she said.

'Hopefully there'll be news on the TV show soon,' said Rich.

'That's great,' said Madison, the words slipping out automatically. Then she gathered herself. 'So who exactly are you talking to? What's on offer?'

Rich lifted his hand and wobbled it to and fro, indicating that things were precarious. 'I'll have firm news soon,' he said.

A few weeks ago, Madison would have been excited but now she just felt excluded.

She rubbed her eyes.

'Tired?' Rich said.

'Yeah.'

'I know how that feels,' he said, with a smile.

She regarded him, the husband who now felt like a stranger. 'I was in East London today,' she said suddenly. She wanted to see how he'd respond.

He raised an eyebrow. 'How come?'

She shrugged. 'I fancied an adventure.'

'That's cool,' said Rich, as his phone pinged. 'Pizza's nearly here. That was quick.'

Their conversation felt so thin, Madison thought. He hadn't asked her anything more. She'd wondered if he would open up the conversation, ask where specifically, and what she'd done – but no. She was normally talkative and found it easy to share, but now that she wasn't, he hadn't even noticed the difference.

They pulled out plates and napkins, working in tandem. The doorbell rang and she heard Rich take the pizzas and hand over a tip. They called the kids to the table – she wasn't about to let them have two nights in a row in front of the TV – and dug into the pizzas.

'Can we go ice skating again?' said Jordan, twisting a string of cheese round his fingers and gobbling it. 'With those free tickets they gave us?'

'Yeah!' said Chloë. 'This weekend?'

Rich chewed a piece of pizza and swallowed. 'We can definitely go again. Not sure about this weekend. Chlo, tell me exactly how it felt being the Christmas Worm. Were you nervous before you went on?'

'Not at all,' Chloë said confidently.

Madison wasn't sure how to take that. Was Chloë pretending to be more OK than she was, or was she simply rewriting what had happened, like so many kids did?

'Good to hear,' said Rich. He turned to Jordan and asked him what he wanted for Christmas. He was so good at chatting to the kids, so good at entering their worlds and getting them to engage, thought Madison. Her own dad had always been loving, but he was from a different generation. He showed his love through actions – she wouldn't have had a heart-to-heart with him.

Leaving her to clear away the pile of pizza crusts and empty boxes, Rich got up and began putting the kids to bed. Once they were tucked up, he padded downstairs.

'Guess you'll be heading back to Marvin's, then,' Madison said. She was keeping her voice cool. She was over trying to lure him home. But her frostiness seemed to be having the opposite effect.

He looked at her, then at his feet. 'I thought maybe we could watch a film or something.'

'Uh, we can,' said Madison, slowly. Her head was spinning. Rich's behaviour was so disorienting. He'd left them last night without explanation, and now he seemed to want to spend time with the kids, with *her* again, like nothing had changed. She wasn't sure what to do. Maybe he was trying to find the right way to open up to her about whatever had been going on. Maybe this was his way of trying. She'd give him a chance.

They went into the living room and sat on the sofa – one at either end. So things weren't back to normal, then. Normally they would snuggle up, or Madison would lie down and stretch out her legs over his.

Rich flicked on the TV and headed to Netflix, scrolling through action films. 'Oh, amazing, they've got the very first *Mission: Impossible*,' he said. 'Shall we watch that?'

'Can do,' said Madison, breezily. She didn't care what he selected. She just wanted to talk, to have time together. She was flicking through the photos she'd taken and felt a flicker of excitement. 'Look at these. Some stuff I saw today.'

He glanced at her phone. 'Graffiti, cool.'

'Look at this one. It's such an incredible mural, the detail on this woman's eye . . .' She showed him her favourite piece.

'Yeah, that's lovely,' said Rich, his eyes glancing back at the TV.

She gave up. It was making her feel worse trying to share this with him when he clearly wasn't interested. She opted for the comfort of familiarity and let him play the film. She'd been hoping he would begin chatting over it – sometimes they both liked to have the TV on in the background and talk through it – but he was silent. What was he thinking? He couldn't possibly be thinking this was normal. The atmosphere between them was so awkward.

Halfway through, he paused it and got up to make a snack.

Madison's phone pinged. A voice note, from an unknown number. She pressed play.

Madison, it's Savine, I am SO sorry to leave you hanging. Her voice was raspy. *Turns out, I had quite a fun night with that guy Nick, but then managed to lose my phone and I only just got a replacement sorted. I know, I'm fifty going on fifteen, but at least it was fun.*

Madison smiled. At least someone was having fun.

Listen, I need to tell you something else.

This was less fun.

I don't think anything was going on between Rich and anyone there. But I saw him leave – he got an Uber, and when it drove away, this other car started up and followed it. There was a woman driving. I couldn't see her clearly, though. Maybe I'm wrong, but there was just something about the way she started the car and drove off straight after him that felt like they'd arranged it.

Madison felt bile rise in her throat.

The message from Savine continued.

It's a distinctive car. White SUV. The number plate is personalized: it's MOM311. I don't want to stir the pot but, yeah, my spidey senses were tingling. Message me if you need me and let's see each other soon, either way.

Rich pushed open the door and sat down with a cheese toastie on a plate. 'Sorry, babe, do you want any of this?' he said. 'I should have asked. Just normally you never want more after a pizza.'

162

'Nah,' said Madison. Her stomach was in knots. Just when she'd been relaxing slightly, her mind was racing again. To fill the silence, she pressed play and tried to concentrate on the explosions onscreen.

At one point, Madison knocked the empty plate to the floor, where it landed softly on the carpet. 'You almost jumped out of your skin!' Rich said.

'It's the film,' said Madison, but it wasn't – her body was full of adrenaline once more.

'Yeah, it's a good one,' Rich said, his eyes glued to the TV. If anything, he seemed *more* relaxed tonight than he had for weeks. Why? Because he'd had an amazing night with his other woman? Because he'd met her to call it off and decided he wanted to return to Madison after all? Who was she, this woman in the white SUV with MOM311 as a personalized plate?

After the film had finished, he stretched out his arms and yawned. 'I need to get to bed. I'm up early,' he said.

'You OK to get the kids after school tomorrow?'

'Yeah. I can take them in if you like.'

Madison narrowed her eyes.

'I mean, if I stay here,' Rich said.

Madison laced her fingers together. The silence hung in the air between them. Wasn't this the moment she'd craved, Rich wanting to come home, all of them under the same roof once more?

'It's your home,' said Madison, but suddenly those words didn't feel true. And she definitely didn't want to sleep with Rich beside her. She looked for an excuse. 'I feel a bit like I'm coming down with something.'

He looked at her as if he was unsure what she meant.

'I'd just hate for you to catch anything when work's so busy.'

'Oh. I can stay on the sofabed. I was thinking . . . anyway . . .'

She had no idea what he had been thinking, but she was relieved that they wouldn't be sharing a bed, and wondered if he felt that, too, or disappointment.

She lingered downstairs as he did his teeth, wondering why he'd decided to stay now. The sofabed was in the little room they used as a makeshift office-cum-dumping ground – the one he'd once said he'd turn into Jordan's bedroom, but still hadn't got round to sorting. She heard him pull it out and settle into it.

Madison padded upstairs and showered before getting into bed and staring at the ceiling. Sleep would not come. The sound of Rich's snores emerged from the other room, which irritated her. He had caused all this worry, yet was out like a light. She listened to Savine's message again. She googled the number plate MOM311. Nothing came up. She researched if you could trace the owner of a car just from the number plate, but you couldn't – not unless you had 'reasonable cause', like the car being involved in an accident. Or your husband might be cheating on you with the car's owner, Madison added.

As the minutes rolled past and she felt even more awake, she got up and went stealthily back downstairs. In the kitchen, Rich had left his plate on the side. She stacked it in the dishwasher. His coat was draped over the back of one of the kitchen chairs. She lifted it up, and then on to a coat hook in the hallway.

Check his pockets, a voice said in her head.

She breathed in and out calmly. She hated this. She hated the snooping and the spying. But he was leaving her with no choice.

She slipped a hand inside his coat pocket, feeling around. Nothing in that one, except a chocolate wrapper. Or in the other. Then she looked in the inside pocket. There was a single white appointment card. The front was printed with an address in Central London: Flat 21, 90 Ryder Street. On the back, a date: 20th December, 7 p.m. Underlined. So here was the private appointment. Another clue. Using her own phone, Madison took a photo of the address, and hid the image in a private folder.

A mysterious car, and an address for the twentieth. She couldn't rest until she knew the explanations behind both.

14

'Maddy, would you *please* try to remain alert at all times? Just because it's nearly Christmas doesn't mean you haven't got work to do!'

Madison jerked upright as Jenson's words cut through her. Everyone else around the boardroom table tittered. She was exhausted. The adrenaline of the last few days was getting to her. She'd barely slept a wink, wondering what the card meant. She would go that lunchtime and see, she decided. Maybe the mysterious car would be parked outside.

'Sorry,' she mumbled.

'It's the extremely important agenda point of *where* we source the mince pies,' Jenson said, scowling.

'That is important,' agreed Madison.

Nathan gave her a sideways glance.

'What?' she whispered to him. 'I love mince pies.'

'Fortnum & Mason for selected people,' decided Jenson. 'And, Maddy, whatever you can find for the rest.'

'You OK?' said Nathan, as they filed out.

'Tired,' Madison admitted.

Nathan smiled sympathetically. 'Fancy strolling out for a sandwich in a bit?'

'Sure,' said Madison. As much as she liked talking to Nathan, though, she wanted to sneak off and find the mysterious Ryder Street.

They wandered to a local shop and queued. Nathan ordered a bagel.

'Hate to say it, but that doesn't look nearly as good as the one I had yesterday,' Madison said.

Nathan took a bite. 'Hmm, it's OK. Where was the wonder-bagel, then?'

'Brick Lane.'

'I love it round there.'

'I hadn't been in literally years,' said Madison. 'But it was amazing. The vibe of it, the street art too.'

'Yeah!' said Nathan, his face lighting up. 'So many different styles of expression. I love it. It's like this amazing free art gallery that anyone can go to.'

'I found something I really loved,' she said, pulling out her phone and showing him the picture, feeling oddly self-conscious as she did so.

'Dreph,' said Nathan.

Madison groaned. 'Does everyone in the world know who this person is, apart from me? Am I that uncool?'

He laughed. 'Stop fishing for compliments! I love the project he did, that's all.'

'What project?'

'He did a series of portraits of Black women – there are nine across London. He said it was ordinary women doing extra-ordinary things.'

'Like who?' said Madison.

'His partner. Friends. The mother of his child. A therapist.'

'That is . . . *amazing*,' murmured Madison.

'They're incredible portraits. I love them.' He looked at her, head tilted. 'You know who else loves them?'

'Who?'

'Jenson. He loves getting out and about with a spray can.'

Her jaw dropped and Nathan guffawed. 'Sorry, I couldn't resist!'

'Oh, my *God*, Nathan, you had me for a moment!'

'I'm good at keeping a straight face when I have to.'

'You lasted a second!'

'Yeah – true. Your face was such a picture!'

Try as she might, her smile kept returning. 'OK, who loves the paintings other than me?'

'Mellow,' he said, with a questioning look. 'Mellow, who still hasn't found anyone she likes to do her design.'

Madison met his gaze.

'I know you didn't reply to my email,' he said, 'and that's cool. But . . . I dunno. Come and talk to me more about it?'

'Why are you doing this for me?' said Madison. 'I don't want to be some sort of charity case.'

'Because I think you'd do a good job,' Nathan said. 'And you deserve it.' He glanced at his phone. 'Look, I have to get back but I'm free this evening. We could have a quick drink . . . or a phone call and go over it again.'

Madison was quiet.

'Just let me know either way,' said Nathan. 'And good luck with the mince pies.'

Madison watched him go, her mind swirling. She checked the mysterious address on her phone: it was a ten-minute walk. She'd have time to check it out and get back to the office in time to eat her sandwich. Maybe the walk would help clear her head about what exactly was going on.

She'd been taken aback by Nathan's offer to meet for a drink. A thought had flashed into her head: did he have an ulterior motive? But that was crazy. He'd been nothing but respectful and friendly towards her. She caught sight of herself reflected in a shop window and frowned. She looked exhausted. And she'd been so sleepy that morning that she'd grabbed the nearest clean clothes, a pair of jeans that had seen better days and a sweater that needed ironing.

She walked briskly to Ryder Street, which turned out to be a grotty backstreet. Number 90 had an inauspicious door and the buzzer was old and cracked. It looked like somewhere you'd put the bins out. Why on earth did Rich have this address on a card in his pocket? She took a deep breath and pressed the buzzer. She waited. No answer. She buzzed again. Still no answer. Maybe whoever was in just wasn't going to open the door, but she had the impression that no one was there, and she was keen to get away from that alley. Her mother would have hated the thought of her scuttling down some back alley to ring a mysterious doorbell.

She emerged back into the faint December sun. She might have found the place but she was left with more questions. She felt grubby, as if she wanted to clean her energy, focus on something positive. She pulled out her phone again and googled the street artist's project. It was called 'You Are Enough'.

She smiled at the nice self-serving reminder. Next she searched YouTube and found a TedX Talk by Dreph, which she listened to on the walk back to the office. Feeling bold and inspired, she emailed Nathan as soon as she got to her desk. *Let's talk. I'd love to hear more.*

Amazing! he replied. *Let's do the rooftop bar at 100 Shoreditch? Here's my number, in case you have any delays.*

She typed his name and number into her phone and prepared to save it. But she paused, suddenly self-conscious. She felt like there was something intimate about saving a man's number in her phone. How long was it since she'd done that? She told herself not to be so silly: she'd probably done it loads with friends, colleagues and other contacts, and this was no different. Was it?

A message from Rich popped up as she was finishing Nathan's name, and the proximity of the two men – at least digitally – made her stomach lurch, though she couldn't put her finger on why. She wasn't doing anything wrong. But a voice lurked in the back of her head: Nathan showed more interest in *her*, it said, not as a mum or a partner, than Rich had, even when she'd given him the opportunity.

Some filming got cancelled, so I could be back early today and spend some time with the kids this evening.

Now she had a dilemma.

Go to meet Nathan, or stay in with Rich and the children? She shouldn't feel guilty for going to see someone about work. But it was in a bar, in the evening when she could have spent the time with Rich and the kids.

She messaged him back: *Great – the more family time we can give them, the better.*

That afternoon, Madison *still* hadn't decided what she was going to do. She wasn't used to being indecisive. She'd built it up in her head: meeting Nathan represented prioritizing herself, new horizons, creativity. The evening with Rich and the kids was family, shared history, the familiar. But why did one have to threaten the other, or so it felt?

Her phone buzzed: a notification from Savine. *Just checking in*, the message said. *Hope you're doing OK.*

I am, answered Madison. *Or as well as I can be in the circumstances. But – if you're free – I could do with some advice.*

Savine rang her about five minutes later.

'Hey, Savine, I appreciate it,' said Madison.

'No worries. How are things?'

'At a weird stalemate,' said Madison. 'I can't read his behaviour. He turned up the evening after the gallery opening and wanted a cosy night in, then stayed over – not with me, I should add. I've no idea how to interpret that.'

'Could be realizing what he stands to lose,' said Savine. 'Is this what you need my advice on?'

'Actually, no,' said Madison. 'It's something just to do with me.' She explained the situation with Nathan, the work opportunity, the clash between family time and meeting him.

'Is this man handsome?' Savine said.

'That's not the point, Savine!'

'Isn't it?' said Savine, with a chuckle. 'Seriously, though, I think you should go for it.'

'But it feels weird meeting someone after work. In a bar.'

'Isn't that exactly what Rich has just done? For his career?'

'Touché,' said Madison.

'Go. Wear something that makes you feel great. You're there because you're talented and creative and he obviously sees that, as anyone with a pulse does.'

'You don't think it crosses a line?'

'Madison, he's asking you to meet him for a work drink, not to run away to Paris for the weekend. Hear him out. Spread your wings.'

So Madison got ready. She put on a smart-casual long-sleeved black jumpsuit that showed a hint of cleavage. Applying her makeup carefully, she chose burgundy lipstick to bring more glamour and an evening vibe to the mix.

Rich arrived home with the kids, and Madison's resolve wavered. She should be spending time with them, trying to show Rich exactly what he was missing.

'You look nice, Mummy,' said Chloë, gawping at her.

'Thank you, baby,' murmured Madison. She waited to see if Rich would say anything, but he was fiddling with his phone.

Then he glanced up. 'My agent thinks we're really close with the show,' he said. 'Apparently they're very keen on me fronting it.' He flashed her that million-dollar smile. 'And then you'd be back working in TV!'

'In design,' said Madison.

'We'd get you something,' said Rich.

Madison felt oddly flat. This was what they'd been working towards, but now she didn't feel the same excitement. 'What is the show concept now?' she asked.

'They're still refining a few elements,' said Rich, 'but the one I like is the idea of upgrading from basic to luxe.'

That was the most information he'd ever given her, but she was underwhelmed.

She peered at her phone. She'd have to leave shortly if she was going to meet Nathan on time.

'We could chat about it tonight?' said Rich. 'Actually it would be great to work up a few ideas for the producer.'

'And I'd come to those meetings?'

'If I can swing it,' Rich said. 'But you know how it is. Until the contract is signed, I can't promise anything.'

'I'm hungry,' said Jordan, trailing into the kitchen.

'Ask your mum what's for dinner, then,' said Rich. 'I'm starving too.'

Madison smiled sweetly, her mind made up. She had the choice between coming up with ideas for Rich, no guarantee she'd even be involved, or talking to Nathan, who seemed to be offering her an opportunity. She was surprised at her toughness. She imagined Savine nodding proudly.

'Dad's in charge of dinner tonight,' she said. Jordan bowled out of the room again, evidently satisfied that food would arrive imminently. Rich was a perfectly capable cook, and she resented the implication that she would already have sorted everything out. She looked at Rich. 'I'm going out.'

'Really?' He looked her up and down, as if he was seeing her for the first time that day. 'Where to? You're dressed up.'

'It's a work thing.'

'With . . . Jenson?'

She shook her head. 'No, a potential new project.'

Rich frowned. 'You didn't mention it.'

'Didn't I?' said Madison, pulling a bemused face. 'I guess maybe I've been a bit distracted recently.'

'So who are you meeting exactly?'

'Nathan,' said Madison. *Let him know how it feels,* a little voice in her head said. *Let him feel insecure, for once.*

'Who's Nathan?' said Rich.

'You know how it is,' said Madison, putting her phone into her bag. 'Until things are finalized, it's best not to say too much.'

'When will you be back?'

'I'm not sure,' said Madison, putting on her boots. 'But you'll be OK to hold the fort with the kids, right?' She didn't wait for an answer, just flashed him a smile, grabbed her scarf and coat and walked out into the chilly December night. She paused in the street to button her coat and fix the scarf around her neck, then rolled her shoulders back and held her head high. She felt powerful. The moon was shining overhead, in a sky that was clear – at least for London – and seemed to be lighting her way along the pavement. The air was cold on her skin, but she was finding it energizing.

In the last few weeks, her life had fallen apart. So why was she starting to feel . . . *alive*?

It was a brisk twenty-minute walk to the bar where she was to meet Nathan, and Madison arrived a tiny bit late. It was a trendy place, the kind she'd used to frequent back in the day. 'Evening,' said the doorman, holding the door open for her, and Madison sashayed inside.

She spotted Nathan instantly. He was in the lobby, sitting on a beautifully shaped solid wood bench. When he saw her, he grinned, stood up and waved frantically with both arms.

Madison liked that about Nathan: he seemed to have the capacity to goof around, and not care about being cool and collected.

'Hey!' he said. 'Great to see you. Did you find it OK?'

'Yeah, sorry to be a few minutes late.'

'I think I was early, don't worry. The rooftop has a private event on, but we can grab a drink over there.' He pointed to a low-lit space with complementary tones of burnt orange, rusty red and bronze, which looked warm and inviting. Madison followed him over. 'Here, let me get you a drink,' he said.

She hadn't been planning on drinking – it was a business meeting, after all – but Nathan was offering her the cocktail menu and saying they were really good, and she thought, *Why not?*

'I'll take a Spicy Margarita,' she said, and he went to the bar to order.

Madison sat back and looked around. The bar wasn't too full, particularly given it was December, and Christmas-party season was in full swing.

'How's the rest of your week been?' said Nathan, setting down two ribbed tumblers, lined with red and white sprinkles and half a red chilli sticking out.

'Wow! Those look beautiful,' said Madison.

'I'll let you judge for yourself, but they're the best I've tasted, and I've tasted quite a few,' said Nathan.

Madison took out her phone to take a picture of the drinks.

'Your kids?' said Nathan, gesturing to her screensaver of Chloë and Jordan.

'Yeah,' said Madison. 'Little monsters.'

'I bet they keep you busy,' said Nathan. 'My mum brought us up single-handedly, and I dread to think of the stress we caused her.'

'Oh, I'm not—' said Madison, flustered. 'It's not single-handed . . .'

'Sorry, I didn't mean that.' Nathan was equally flustered. 'There's a ring on your finger, so, I presumed, yeah, umm.'

'Right!' said Madison.

'Has Jenson been behaving himself?' said Nathan. 'Mince pies all sorted?'

Madison laughed and sipped her drink, grateful for the change in subject. 'Wow! The chilli, lime and sea salt on the rim is divine! Who would have thought? But, sorry, erm . . . yes, mince pies all sorted, I had to sample a few and it's safe to say I don't want to see or taste any more for a while.'

He winked. 'Hope you put them on the company account, then.'

'Duh! Of course.'

'How are things at the new site?'

'In-hand, miraculously,' Nathan said. 'Then I'll be off to the next thing.'

'Did you always want to be an architect?'

'I guess so,' he said. 'When I was little, I used to imagine designing all sorts of weird and wonderful buildings – magical castles, underwater cities, that kind of thing.'

'Fancy pitching one of those to Jenson?'

'To be fair, it's not a bad idea. He'd probably love a magical castle.'

'And I'd be left sourcing the drawbridge,' quipped Madison.

'No doubt embossed with his initials,' added Nathan.

Madison threw back her head and laughed. It was so easy to spend time with Nathan, she reflected.

'*Soooo* . . .' he began. 'Let's talk Mellow.'

'Just when I'm starting to feel mellow?' She picked up her cocktail.

'All part of my plan.' He smiled. 'Look, I'm not going to push this but she really would love to meet you.'

'You've told her about me?'

Nathan looked directly at her. 'Er, yeah?'

Suddenly Madison was burning with curiosity to know what he'd said. Her imagination was running wild. *There's this really cool woman at work,* she imagined him saying. *Reckon she's about thirty-two, and she's just got such great style, great taste, and she's really funny . . .*

Madison forced herself back to reality. She was behaving as if she were back in school with a crush on someone. And she *didn't* have a crush on Nathan. She was probably just responding to a man paying her attention in a way that, recently, her husband hadn't.

He cleared his throat. 'Just that you're looking to get back into design, and that I think you'd really get on with her.'

Maybe it was the drink, but Madison was suddenly bold. 'OK,' she said. 'OK, set a meeting up.'

'Yeah?' said Nathan.

'Yeah,' said Madison, swiftly followed by 'Oh, God.'

He laughed. 'You're acting like it's going to be an exam. You never know, it might even be fun. Kick some ideas around.'

'Ideas are the problem,' she admitted. 'They used to come all the time. Like, sometimes it was really annoying – I'd be drifting off to sleep and then be thinking about someone's bathroom, what I'd do if I had the chance to design or redesign it.'

Nathan's laughter deepened. 'And where exactly did that impulse come from?'

'I think my parents' house,' mused Madison. 'They kept it pretty much exactly the same as when they'd moved in. Bland magnolia walls with the only colour coming from a few paintings from my grandma. My mum had green fingers so we had lots of plants, but I always wanted more vibrancy and pattern. It was a nice house, but they always played it safe. And I was always *so* desperate to put my mark on it!'

'And did you?'

Madison widened her eyes. 'Well, there was the one time when I took matters into my own hands and painted my bedroom as a teenager . . .'

'How did that go down?'

She shook her head. 'Bad. I did one wall lime green and another in what I thought would be a cool tangerine contrast – stop laughing! Citrus colours were trendy!'

'I'm here for it, to be honest,' said Nathan, holding his hands up.

'But the trouble was, I picked the wrong shade, so it was just this really *bad* shade of peach. Although the colour co-ordination was the least of my parents' concerns . . .' She winced, remembering. It had been one of their few bust-ups. She'd been set to work repainting the room in a sensible shade, and not even Finn had been permitted in the house to help her.

'Maybe this is the project to resurrect that vision,' said Nathan.

'Maybe,' said Madison. 'Actually, if you did it in the bathroom, with, like, different plants to break it up, maybe lean into a couple of gold flourishes, clean white porcelain, but gold taps, maybe you could give a sort of tropical feel to it . . .' She narrowed her eyes. 'And the floor, I'm thinking go all out and have black and white tiles. So it's this clash between something wild and bright with the citrus colours, and something totally classic with the black and white . . .'

Nathan was gazing at her, his head tilted to one side.

'What?' she said, embarrassed suddenly.

'Nothing,' he said. 'But that doesn't sound like a woman who's short of ideas.'

Madison took a sip of her cocktail. True. That had felt like old times, when an idea just popped into her head and she had run with it, mentally trying different colours, patterns and textures, without second-guessing herself.

'When you talk about stuff, you're just so—' Nathan broke off.

'What?' she said again, licking salt off the rim of her glass.

'Just so . . . alive about it,' he said. He cleared his throat. 'If I fix something up for next week, then? That sound good?'

'Definitely,' said Madison. She reached for the water jug, poured herself a glass and had a few sips. Was it just her, or had that comment from Nathan felt like it crossed a line? Or come near to a line? She'd felt a jolt of electricity run through her, no doubt intensified by the drink. 'Excuse me,' she murmured. She went into the loos and sat down in one of the cubicles. What was going on? In this bar, she'd become aware of how attractive Nathan was. She'd been having such a good time with him, laughing and sharing ideas. *This is how I want to feel with my husband*, she thought, despair flashing through her again. But was something else going on too?

She'd been with Rich for so long that she'd never thought of how it would feel to be single again. But Nathan was making her feel *attractive* in a way she hadn't for months – if not longer. And it was because he was paying her attention, asking questions that weren't to do with running the household. It was time for her to leave, she thought. Even though she would never *dream* of crossing a line.

She reapplied her lipstick and went out.

Oh.

One of the barmaids had come over to their table, and was standing by it, holding their empty glasses. Nathan was smiling and looking up at her. She was really young, early twenties at most, her figure perfectly toned, wearing a dress that hugged her body in the right places. *Well, if you've got it, flaunt it*, thought Madison. After two kids, only Spanx could help her look so . . . so tight and smooth.

If you were single, this is what it would be like, said a voice in her head.

A shiver of fear went down her spine. Now she was hovering halfway between the door to the loos and their table. She felt like Nathan's auntie, interrupting him at an awkward moment. He looked up, saw her and smiled.

Madison had no choice but to go back over. The barmaid turned to face her, hand on hip, and Madison could have sworn she was using all her strength not to look her up and down. 'Frankie here was wondering if we want another drink,' said Nathan.

'Ah, not for me,' Madison said. 'Best call it a night.'

'You sure?' said Nathan.

'Definitely,' said Madison. 'Don't want to turn into a pumpkin or anything.'

He chuckled. 'That was midnight, not eight p.m.'

'I like to be on the safe side.' Madison glanced at the waitress. 'Could I pay for mine, please?'

'No need, he's already done it.'

'Oh,' said Madison. 'Oh, well, let me give you the money? These are expensive.'

He waved her away. 'It's all good. How are you getting home?'

'I'll order an Uber – should be one here quickly.'

Frankie was still hovering over them, clearly keen for Madison to leave. That was probably why Nathan had paid. Yes, he was helping her out, but of course he'd want to be free to enjoy himself – especially with the attention of a gorgeous waitress. She put on her coat and scurried out, waving goodbye.

She'd talk to Rich, she decided, because she *deserved* attention from him. At the very least, she wanted to know *exactly* when he was going to be with the kids instead of her having to juggle everything. She had a very important meeting next week, and she was going to prepare for it.

She slipped the key into the lock. She'd push for answers. She was sick of this. The house was quiet and still – the kids had already gone to bed.

'Rich?' she called. She heard movement in the kitchen. She padded towards it. 'We need to tal— Oh, God, it's you!'

Instead of Rich, his mother was perched in the kitchen. There was a mound of gleaming washing-up stacked on the draining-board. Her heart sinking, Madison knew this meant *she* had done it. Tina insisted on scrubbing everything by hand, instead of bunging it in the dishwasher

'Where's Rich?' Madison said, forcing her voice to stay calm.

'He had something very important to discuss with his brother,' said Tina.

Madison knew from her tone that Tina was annoyed. 'He didn't say.'

'He called me and told me you'd darted out to meet someone.'

Madison flinched. That wasn't the full story. 'I'd made an arrangement with a work contact. I asked Rich to cook and put the kids to bed.'

'And I jumped in to do that!' said Tina, indignantly. 'What on earth is going on between the two of you at the moment?'

Madison ground her teeth in frustration. She wasn't about to spill her marital secrets to Tina – Rich was her son, after all – but she wasn't going to be painted as the bad guy here. She barely knew where Rich *was* most of the time. 'Well, I'd like to know that too, Tina,' she said evenly. 'And I'd also like to know why Rich felt his brother couldn't come round here.'

Tina tutted as if the idea was preposterous. 'They have something important to talk about. Maybe it's not in front of the children.' Tina didn't have to voice what she was thinking. The traditional views still ran through her. Even though she supported Madison working, there was always a limit. Always a difference. Madison's *priority* couldn't be work, or indeed herself, but for Rich it was somehow OK.

'Let me get you a taxi home, Tina,' said Madison, wearily, pulling out her phone to order an Uber.

Tina nodded briskly. 'Rich mentioned that we'll be having Christmas around here.'

'Will Lloyd and Jamila be coming?'

Tina shook her head. 'They're in the Maldives.'

'How lovely,' Madison said, forcing a smile and trying not to show the annoyance on her face. 'Well, Christmas all together.'

First she'd heard of it. Sometimes they'd alternated between Tina and her own parents, and more recently she and Rich had hosted, but this was yet another thing that had been sprung on her, without a proper discussion. She would bear the brunt of all the organizing. In previous years, she'd relished that, even shooing Rich away. Usually she looked forward to Christmas, but not this year, and Rich hadn't even confirmed to her what would be happening. Now she was faced with cooking and making sure everyone was happy. Perhaps even without realizing it, she wondered what it would be like to have Christmas with just her and the kids. Or even having Finn and his husband round.

Mercifully, the Uber came quickly. She hugged Tina and walked her to the door.

She checked her phone. She had a message, but not from Rich: Nathan asking if she was home OK. *Yes, thank you x*, she typed back, then deleted the kiss. She wasn't going to message Rich. She wanted a face-to-face talk with him. She was furious he'd wriggled out of being at home. Had he really been seeing his brother, or was it some form of retaliation for *her* having her own plans? Either way, their situation felt even more toxic. But look how far she'd come from her first few days without Rich when she'd completely melted. Here she was, just back from a work meeting, preparing to meet a model next week. She wasn't crying. She wasn't a mess. She was *angry*.

So, what was the next stage of the plan? She wanted to corner Rich. Where would he be this weekend? Rich went religiously to the gym on Sunday mornings, always pestering Madison to go too, which she'd found mildly annoying but also kind of sweet and supportive. Generally she'd snatched those precious few hours to catch up on housework, or maybe grab a coffee with a friend. Perhaps this Saturday, though, she might take Rich up on his suggestion.

15

Sunday rolled around and, after dropping the kids at her dad's, Madison returned home to cobble together a gym outfit. She pulled open the wardrobe doors and frowned. She found a couple of pairs of leggings and pulled them on, before – with difficulty – pulling them off again. She'd managed to persuade Savine to come with her, promising her it would be fun. She was worried she might lose her nerve if she went on her own.

'I'd like to be able to breathe during this,' she muttered. Jess was always sloping around in luxe gym gear that looked fantastic. But Madison just had to get in there in something convincing enough, and then she could find Rich.

From the very back of the wardrobe, she pulled out a pair of paint-spattered jogging bottoms. She'd last worn these when she was painting the bedroom. Happier days. But there was no time to get distracted. She grabbed the first plain T-shirt that came to hand and pulled it on, then dragged a hoodie over the top. OK, with a pair of trainers on, she looked plausible. She grimaced at herself in the mirror. Madison was not a gym bunny. Get her on the dance floor and she'd keep going for hours, but heaving weights around with a load of grunting men and ultra-toned women? Where was the fun in that?

Putting on her biggest sunnies, she drove to the gym and parked outside. The very sight of the building was giving her the heebie-jeebies. She spotted two immaculate women heading inside, sipping green smoothies, and a very lean middle-aged man in Lycra doing squats outside. *Why couldn't he at least wait to be in there?* she thought churlishly.

A sleek red convertible pulled up, and Savine got out. 'Yeah, it's my mid-life crisis treat,' she said, clocking Madison goggling at the car. 'She's a beauty, right?'

'She is,' said Madison. 'Where's your trainers, though?'

Savine was wearing high-heeled boots. 'Uh, I thought we were just going for a look around?'

'Yeah, but we need to look the part.'

'Who says I can't get on the treadmill in these? Now, come on, let's get this over with.'

They went into Reception, and Madison rehearsed her plan. She was simply going to ask to have a brief look at the facilities. There was no way they could deny her that.

'OK, sure,' said the receptionist. 'We just need you to fill in some forms and then we can give you a quick tour. I'm sure Clive will be delighted to show you round.'

'OK,' said Madison, her heart sinking at the sight of a hefty form coming her way. 'Are you sure I can't just pop my head in and have a look?'

'Insurance policy,' said the receptionist, briskly, handing her a pen.

She scribbled down the details as quickly as possible, ticking some random boxes about what she was interested in. Flexibility? Sounded good. De-stressing? Yes, please. Cardio sounded a lot like sweating. She didn't tick it. Getting stronger? She hesitated over that one. Well, why not?

'Thank you,' said the receptionist, as Madison handed her the form. She looked at Savine, who was tapping one foot. 'Have you done your form too?'

'Oh, I'm just here for moral support.' Savine's steely tone caused the receptionist to nod and say no more.

'And now here's Clive to take you on your tour.'

Clive, God bless him, was a man of senior years, who wore a manic and enthusiastic grin with a Mr Motivator T-shirt that had seen better days. 'Welcome to the gym!' he said, beaming at them. 'A quick rhyme before we start?'

'Clive, please,' murmured the receptionist. 'You know management had a word with you about that. You're meant to stick to the official script.'

'And we don't have long,' cut in Savine.

Clive looked so crestfallen that Madison felt a pang. 'Well, I'd love to hear the rhyme,' she said. 'I think more gyms should have rhymes.'

The receptionist groaned. 'Your funeral,' she said. 'But, Clive, please can you do it through the doors?'

Clive gave a theatrical bow as he opened the door into a high-tech gym, ushering Madison and Savine through it. Madison felt as if she'd stepped into a spaceship: there were machines everywhere, which looked hopelessly complicated. She could hear weights clanking and feet pounding on treadmills. There were screens everywhere she looked: screens showing fake cycling routes, screens with flashing numbers, screens showing non-stop music videos featuring a series of writhing women. Madison was overwhelmed. *Look for Rich*, she told herself.

Clive cleared his throat to get her attention. 'Spectacular, isn't it?' he said. Then he launched into the rhyme: 'Why wait if you need to lose weight? Spinning's the thing if you want to get thin!'

Madison cringed and Savine started to laugh, but deftly turned it into a cough.

'That's what the normal gym slogans say, but I have a different way of looking at things.' Clive paused, eyes searching the ceiling for inspiration. 'Aha, yes, I've remembered it.' A cough, and he was off: 'Why not look instead for how it makes you feel? Not judging from the outside, but looking from within . . .'

The rhyme went on for several verses, Clive's eyes shining. Madison and Savine applauded politely at the end.

'That was amazing,' Madison said.

Clive beamed. 'Thank you so much!' he said. 'What a charming young lady you are. Now, let me show you some of these machines.'

'Oh, I can just have a quick look round by myself,' said Madison, but Clive was crestfallen again, then muttered about how she was his responsibility as long as she was on gym premises and not a member. His eyes brightened at the word 'member'.

'We have three membership options,' he began. 'Bronze, silver and gold, each with benefits. It just depends on what suits you as you embark on your fitness odyssey.'

A fitness oddity, more like, thought Madison. This whole place was beginning to feel like a cult. The shiny-eyed disciples on their treadmills, Clive trying to recruit her, like those Jehovah's Witnesses outside the station. He took them from machine to machine, giving detailed descriptions of exactly what muscles each would work out.

'I'm going to sign up,' muttered Savine. 'Have you seen the

guys in here? I could just sit on one of the machines and lie in wait.'

The only guy Madison was looking out for was Rich, and she hadn't seen him.

Savine nudged her. 'Look, there's a special room where they keep the hottest ones.'

She gestured towards a room filled with weights of all shapes and sizes, and muscled men standing in front of mirrors.

Something told Madison that that was the kind of place she might find Rich. He was a fan of a biceps pump. 'Can we look in there?' she said casually.

Clive grimaced. 'The lion's den!' he said. 'We can walk past.' He glanced at the form she had completed. 'It doesn't say you're interested in weights.'

'I'm feeling inspired,' lied Madison, smoothly.

'So am I,' said Savine, eagerly.

'Free-standing weights are a *whole different ball game* from the machines,' said Clive, but Madison was already on her way to the room.

She peered through the window. It was hard to see anything as the lighting was dim, but, with a jolt, she recognized Rich, standing with his back to her, his muscles flexing as he heaved the heavy weights. She was relieved to see him where he was meant to be, then nervous at the prospect of starting a conversation with him. The man turned around and Madison blinked, realising it wasn't Rich after all.

She felt panicked that she couldn't recognize her husband. Her mind was playing tricks on her. Suddenly the plan wasn't as good as she'd thought. Maybe Rich had been saying he was off to the gym when in fact he was liaising with his mistress. She swallowed the thought, but her stomach was now clenched and anxious. Clive showed her around the rest of the gym, introducing her to his favourite treadmill, Terence, and the most temperamental machine, Angela, which had an out-of-order sign slung across it.

'Terence just keeps going,' said Clive, patting the treadmill proudly.

Isn't that the point of a treadmill? thought Madison, resisting the urge to say, 'It has one job.' She felt curiously sympathetic to Angela, tarred as the troublemaker. Her hormones must be playing up.

By now they'd toured the whole gym and there was no sign of Rich.

'You OK?' murmured Savine. 'We can get out of here.'

Madison glanced at a clock on the wall. If she could wriggle out of this now, she could grab forty minutes in a café to scribble some ideas for the meeting with Mellow. 'Thank you so much for your time, Clive,' she said, making her voice assertive.

'You are *so* welcome!' Clive grinned. 'The best is yet to come! This way!'

Is it really? Madison thought wearily. She looked at Clive, his happy face, his well-loved Mr Motivator T-shirt. All she wanted to do was leave. But she could humour him for a moment more, surely. He reminded her a bit of one of her dad's friends, and that alone was enough for her to follow him meekly through a set of doors, then through another into—

'Surprise!' said Clive, as he pulled a party popper and Madison screamed, putting a hand to her thudding heart.

'Oh, my *God*,' said Savine, walking in behind her, still in her high-heeled boots.

Five grey-haired people, all in brightly coloured Lycra, were beaming at them. Had Madison made it to the inner sanctum of the cult, without even realizing it?

'You're actually our hundredth new-customer enquiry,' said Clive, tears of joy in his eyes. 'And that means *not only* do you get thirty per cent off your membership *but* you get to join a complimentary class, and I thought, Why not try my Sunday morning Stretch 'n' Flex?'

Madison turned to survey the other people in the room. They'd surrounded her. She was standing in the middle of them, all shiny-eyed and smiling, with deep creases and laughter lines.

'Oh, wow, this is something,' said Savine, grinning. 'Morning, everyone!'

'That is a very kind invitation,' Madison began, 'but I actually need to . . .'

'Go?' said one lady, with a pink stripe running through her buzzed grey hair. She tutted. 'Let me ask you, young lady, can you touch your toes?'

'Of course I can,' said Madison, huffily. 'Look.' She reached down . . . and her toes remained resolutely out of the way of her fingers. Not far, but very definitely not there.

She glanced up to see the old lady staring at her, an eyebrow arched.

'I'm not warmed up,' muttered Madison.

'My name's Gladys. I'm seventy-four. And I'm not warmed up either.'

Gladys took a slow, elegant movement forwards, and her neon-pink nails landed neatly on her trainer-clad feet. 'So, young lady, I challenge you to stay.' She winked at her. 'See if you can touch them by the end.'

Savine hooted with laughter and leaned into Madison. 'I

reckon we should do it! Come on, might be fun! And God knows I definitely can't touch my toes.'

Despite her gnawing anxiety, Madison found herself chuckling and putting down her bag. 'All right,' she said. 'Challenge accepted.'

Savine whooped, then made a show of taking off her boots and telling everyone please not to judge her as she was due a pedicure.

As Madison took her place on a mat, an elderly gentleman mumbled, 'You're lucky Gladys didn't put her leg behind her head! That's what she normally does to newbies!'

'Oh, my G-God, are you serious?' stuttered Madison, looking at Gladys with fear and respect, as Clive guided them in a series of gentle forward and sideways bends, to get them warmed up. It felt so good to move, she realized, beginning to ease out the aching knots in her back.

There was a clatter as the doors opened. 'Sorry I'm late,' said Nathan, and Madison's heart dropped.

16

'Five extra push-ups for you!' said Clive, tutting at Nathan. 'You'll be giving the wrong impression to our new recruits! I run a tight ship here.'

Nathan and Madison made eye contact. He looked surprised to see her, but his face broke into a smile and he mouthed, 'Hi.' Madison gave a small wave back. Inside, she was cringing. She could just about cope with doing this in front of a room of grandparents. But Nathan? Nathan seeing her attempting a Downward Dog or whatever other horrors awaited? She shouldn't care, but she did.

Please, dear God, do not let him set up a mat directly behind me. She was grateful when he joined the end of the row.

'OK, everyone, all fours!' said Clive. There was the sound of clicking and groaning as people did as they'd been told, and Clive put on some music – Madison was relieved by the new soundtrack.

'Who the hell is that?' whispered Savine, leaning into her. 'Who?'

Savine rolled her eyes. 'Don't play innocent with me, young lady! That very cute guy you seem to know?'

'We're going to start off being kitty cats,' said Clive. 'Think about how that nice pussy of yours' – *Jesus Christ!* thought Madison – 'can bend and flex its spine! You never saw a cat with a stiff back.'

'That's Nathan,' hissed Madison to Savine, wiggling her spine up and down. In front of her, Gladys was arching her back in a faintly alarming manner.

'*The* Nathan? He's *so* cute,' said Savine. 'And his lower back strength looks wonderful. Which bodes well.'

'Stop it, Savine,' said Madison, who was getting the giggles.

'Girls, could you try to keep up, please?' said Gladys, her voice severe.

'Sorry,' said Savine.

'And now on to the bumping crabs,' said Clive. This manoeuvre involved moving sideways on all fours.

Madison cleared her throat. 'Why is it called bumping—'

The gentleman next to her toppled over and looked mournfully up at her. 'That's why, my dear. Some of us aren't quite as stable as we used to be.'

Madison helped him up. As she did so, Nathan glanced at her, and caught her eye. She could tell he was about to laugh.

Savine had pretty much given up, it appeared, and had rolled on to her back.

'What are you doing?' hissed Madison. 'Get up!'

'I can't,' Savine spluttered. 'I'm laughing too much. And I'm calling this the Overturned Beetle.'

What *were* the names of these positions? Madison was pretty sure Clive was making it up as he went along. She'd done a bit of YouTube yoga in lockdown, but she couldn't remember the Angry Spider, the Fried Potato or the Curious Chicken being *classic* postures.

But something was happening. As she moved into the

positions, she found she could do more than she'd thought. She even managed to raise herself into a kind of side plank, with her knees down, which Clive called the Sulking Walrus.

'Look at you go!' said the man next to her, and she buzzed with achievement.

The rest of the class were vocal in encouraging each other, bantering, and making clear to Clive what they did or didn't like, so the room had a buzzing, festive atmosphere.

'I'm calling this one the Cheeky Robin, working to a Christmas theme,' said Clive, as they tried to come into a ball shape on the floor, balancing on their toes, some with hands down, others daring to hold them up.

'If I need a hip replacement after this, I'll be presenting you with the bill,' called Gladys.

'Get Santa to bring you a new one!' retorted Clive, with a wink at her.

'There's something going on between those two,' whispered Savine. 'The chemistry is *red hot*.'

Before Madison knew it, the class was nearly over. How had the time gone *that* quickly? She was moderately out of breath – those animal shapes were harder than they looked – and she dreaded to think what her hair was doing, but her body felt loose and flexible.

'Before relaxation, it's time for the Double-headed Sea Monster,' said Clive.

There were oohs and aahs of excitement.

Madison looked sideways, unsure what was happening. The others in the class were getting up and reaching for one another, and before she realized what was happening, they were in pairs and the only person left was – Nathan.

'I'm sitting this one out,' said Savine. 'Quite enough

excitement for me. So that means . . .' She reached out a hand and gently pushed Madison in Nathan's direction. 'You two are together.'

Madison went to stand beside Nathan. 'What is this move?' she murmured.

'No idea,' he said. 'But I've tended to find that the more elaborate the name, the worse it is.'

'Gladys will demonstrate,' said Clive.

Gladys sat on the floor with her legs bent, and Gregory sat opposite her in the same position. They clasped wrists.

'Now, both lean back,' said Clive, and they did so, their hold on each other tightening. 'Now, Gladys, allow yourself to be pulled forwards,' instructed Clive. Helped by Gregory leaning his weight back, she slowly folded forwards.

'Feels delicious on your back,' she called.

Madison looked at Nathan, aghast. She couldn't do this. It was way too intimate. She would look ridiculous. Her T-shirt would probably ride up. He'd probably be unable to pull her forwards. She wished she'd put on an extra swipe of deodorant.

'If you're not comfortable . . .' Nathan began.

'Get on with it, you two!' shouted Gladys, to Savine's amusement.

Nathan scrambled on to the floor and sat down, and Madison sat opposite.

He stretched out his hands and clasped hers. Her heart began to beat faster.

'Both lean back,' said Clive.

'It's OK, I've got you,' said Nathan, as they leaned back and the weight on their arms increased. 'Just trust yourself.'

Madison breathed in and out, and realized they were

perfectly balanced. They made eye contact for a moment, and then she glanced away.

'First partner roll forwards,' said Clive, and Nathan began pulling her arms, encouraging her to round her upper back and lean forwards. The stretch was intense, yet gentle, and Madison felt the tension in her lower back begin to dissipate. She shut her eyes and took some deep breaths.

'Time to swap over!' called Clive.

Madison returned to the upright position and shook out her arms, then clasped Nathan's hands again. 'It really does feel good,' she admitted.

She began to lean back, and watched as Nathan bowed forwards. *Don't let go,* she told herself, fearful of being unable to hold him. But, to her surprise, she was stronger than she'd thought. Her core was engaged, her arms strong. Savine darted into her eye-line and gave her a comical thumbs-up.

Clive called time, and Nathan sat up. Madison and he glanced at each other and laughed. 'It's fun, isn't it?' he said, his face now glowing with sweat.

'Yeah,' she said. 'It's like being a kid again.'

When she looked down, she saw they were still holding hands. 'God, sorry,' she said, letting go and feeling flustered.

Clive guided them through a final relaxation for a few minutes, during which they imagined their thoughts to be clouds drifting across a blue sky. Madison focused on the thrum of the blood in her veins, on the feeling of sweat cooling on her skin. All too soon, the moment of peace was over.

Gladys stopped her on the way out. 'Toes?' she said. Madison bent down, and found that her toes were within reach.

'A Christmas miracle,' said Gladys. 'Will you come back again?'

'You know what?' said Madison. 'Yeah. I will.'

'And me,' said Savine. 'I'm converted.'

Madison, Savine and Nathan walked back into the main area of the gym.

'So how on earth did you get roped into that class, Nathan?' Madison asked.

'They got me on the introductory tour,' he said. 'I just couldn't say no. Clive seemed such a sweet old man.'

'I think it's their preferred method for recruiting new victims,' said Madison.

'Play the innocent-old-people card?'

'Oh, yes.'

'I'm going ahead to get into the car,' said Savine. She gave a cheeky sideways glance at Nathan. 'Nice to meet you.'

Madison was suddenly conscious again of what she was wearing. 'God, what must you think of me! I promise I'll look way more professional than this for our meeting.'

He shook his head, puzzled. 'Nah, Madison, you look great.' Then he shuffled his feet from side to side. 'Got to go. See you next week.'

The positive energy from the class powered on into the rest of the day. It had been amazing to do something new, something unexpected. If someone had suggested the class to her, Madison knew she would have dismissed it and come up with a list of reasons why it wasn't for her. She'd have told herself she couldn't do it, that it would be embarrassing. But it had been great. Maybe, just maybe, she could apply the same feeling elsewhere in her life.

At home that afternoon, Madison made gingerbread men with the kids and star-shaped biscuits that went down a storm. After they'd gone to bed, she pulled out her laptop and a notepad, and began scribbling down ideas for designs. If she could nail a Double-headed Sea Monster, surely she could smash this meeting.

17

Madison glanced at her phone to see a notification from Nathan: *We're outside.*

She stood up from her desk, rolling her shoulders back and exhaling. She'd worn an off-the-shoulder jumper, jeans and boots. Her hair was out for once. After the mini sweat session yesterday she'd decided to give it more love and had taken time to wash, condition, blow dry and plait it. She'd been chuffed with her defined curls in the morning, which she'd had to force herself to stop touching all day.

'Just off to get the mince pies,' she called to Jenson, but he didn't hear her. She sometimes wondered if he noticed whether she was in or not. He never saw her unless he wanted an audience.

She took the lift down to the entrance and emerged on to the street, where Nathan was waiting with Mellow. The sight of her took Madison's breath away. She was even more beautiful in real life than she was in magazines, wearing a simple wool-blend, knitted cream maxi dress with chunky brown boots and a brown Aviator jacket, which she managed to make look *über*-feminine. The tips of her jet-black dreadlocks had been dyed cherry red. Together, she and Nathan looked like a model couple, Madison thought, and wondered if anything *was* going on between them.

'Madison, this is Mellow,' said Nathan, sounding slightly nervous.

Madison beamed. 'It's so good to meet you. I'm looking forward to talking about the designs for your house.'

Mellow smiled back, appraising Madison. She was a cool customer, Madison thought.

'So where are we going for lunch?' Mellow asked Nathan.

'A sushi place, just round the corner,' said Nathan. 'If that's OK by you?'

Mellow gave a single nod, and they began walking.

'So, have you lived in the house long?' said Madison.

'About six months,' said Mellow.

'And how's that been?'

'Fine,' said Mellow.

She wasn't giving much away, Madison thought uneasily. Maybe she was used to guarding her privacy. She tried again: 'I always think it's best to really *live* somewhere before you start making any design changes. See the light at different times of day. Decide what bugs you about the kitchen layout.'

'I basically live out of a suitcase,' said Mellow. 'I feel like I'm almost never there.'

'Oh, of course,' said Madison. *Why didn't I think of that?* Of course Mellow would be travelling all over the world. Nerves gripped her. Mellow was so young, and so cool, and Madison was already feeling out of her depth. Just breathe and relax, she told herself.

'Here we are,' said Nathan, as they arrived at the restaurant. The interior was furnished with different shades of burnished metal, studded with hot-pink flower arrangements.

'Cool,' said Mellow, and Madison took that as a hint as to her design tastes.

A waiter dressed in dark grey came over and took Nathan's name, heading off into the depths of the restaurant, then coming back with a frown. 'I'm sorry, sir, we don't have a record of your booking.'

'I made it yesterday,' said Nathan. 'Via the website?'

The waiter's face fell. 'Ah. I'm sorry. We had a problem with reservations feeding through.'

'But there's space?'

He shook his head. 'I'm sorry, we're completely full.'

Nathan groaned.

'We can offer you a complimentary drink when you next book,' said the waiter. 'And I can only apologize for the inconvenience. Really, I'm sorry. If there was anything I could do to make it happen, I'd do it, but we're completely full for lunch.'

'Don't worry about it,' said Nathan. 'Not your fault.'

With that, they were back on the street.

'Should I have pushed harder?' said Nathan.

Mellow shook her head. 'Nah. I can still remember enough of waitressing to know how bad it was when customers gave you hassle for stuff beyond your control.'

Madison liked that.

'But I've literally got an hour,' said Mellow. 'So . . .'

'I need to find somewhere soon?' said Nathan, pulling out his phone and searching frantically. Mellow stared around, tapping her foot.

Back to being the star, thought Madison, wryly.

'OK, so there's this fusion place round the corner,' Nathan said, showing Mellow his phone.

She wrinkled her nose. 'Let's see the reviews.'

Nathan tapped the screen rapidly. 'Yeah, they're mixed, just looking at Tripadvisor. Some of the recent ones are quite bad . . .'

'What about the Greek one?' said Mellow, leaning over and peering at the screen.

'Let's see how long it takes . . . Nah, that's a twenty-minute walk. We'd be sitting down with menus and you'd have to go.'

'Could get an Uber?'

'Not in this traffic, Mel.'

Mellow now had her phone out, too, and was searching through restaurants.

'No, tried it . . . I think that one got a bad review? And this one, I didn't like the other place . . . Hmm, this could be an option . . . Wait, no, someone's left a review saying there was a weird *smell*?'

Madison was stressed out watching them scroll through their phones – and she was watching their precious time ebb away. 'How about we just walk around, take a few turnings and go to the next place we come to? Me and my friends have stumbled on so many good places that way,' she said.

Nathan and Mellow looked at her. 'Seriously?' said Nathan, but she thought she detected a smile in his voice.

'But what if the place is terrible?' said Mellow.

'What if it's amazing?' said Madison. 'Yes, we had a few disasters, and a few mediocre meals. But we also found the best falafel ever.'

'Where was that?' said Mellow.

'You know what?' said Madison. 'We never found it again. And that place may well have disappeared. But, in a funny way, that's what made it all the more special.'

'The case of the disappearing falafel,' said Nathan, and Mellow smiled properly.

'And the clock's running down,' said Madison. 'You'll never

discover anything new, if you're not willing to do something different.'

Suddenly Mellow laughed, her face transforming completely. 'OK, let's do it,' she said. 'I vote we go . . . left down here.' She pointed to a backstreet. 'Two rights and another left?'

'Lead on,' said Madison, feeling the tiny buzz of adventure she'd experienced so often as a teenager – while praying with the perspective of a forty-year-old mother of two wanting to change her career that the first place they saw wouldn't be terrible. They went down the alley, then turned left into a broader street, then went along another alley. Madison cringed as she saw Mellow's expensive jacket brush against some bins. It wouldn't be ideal if she covered her prospective client with bin juice before their meeting: first rule of business 101.

And then they did their last turn, and—

'There!' said Mellow, pointing.

It was a sweet little Italian restaurant, titled Giovanni's.

'Italian good?' said Nathan, to Mellow.

'The rules are we have to go wherever,' Mellow insisted, and in that moment she reminded Madison of her own daughter and of herself as a teenager.

Mellow sashayed into the restaurant, to be welcomed by a spotty young waiter who goggled at her and asked – tongue-tied – if she wanted 'a three for table', stammering and correcting himself, 'Uh, a table for three?'

'Yes, please,' said Mellow, and they perched at a corner table, with a red-and-white checked cloth.

'Look at all these photos on the walls,' said Nathan.

They featured the same man, round and beaming, with the great and the good – actors, sports stars, even royalty. 'Wow,' said Mellow. 'I'll have to see if he wants a picture with me.'

Nathan and Madison made eye contact briefly, and Madison pressed her lips together to avoid laughing.

Then Mellow nudged Madison. 'Got you there.' She cackled. 'Bet you were thinking I'm a right diva. So – do we choose the food randomly as well?'

'Can do,' said Madison, and she watched as Mellow shut her eyes and poked a finger at the menu.

'Gnocchi with four-cheese sauce. Good job I'm not doing runways any more.' She grinned.

Madison ended up with a Neapolitan pizza, and Nathan with a Caprese salad, which he moaned wouldn't be enough, until the other two said they'd share.

'And if the food could come quickly that would be fab,' said Mellow, batting her eyelids at the waiter. 'Listen, Madison, we don't have long. I'd love to hear about your designs.'

Madison took a deep breath. She'd been preparing for this, pulling together mood boards and possible colourscapes. 'I'm thinking something really fresh and modern,' she said, showing Mellow what she'd prepared on her iPad. 'This beautiful light wood. Exposed brickwork. Maybe some black-and-white shots on the walls. We can go super-high-end with the materials, really show them off. I was also thinking about burnished concrete.' She showed Mellow a few designs that featured it. It was a funny one, she thought. It had become really fashionable in recent years, and if it was done in the right way, it resulted in a glossy, textured sheen that could look great alongside other materials. It wasn't up Madison's street – she would always find it a bit cold – but it could be perfect for someone like Mellow.

Mellow was looking at her designs and nodding, but without the enthusiasm Madison was looking for. Maybe she was a slow burn.

'In terms of textiles, I was also thinking we could look at neutrals, but warmer than greys,' Madison continued. 'Like, creams through to beige through to taupe. And play about with the textures there: we could go anything from sheepskin to some ruffled cushions, so we're getting interest.'

At that moment their food arrived, and Mellow's eyes lit up at the sight of a steaming plate of gnocchi. Madison recognized a woman who just wanted to eat, so she stopped talking about her ideas and tucked into a pretty good pizza. Nathan had definitely drawn the short straw with a lacklustre salad.

'You win some, you lose some, Nate,' said Mellow, raising a hand to her perfect pout – Madison suspected she was stifling a burp.

'So maybe we could talk about the finishes?' said Madison. 'Chrome, or maybe copper?'

Mellow glanced at her phone. 'I really do have to go. Listen . . .' She hesitated. 'I like *you*. And I can see that these are good designs. They're cool. They're modern, but timeless as well. It's not gonna be doing my head in after a few months. But I spend so little time at home that when I'm there . . . I really want it to *feel* like a home.'

She looked at the restaurant. 'Like this place. I know the tablecloths are awful' – Madison cringed – 'and the bathrooms probably haven't been switched up since the forties. But the maps of Italy on the walls, the photos of the owner with all those people, even those weird little lace curtains in the window I kinda like. Feels like someone actually lives here. And I guess that's what I'm really looking for.'

'Then I need to come to your place,' said Madison, seizing the chance. 'If you want me to design a home, I need to see what I'm working with.'

Mellow nodded. 'Fair. Let me work out timings. I'll be in touch.' With that, she scrambled out from the table and away.

Madison exhaled. 'I've no idea how I think that went,' she said to Nathan. 'I feel like I messed it up, trying to second-guess what she'd want. What's cool.'

'You didn't mess it up,' said Nathan. 'She likes you. I know her, and if she wasn't feeling it, she wouldn't have waited for her food to come. So let's see.'

'Shall we get the bill?'

They waved the waiter over, and asked for it along with a takeaway box.

'Your friend, she already paid,' he said, blushing furiously.

Nathan grinned. 'That's Mellow for you. A mass of contradictions. Total diva, but I wouldn't still be friends with her if she wasn't a total sweetheart as well.'

Madison looked at her phone. She was running out of time to get back to Jenson, and she still had to buy some mince pies en route or think of a speedy lie to cover her back.

'Got to dash, Nathan,' she said. 'But let me know about another meeting?'

'If I don't see you before, Merry Christmas,' he said. He reached out his arms and suddenly they were hugging. It felt so good to be held.

Madison pulled back. She had a crush on Nathan, that was becoming clear, but nothing more. 'Merry Christmas to you too,' she said, turned away and walked as quickly as she could back to the office.

She needn't have worried: Jenson had left her a note saying he'd be out for lunch. She knew that meant he wouldn't be back in the office until much later, if at all, red-faced and full of his own genius.

One other thing was playing on her mind: a return to the mysterious address she'd found on the card in Rich's pocket, Flat 21, 90 Ryder Street. It would be almost impossible to get there later, with the kids. Her dad couldn't look after them, and she wasn't going to ask Savine to spy on her behalf again. If she took a swift afternoon break, maybe she could walk there again, ring the buzzer and see if anyone answered.

Her mind made up, she waited until half past three, inventing a fake parcel that needed urgent posting, if anyone asked. She returned to the alleyway, and was standing outside the door and preparing to ring the buzzer when the door opened and a man with a beanie hat and sunglasses emerged, looking startled to see her.

She caught the door before it could shut behind him and stepped inside, her heart in her throat. She was standing inside an unassuming lobby. There were pigeonholes for the post, a staircase and a rusty lift.

She looked at the pigeonhole for the address on the card. Empty. *Damn.*

Slowly, she walked up the stairs – nothing on the first floor or the second, but on the third she worked out which flat must be number twenty-one. There was no identifying name. It was completely blank, but the door opposite was twenty, so this had to be twenty-one. She raised her hand to knock, then lowered it. Was she putting herself in danger? Who was behind that door potentially?

Steeling herself, she gave a brief knock.

The sound of footsteps from within, and then the door opened.

18

A young woman, her face looking as if it had been carved from marble, stood before her.

'Yes?' she said to Madison. 'I don't think you have an appointment. Dr Farquhar is out until six p.m.'

'Dr . . .?'

The woman nodded. Madison noticed she was dressed in a smart navy tunic and trousers: a uniform. Her mind was racing. Why was Rich seeing a doctor secretly? Was he ill? Was this what he had been hiding all along? She felt sick.

'What kind of doctor?' she squeaked.

'I'm sorry, we cannot disclose any details,' the woman said.

'Could I just come in and sit down for a moment?'

'I'm afraid not. The clinic is appointment only, strictly, and you do not have an appointment with the doctor. In fact, I am unsure how you even gained access to the building. I'd suggest you leave, as we take security very seriously.'

With that, the young woman gave an icy smile and shut the door in Madison's face.

Madison didn't dare knock again, but her head was whirling. She went back down to the ground floor and leaned against the cool wall in the lobby, trying to gather her thoughts. Had she been completely wrong? What condition did the clinic treat? Her mind was racing to the very worst possibilities. Had Rich been having some kind of treatment, and was that why he was staying at his cousin's?

'All right, dear?' said a wavering voice, with an East End accent. Madison followed the sound, and saw that one of the doors was ajar. A tiny old lady was peeking out, her face fully made up, with thick black eyeliner and shocking pink lipstick. She was wrapped in a leopard-print dressing-gown.

'Bit wobbly,' said Madison. 'Just need five minutes . . .'

'Oh, take your time,' said the old woman. 'Nice to have a bit of life in here. I'm Ethel, by the way.'

'Madison. What's in this building?'

The old lady sighed. 'Used to be full of people living in flats – there was a real community of us. Soho in the seventies, what a place to be! But a lot of properties have been sold off to investors, lying empty while they decide what to do with them. Breaks my heart.'

Madison nodded.

'And there's the odd office. Funny little businesses. Obscure legal firms. Probably dodgy. The only real excitement I get is watching out for the stars!'

'The stars?' said Madison, doubtfully, wondering if Ethel was quite all there.

'Oh, yes. They scuttle in, up to the doctor's, and then they scuttle out again. And then I'll see them a few months later when it's all sprouting!'

Madison was wondering if she really was OK. 'What's going on there?' she said carefully.

'It's hair transplants. Isn't that lovely? Dr Farquhar is one of the best in the world! And, of course, they don't want anyone to know they're having them, just that their hair has suddenly miraculously regrown!' She let out a giggle. 'But I can tell you a list of everyone who's been through that door. It's like a red carpet in here.'

She proceeded to reel off a parade of well-known actors and musicians, including some A-listers that had Madison's mouth dropping open.

'*Really? Him?*' she gasped.

'Oh, yes. After his divorce.' Ethel tapped her nose. 'And then he got cast in that superhero film, so the transplant must have done the trick.'

Quickly putting things together, Madison pulled out her phone and flicked up a picture of Rich. 'What about him?' she said. 'Has he been in?'

Ethel looked at the screen. 'Oh, yes,' she said. 'Quite a few times now. Sometimes late at night. Dr Farquhar sees them any time they need to come. Very handsome chap! No idea why they all feel like they need hair when they look lovely just as they are.'

'Ethel,' breathed Madison. 'I cannot thank you enough.'

'What have I done?' said Ethel, clearly surprised. 'Well, you're most welcome, dear. And you must pop in again. It's rather nice having a bit of company.'

'I will,' said Madison. 'Happy Christmas!'

'Same to you, dear,' said Ethel, and retreated once more into her home. Madison noted she lived at flat eighteen. If she ever needed to visit again, she now had a buzz friend.

Outside in the street, Madison took deep gulps of air to steady herself. She didn't know whether she was going to laugh or cry. So Rich wasn't ill. And maybe there was no other woman. He was planning on a hair transplant. Relief was tempered with . . . a kind of sadness. Why wouldn't he tell her? Was he really so insecure about how he looked? Why the secrecy? Why had he felt he couldn't let her in? And more than that, wouldn't it cost the kind of amount that should be discussed with your partner?

But enough was enough. She wasn't going to let some follicles be the cause of their marriage breaking down, no way.

She messaged him: *See you at the show tomorrow night? And it would be really nice if you were back home for Christmas. x*

The choir show was one of her favourite dates in the festive calendar: the moment when their hard work paid off, and the community was brought together by music. She often spotted her mum's friends in the crowd, faces a little more lined every year but their hugs as strong as ever. The choir meant continuity too – she and her school friends had sung in this concert every year, including one memorable occasion when Abiola had come straight from delivering her first baby. She'd been so exhausted and so exhilarated that they still weren't sure how she'd got through it. This year, Madison had invited Savine – she felt like they were becoming real friends.

Madison was feeling good. She'd dressed in white, as instructed by Valerie, and done her hair and makeup just right. She'd been practising her solos, and her voice was like honey. The kids were smart and excited, and she was excited too to show Chloë that it wasn't just her dad who was a performer. She'd arrived early to practise their final positions, and now the mall was filling up, the crowd chattering happily.

Jess, Abiola and Ladene were beside her, the banter between them flowing smoothly, the in-jokes just the same as they'd been back at school.

211

'And we're gearing up for our winterval lunch too, ladies?' said Madison.

'Of course we are!' said Jess, indignantly.

Their winterval lunch was a long-standing tradition – they met between Christmas and New Year for a girls' lunch that generally rolled on into the evening, fuelled by Prosecco and gossip.

'It's the only thing that's keeping me going through the Christmas Day shift,' said Abiola, and they all sympathized.

'You're a Christmas angel,' said Jess.

'Also, Boxing Day's the best anyway,' said Ladene. 'I'm going to a day rave in Camden if you need to let off any steam.'

Abiola chuckled. 'Yeah, might be chilling in my trackies and eating leftovers, but I do appreciate the offer.'

'I'll need the winterval lunch to offload any criticisms Tina makes about my cooking,' said Madison. 'As much as I love her, the woman has opinions about the right way to cook a turkey and she's not afraid to share them.' She thought she detected a few glances between the girls.

'So . . .' said Jess, carefully. 'You're having a big family Christmas?'

Madison nodded. 'We are,' she said. 'And, turkey criticism aside, I can't wait.'

Jess beamed. 'I knew you guys would work things out. You'll be stronger than ever.'

'Let's hope,' said Madison. 'Thanks for keeping the faith, Jess.'

Peeking out from behind the screen she saw Rich arrive, with Chloë and Jordan, all of them so well turned-out.

How could he think he needed a hair transplant? thought Madison. She still found him *so* attractive. She pulled out her phone and messaged him. *Just seen you get here. Looking good. Hope you all enjoy the show. X*

She saw another message from Savine: *I managed to get here! Just squeezed in at the back but can't wait to see you in action. You'll be amazing.*

Madison just had time to respond with a heart before they were lining up and walking out from behind the screen on to the stage. Finn was taking his place at the piano, Valerie was shushing them all, and Madison felt Christmas excitement fizz through her. She lost all sense of time as they were singing: everything from gospel to carols, to slower songs, to newer pop songs like 'Oh Santa!' by Mariah Carey, featuring Jennifer Hudson and Ariana Grande (Finn's influence, no doubt about it). Then it was time for Madison's solo in 'Silent Night'. It had been her mum's favourite carol. Every time she sang it, she felt close to her.

Madison stepped into the spotlight, then adjusted her position to avoid the dazzling white glare of numerous lights in her face. *Shake it off,* she told herself. This is the shopping centre, not Broadway. She reminded herself of the family waiting for her out there, of friends old and new who were willing her to do well. *This is for you, Mum,* she thought, as she opened her mouth and let the first lyrics fly. She knew her voice sounded good, cleanly hitting the high notes, and the emotion poured through her. The rest of the choir came in to support her, their voices a soothing harmony to her high notes. She was thinking of nothing now, just enjoying the music, and all too soon they arrived at the end.

There was a moment's pause before applause broke out. At the back of the crowd, she spotted Savine clapping wildly as she got to her feet, prompting those around her to stand too. Madison's attention was caught by someone whooping, and she looked to the front of the audience where she saw Rich standing with Chloë on his shoulders. Madison gave her a tiny wave. As she searched for Jordan, Rich pointed down, as if to say, 'He's here,' before Jordan stretched up his arms and gave her a thumbs-up. Her heart swelled.

After the concert, there was mulled wine, and Madison was surrounded by people wishing to congratulate her. Savine had had to rush off, but Madison didn't mind – she was just grateful she'd come to support her at all.

Her dad was there with a few of his friends, and he pulled her into a hug. 'Your mother would be so proud,' he said, eyes glistening. She squeezed his hand and swallowed her tears. There was no need for more words between them, and more people were clamouring to congratulate her.

'Smashed that, didn't you?' said Finn. 'And the rest of you girls too; not a bum note between the lot of you.'

'Although there'll be no slacking off next term,' said Valerie. 'But yes. Well done.'

They exchanged glances: they must have been *really* good if she was dishing out the compliments.

Rich and the kids appeared, Chloë and Jordan hurling themselves at her. 'Mum, you were amazing!' said Jordan. Chloë's eyes were round and bright with excitement.

'You were incredible, babe,' said Rich.

Madison smiled at him. Then slowly, hesitantly, she leaned forward and kissed him on the lips. 'Thank you,' she murmured. 'Feels like Christmas has properly begun. And I think it's going to be a good one.'

She sensed Rich was taken aback, perhaps shocked by her actions, but then he seemed to relax – he smiled at her.

*

In the car on the way home, the kids chatted non-stop about what they wanted from Father Christmas.

'Remember, you have to *choose* what you *most* want,' said Madison, in a futile bid to manage expectations.

'But I'm sure he'll bring loads,' added Rich, quickly, and she didn't have the heart to disagree. The kids had been through this disruption too: she and Rich owed them a great Christmas.

At home, with Chloë and Jordan in bed, she poured two glasses of wine and passed one to Rich. 'Look,' she said, taking a deep breath. 'I know there's been stuff going on. I know you haven't been happy.'

He looked at her, taking a slow sip from the glass.

'But I want you to come home for Christmas,' she said. 'Like, properly. Wake up together on Christmas morning. Be with the kids. And then I want us to talk. Work through whatever's been going on.'

Rich was nodding, her words sinking in. 'I know, Madison,' he said. 'And I know I've been letting you down. But I'm working to be better. I promise.'

She reached for his hand. 'All I want, Rich, is for you to let me in. For us to tackle this as a team. Like we used to?'

He squeezed her hand. 'I don't deserve you, you know that?'

'Well, obviously,' she said, her tone light. 'I just want things to go back to how they were.'

A cloud passed briefly over Rich's face then, but was gone so quickly that she wondered if she'd imagined it.

'I'm filming tomorrow,' he said. 'But I'll be back for Christmas Eve. I promise.' He glanced at his phone. 'And I really should go. I've got an early start.'

She walked with him to the front door.

'You really were spectacular tonight,' he said. 'A star. Made me fall for you all over again.' He leaned forwards and kissed her.

Madison waited for her heart to flip, like it used to, but a quieter emotion was in play. She couldn't put her finger on it. Maybe this was security. Comfort? You couldn't expect someone to make your heart flip after years and years of marriage. Was it relief at knowing she had him back? After all her insecurity that his head had been turned by some glamorous young celebrity, surely she'd dreamed of him seeing her as the star of the show again. She was probably exhausted, wrung out by what she was feeling.

It was *nice*, she thought, closing the door. And right now, nice was good enough. They could build from nice. She went to bed that night, imagining how Christmas would be. They'd always loved Christmas. Waking up together, the kids opening their presents in a frenzy of excitement, her mum and dad coming round, Tina too. It was a day full of warmth and chaos, and she wouldn't have it any other way.

19

'Madison, you are not a Duracell bunny, slow down.' Rich walked over to her, chomping a slice of toast.

'I just feel caught off guard this year. There's so much I haven't done.' It was Christmas Eve, and Madison still had loads to do.

Rich had arrived back early that morning, complaining about Marvin having people round till late, and had been napping on the sofa, which was where Madison had found him. He'd brought his suitcase with him, she noted. It felt both weird and entirely normal having him at home.

'And the world continues to spin. Just slow down, OK? Have we got the food sorted?' Rich said.

'It's coming at eleven,' Madison said, as calmly as possible.

Rich nodded. 'OK. I'm going to nip out and get a few last-minute stocking fillers for the kids.'

'Don't go crazy,' Madison pleaded. Of course she wanted them to have an abundance of gifts, but she wasn't keen on spoiling them rotten. She wanted them to learn the value of money.

'Sure, but Lloyd gave me some cash and told me to buy something nice for them.'

Madison pressed her lips together. It was his brother's

money, she told herself. Instinct said they should talk to the kids about what they wanted, maybe even start them in the habit of saving, but it was Rich's first morning back in the household and if he wanted to spend the cash on presents, she wasn't going to fight it.

'Chlo was talking about a few books she wanted,' she said.

'I'll get something fun,' Rich said, pulling on his trainers, then leaving the house.

Madison contemplated his suitcase, left in the living room, half open and bursting with stuff. She was tempted to rifle through it, but she told herself not to. Last time she'd done something like that, she'd jumped to completely the wrong conclusion about what she'd found. Now was the time to start trusting Rich again.

Sitting on the edge of the sofa, she tried to feel satisfaction in her twinkling Christmas tree, adorned with white lights and strategically placed gold and silver baubles. A Black fairy holding a large shiny star sat at the top. Neatly wrapped presents spilled out from underneath the tree – she'd been up late last night wrapping them, including one for Rich. She'd thought carefully about what to get him and decided on a nice watch from an up-and-coming designer. He'd always liked being ahead of the pack, and if Rich was going to front his own show, it would be a great way to support another rising star too.

The subtle whiff of orange and cinnamon from the potpourri bowl on the coffee table cemented the Christmassy feel of the room. Gold tinsel woven down the banister in the hall was a tribute to her mum, who loved the stuff a bit too much. She'd wrapped it round picture frames, the TV and even worn it as a necklace on Christmas Day. She'd never got the 'less is more' memo.

Madison's eyes were drawn to the photograph of her kids sitting on her mother's lap. She walked across to the mantelpiece and picked it up. Her heart felt heavy with sadness, but Madison focused on gratitude: *I'm so glad you got to see me walk down the aisle, so glad you met my children, that they will always know you.* She touched her Angel Gabriel necklace. *I know you're watching over us.*

She wanted to ask her mum if she was doing the right thing, if she thought she could trust Rich again. Suddenly, as if her mum was speaking right into her ear, she heard her say: *You need to trust yourself, Madison.*

Madison shook her head, her heart beating fast. She wasn't sure if she believed in an afterlife. Her mum continued to be present in the love she'd poured into those around her. But sometimes, very occasionally, she thought she heard Selina's voice in a way that felt . . . different, somehow. As if her presence truly was there.

There was a thudding above her head, and before Madison could look for more messages from her mother, she realized it was Jordan, once again using his bed as a trampoline. She had no energy to tell him off – glancing at the clock, Madison chose the Christmas gospel soundtrack, cranked up the volume and got to work in her yellow Marigolds, cleaning the kitchen to satisfy even Tina's high standards.

She heard a knock at the door as she was pushing the stools back under the breakfast bar. 'That had better be Santa with the food delivery,' she called upstairs to the kids, opening the front door to reveal a mountain of crates on the step. *Oh, God.* Why couldn't it have been Tina's turn this year? She unpacked all the items on to the kitchen counter and began to put them away.

Her phone buzzed with a message from Rich. *What do you think to this?*

It was a picture of a drone.

Jordan's already getting a new game for the Xbox, she typed back. *That's another big and expensive gift?*

I think it's cool!

Madison put down her phone and counted to ten. A bolt of irritation jolted her. Why had he asked her opinion if his mind was already made up? She suspected that Rich was more into the drone for himself than he was for his son – he'd always loved a gadget. Maybe she was being churlish, though.

If you think he'd really like it, cool – just make sure you get something else for Chloë or we'll have WW3 taking place.

Rich sent her a thumbs-up.

Madison hesitated before typing, *Any idea when you might be back? Got to get started on a mountain of cooking, but the kids could do with a run around in the park.*

V soon!

But very soon wasn't soon enough, and it wasn't long before the kids were bouncing off the ceiling with energy. She was going to have to take them out.

She called upstairs and they came bounding down. Madison helped them put on their coats and gloves, with serious warnings not to lose the gloves.

Outside it was chilly but sunny, the colours of the leaves on the trees and ground ranging from dark green and burgundy to mustard yellow and brown. Madison watched her children play, their giggles infectious, and consciously tried to remain in the present moment.

When her fingertips began to sting, she called them and marched them home, arriving to see Rich's car in the driveway.

'I thought I was taking them out?' he said, as they came through the door.

'Yeah, but you didn't get back in time,' Madison said.

'But we didn't say a time?'

'I know, but we waited about an hour after your message. You know how they get, Rich, especially when something exciting is happening.'

Rich rubbed a hand across his face. 'I can't do anything right.'

Madison searched for her reserves of patience. 'There's a whole kitchen full of things you could do right, and I could really use a hand.'

'Let me cook something for you all,' he said.

'Yum!' said Chloë. 'I'm starving.'

'And look what I've got for your mother,' said Rich, taking Chloë's hand and leading her into the kitchen.

A huge bunch of flowers was on the kitchen worktop. Madison gasped. It was a stunning bouquet. She reached for the card. *For My Star, Madison Monroe.* Tears pricked at the back of her eyes, and she swallowed a lump in her throat.

'You like them?' said Rich.

'They're beautiful.'

He smiled, evidently pleased with himself. 'I remembered you love roses' – he raised his eyebrow – 'but these aren't just any roses . . .' he said, mimicking the famous British super-market motto as he turned over the card in her hand.

The beautiful array consisted of mauve memory roses, as well as black orchids, black and sunset calla lilies, Scottish thistles enhanced with gold wire and other flowers she had never heard of before.

Madison was grateful but she wasn't going to forgive him on

the basis of a bunch of flowers, no matter how different they were. Nonetheless, she appreciated the gesture and she would match his positive energy.

He reached over and switched on a soundtrack of nineties R & B classics, then began pulling down pots and pans, whistling. 'Where's the butter?' he said, peering into the fridge.

'Here,' Madison said. 'But listen, babe – can you not use up too much of anything? It may look like we've got enough to feed an army, but this is a finely calibrated operation to get Christmas Day done.'

'Absolutely,' said Rich. 'Maybe it's quicker to tell me what I *can* use.'

'Sure,' said Madison. She felt awkward, as if Rich was a house guest, not her husband. She pointed out the 'normal' food supplies, and he set to work putting them on the newly cleaned work surface.

'I'll look after the kids for a bit. You go and chill,' he said, grating cheese.

She smiled. 'Thank you.'

Jordan sloped into the kitchen. 'What are you doing, Dad?'

'Making us a Christmas Eve feast,' he said. 'Come here, you.' He grabbed Jordan's hand, and they boogied around the kitchen together, Jordan laughing his head off.

Chloë pretended to disapprove but was clearly desperate to join in. 'You're so silly!' she shouted.

'Silly is good. Come on, Grouchy.' Rich twirled Chloë around.

Madison cracked a smile. *This is the man I know,* she thought, and broke into a volley of sneezes.

'Bless you!' said Rich. 'Hope you didn't catch a cold in the park. Shall I make you a hot toddy?'

'It's too early for that.'

'It's Christmas Eve – anything goes.'

She smiled again. She could tell he was making an effort. 'That would be nice.' She took a seat and watched him prance around the kitchen as he made the drink. 'Thanks, babe,' she said. 'I might just have a quiet half-hour with this.'

'Take all the time you need,' said Rich.

Madison padded up to their bedroom. Rich had moved his case up there, and it was half unpacked. Some of his things were hanging in the wardrobe, she noticed. Others were crumpled in the laundry basket. She went to the bathroom and saw his toothbrush beside hers.

So he's really back.

In their bedroom, she quietly shut the door and sipped the hot toddy, listening to Rich and the kids messing around downstairs. It made her smile to hear them. She tried to shut her eyes and catch some much-needed rest, but her mind kept wandering.

And, for once, it wasn't wandering to where Rich was and what he was doing.

It was wandering to thoughts of how to impress Mellow.

Giving up on sleep, Madison pulled out her iPad and began looking again at interiors online, jotting notes for what she thought might work. She found herself looking all over the world, then going back to vintage interiors, wondering what would make Mellow feel at home.

She also decided she'd tell Rich what she'd been up to. She was sick of the secrecy. She'd do it as they were preparing the kids' stockings: it had always been a moment they loved, a chance for a glass of something nice, just the two of them. The hot toddy was a bit too strong, she decided. The few sips had gone straight to her head.

She made her way back to the kitchen, where Rich's cooking had exploded all over the work surfaces. She'd just cleaned them meticulously – could he not have been a bit more careful?

The kids were grinning wildly and chomping stacks of savoury pancakes, so she focused on their joy and hoped Rich would clear up properly, without being prompted. She pulled out her phone and messaged her dad. *You sure you don't want to come round today or tonight?*

All good, my daughter, came the reply. *You know I like a moment to visit your mother.*

Since she'd died, her father went to her grave frequently. And each year, he'd gone to lay a festive wreath and spend some time there on Christmas Eve. He said Christmas Day could get so hectic that he didn't have time to think of her properly.

Say hello, typed Madison. *And make sure you wrap up warmly!*

I've kept myself alive for seventy-four years, sure I can manage a few more, her dad typed back. *But thank you. I've got my hat and gloves all ready.*

See you tomorrow, she messaged. *And if you do want to come over later, that's fine.*

Going to Hector's later, her dad replied. *Boys' night.*

Madison chuckled. Truth be told, she was delighted that her dad was socializing a bit more again. The first couple of years after her mother's death, he'd been a shell of himself. She felt the weight of responsibility for him shift a little.

The rest of Christmas Eve was boisterous. Madison banished Rich and the kids to the sitting room so she could make a start on the food for the next day. She cleaned and seasoned the chicken, turkey and salmon. She soaked the saltfish and made a big pot of rice and peas. It was early evening before she knew it. She ventured into the living room with bowls of popcorn for everyone, *Home Alone* blaring.

'Mum, what did you buy me for Christmas?'

Madison looked at Jordan with a raised eyebrow. 'You really want to know the day before you get to open it?'

He nodded, shook his head, then nodded again.

'Dad says it's going to be the best Christmas ever!' said Chloë, her eyes wide.

Madison frowned at the smear near her mouth. 'Have you been making an early start on the chocolate?'

'Just a bag of the little coins,' said Rich. 'I said no to everything else.'

Madison wasn't about to start shaming her daughter for enjoying a treat. 'Any left for me?' she asked, unwrapping the gold foil and putting a couple into her mouth, savouring the sweetness. It was time to press some sort of order on this scene, she decided. Otherwise the kids would be up late, too excited to sleep, and grumpy tomorrow.

She picked up the remote and turned the TV down a notch or two. 'Why don't we sort out the goodies for Santa?' she said. 'Those reindeers get tired with all the deliveries.'

Jordan rolled his eyes, big enough to know the truth, but sworn to secrecy. Chloë leaped to her feet and raced to prepare a variety of snacks for the magical flying visitors.

'Got her mum's eye for hostessing,' said Rich, as they watched Chloë leaving carrots for the reindeer, a clumsily assembled cheese sandwich for Santa, then writing a welcome note.

Madison laughed.

'Santa might appreciate a few chocolate coins too, Chlo,' said Rich, winking at Madison and handing Chloë a few more.

After they'd wrangled the kids into bed, they began adding

the last presents to large red stockings, stitched with a pink C and a blue J, which Madison had made when they were toddlers. Madison finished off by filling the stockings with chocolates and sweets, being careful to put the same number of treats in each – there would be hell to pay if any present unfairness was perceived.

Chloë and Jordan reappeared back downstairs multiple times, nearly catching them in the act, to see if Santa had been and finally fell asleep way later than Madison had hoped, but that was Christmas for you.

'Glass of something proper?' said Rich, in the kitchen, reaching for the cheese sandwich. 'Could make you something spicy?"

Madison remembered the drink she'd had with Nathan, and felt guilty. 'Yeah, that'd be lovely,' she said, as Rich pulled out bottles, and made her a spiced rum and Coke. She took a sip and winced. 'Tiny bit strong,' she admitted, and added more Coke.

Rich poured himself one and clinked his tumbler to hers. 'Here's to a family Christmas.' He smiled.

'So,' she began, sensing the atmosphere was relaxed. 'There's stuff I've been wanting to talk to you about.'

'Yeah?' said Rich, and she sensed his nervousness spike.

'About what I've been up to these past few weeks.' She swallowed. Now she was nervous too. 'I guess it's given me a chance as well to think about . . . our future. What I want to be doing within that.'

'Sure,' said Rich, slowly.

'I got this opportunity, through a work colleague,' said Madison, 'to pitch for a design project. You know how I've been hating my job, hating Jenson, so much.' The words were tumbling out of her now. 'And this opportunity, it could be really good. It felt great to be using that creative muscle again, and we're going to have a meeting next week, where I get to go to the client's house—'

'Madison, woah,' said Rich, frowning. 'Hold up. So you've been having these meetings, and it's about a potential new job?'

She shook her head. 'Not a contracted job, it'd be freelance, but it's the first time I've felt excited about anything in ages.'

She pulled out the iPad. 'Look, I've been working up these designs.'

Rich took a glance. 'I didn't realize you hated your job with the hotels that much.'

How could you not have known? Madison thought. She came back every day she worked there feeling grey and defeated. 'Well, yeah,' she said. 'I've felt like that for a while now. Maybe it took the prospect of something new to make me see just how uninspired I was feeling. I guess you needed some time out to focus on the future, and I suppose I've been doing the same. Maybe we were drifting along on autopilot. Maybe this is the chance we needed to reinvigorate things.'

Excitement was building in her.

Rich was rubbing the side of his beard.

'These past few weeks, at first it was so awful, but I've been pushed out of my comfort zone, and I was doing stuff that *inspired* me, like going to see street art, going to galleries' – her neck grew hot at this particular admission – 'and I began to feel like myself again. And now that the kids are a bit older, now we're not crisis-managing every day with them, maybe it's time to think big about what's next for us.'

There was silence.

She waited for Rich to speak, to smile. To do *something*.
'You OK?' she said.

'Just taking this in. I need another drink.'

He went to the kitchen, came back with a bottle of Jamaican
beer and took some gulps. 'Look, Madison, I know the last few
weeks have been really hard on you. Don't think I don't feel
guilty about that. And I've been thinking about our future too.
The show is – I promise – so near to coming off. And then it'd
mean more money. An easier life.' He paused. 'You wouldn't
have to work that hotel job any more. Not if you didn't want
to. And we've spoken about you doing something on the show.
I'm still hopeful about that.'

Now it was Madison's turn to fall silent. She felt her stomach
plunge with disappointment at what he'd said about the show:
it was starting to feel like carrot-dangling because it was so far
from definite.

'But there's no actual job offer being formulated for me. I
need to be clear. One minute you're encouraging me to come
to producer meetings and think of designs. The next minute,
you're only hopeful.'

He blew out his cheeks. 'You know how these things are. I'm
doing everything I can to make it happen. What I'm saying,
though, is that once I've got the gig, we'll have the extra income
so that you won't *need* to work at Jenson's.'

'I don't even know what the show is.'

'I think I can tell you now.' He smiled. 'It's called *Rags to
Rich's* – get it? At least that's what it'll be called if I front it.
And it's about how to increase a property's value. So we go in,
we look around the home, we talk about what design features
will add the most value. And there's going to be this really
funny segment where we look at luxurious items from around

the world – the most expensive wallpaper, gold bath fittings, that kind of thing.'

'OK . . .' she said. 'So who's going to be on this show?'

He shrugged. 'I guess people looking to invest in property. People looking to be smart with their money.'

Madison nodded slowly, but the idea was leaving her cold. She fundamentally believed that good design wasn't a question of money, or what it added financially to a property. She didn't want viewers to feel they couldn't make their homes more special because they couldn't afford the priciest options. Good design was practical and beautiful, and made everyday life a bit better. Yes, of course money came into it, she wasn't that naïve, but had Rich forgotten she'd done up their own home on a shoestring budget and he loved every inch of it?

Rich stretched and yawned. 'Shall we hang these up and get to bed?'

'Sure,' said Madison.

They hung the kids' stockings over the fireplace and Rich padded upstairs. 'I'll just take a minute to clean up a bit.' She needed some time to herself. She felt a plummeting disappointment. Rich was back, and apparently trying hard, but it felt like he just didn't *see* her. He'd expected she'd be on board with his vision for the show, when in fact she stood for something completely different. And instead of noticing her hesitation and talking more to her, their conversation had reached a dead end.

'OK, babe,' said Rich. 'Don't be long, though.'

Madison went back into her Zen living room and gazed at the perfect Christmas scene. She tried to feel happy. Rich was back, so the family was together again, but she felt far from calm. She went into the kitchen and gulped a glass of water. OK, things weren't perfect, but she needed to try. She refilled the glass, this time drinking slowly to bide her time and think. She wiped down the kitchen counter, placed dry spoons in the drawer – and stopped. She was procrastinating. She went upstairs, and Rich was already snoring in bed. She felt relieved he was asleep, even though earlier in the day she'd wondered if, when they were lying side by side again, she'd be in the mood for sex.

But now she lay awake, staring at the ceiling, as the hours passed, replaying the conversation. He hadn't even taken an interest in her designs for Mellow or asked who they were for. Where was his curiosity, his encouragement of her vision, interests and next steps? She was beginning to feel she wanted to do her *own* thing, not be a sidekick on Rich's show.

20

'Merry Christmas!'

Madison woke with a start to Jordan and Chloë tumbling in and jumping on the bed.

'What time is it?' She looked around, disoriented. Last time she'd checked, it had been three a.m.

Rich propped himself up on the pillow, yawning, and Jordan pushed his Spider-Man watch in her face. 'Present time.'

Madison moved his hand back to see the watch face clearly. 'It's six o'clock!' She'd had three hours' sleep. Christmas Day loomed like a marathon.

'Come on, son, let's see if Santa's come.' Rich got out of bed, flung on his onesie and looked back at Madison. 'Yes, it's new. You like?'

Madison rolled her eyes at the sight of her husband in a Spider-Man onesie and durag, and wondered if this was the result of yesterday's spending spree.

'Spider-Man! Zap, zap.' Jordan pointed his hands in different directions pretending to release his web as he darted out of the room, closely followed by Rich.

The thought of having to spend all day in the kitchen filled her with dread. *Lord, I know I don't pray to you enough, but please can you give me the strength to get through today.*

She still felt unsatisfied by last night's conversation. She had wanted it to be a breakthrough moment, of them *both* sharing their dreams and ambitions for the future. Maybe if she'd spelled it out to him, he'd have listened, but why should she have to do that? He should be excited about her opportunities whether they involved him or not. She'd spent the last few weeks craving Rich, feeling the pain of his absence, and now she was feeling . . . *not much at all.*

A soft knock at the door and Chloë wobbled in with a cup of tea. 'Dad said to bring you this.'

'Thank you, baby.' Madison patted the bed beside her, and Chloë crawled in for a hug. 'So, since the boys are downstairs, how about some girl time?'

'*Yesss!* Can you paint my nails?' she pleaded.

'Sure. Let's jump in the shower and get dressed first.'

An hour later, they were both showered and dressed in tacky Christmas jumpers. Chloë picked out red glitter nail varnish, and Madison carefully painted her little nails. She was only allowed to wear it in the school holidays.

'Oh, look! I'm all sparkly. Thanks, Mum.' Chloë wiggled her fingers, stood up and fanned them, jumping up and down. Madison looked at her daughter and wished she could absorb some of her energy.

'*Muuum.*' At the slow, dragged-out sound, Madison stopped what she was doing and gave Chloë her full attention. 'Does Jess like me?' Chloë was still jumping up and down, her hands flapping beside her, but she looked sad.

'Of course she does. Why do you ask?' Chloë shrugged. 'Stop jumping for a second.' She did as she was told, and Madison asked again. 'Why do you ask? What's up?'

'We haven't had best-friend time for ages.'

'We've both been busy. It's not for ever. Are you missing Sienna?'

'Kind of,' Chloë said.

Madison remembered what Jordan had said about Sienna's behaviour and wondered what was going on between them.

'Let's all hang out together soon, OK? Film night.'

'The daddies too?'

'Yes, baby.'

Madison looked at her daughter, sensing Chloë's insecurity. More than anything, she wanted to give her the confidence to trust her own instincts and never settle for less than she deserved. She knew this meant leading by example. 'Come with me,' Madison said. She got up, and Chloë followed her to the mirrored wardrobe. Madison sat cross-legged in front of it and gestured for Chloë to do the same. 'I'm going to say some words and I want you to repeat after me, OK?' Chloë nodded. 'All right. I love myself . . .'

'I love myself,' Chloë repeated.

Madison continued, clapping out a beat with her hands. Chloë joined in, repeating every line. 'I love myself. My family love me. I am nice to people and people are nice to me. If people don't like me, that is fine, 'cause I like me and the people who are nice to me.'

They repeated the affirmation again, and Chloë turned to her mother, smiling. 'Thanks, Mum. I love it.'

'You're welcome, baby. I want you to say that to yourself every morning, OK?'

Chloë beamed and hugged her tightly.

'Right! Shall we see what the boys have been up to?' Madison said, with new-found energy. Chloë responded with star jumps on the bed. She jumped off and they headed downstairs.

On their way, Madison retrieved some tinsel from the cupboard under the staircase and wore it as a necklace. Chloë ran into the kitchen ahead of her and, when she saw it was empty, went into the living room. Rich and Jordan were sprawled on the couch playing a computer game. From the doorway, Madison threw Rich daggers with her eyes. He clocked her disapproval. 'Sorry, babe, one more level and then I'll get breakfast all set.'

Madison forced down her frustration and smiled at him. 'That would be great. Thank you.'

A series of bleeps and groans from the boys, then Rich got up and set to work in the kitchen. For breakfast, they ate ackee without the saltfish, fried dumplings and baked beans. It went down a treat, and Madison tried to put everything else out of her mind as they turned their attention to the presents under the tree.

Madison captured the kids' reactions on camera, so she could embarrass them when they were older. Their level of joy was so cute. Jordan loved his new drone and the Xbox game, and Chloë was thrilled with her tap shoes. While the kids were busy ripping open gift after gift, Madison handed Rich his first present. He placed it to his ear and shook it. Madison rolled her eyes. He did that every time and never correctly guessed what the gift was. He unwrapped it and she watched his face light up.

'Oh, this is so good. When did you capture this?' He stared at the blown-up picture in a frame of him and the kids laughing as they kicked leaves in the park.

'About three months ago.'

'Good thing you always have your phone in your hand.' Madison chose to ignore what felt like a back-handed compliment. 'Thank you, hun, I love it.'

She smiled as she handed him another gift. He ripped off the paper, opened the box and looked at her with his mouth open. 'This is a beauty.' He removed it from the box and placed the watch on his wrist. Madison smiled. It gave stylish, professional and self-assured energy, she thought.

She handed him a slim envelope and his eyes widened. 'Hun, you're spoiling me.' He ripped open the envelope. 'Oh, tickets?'

'Yeah,' she said. 'It's an acid jazz band night at the Royal Albert Hall. It'll be our first date night in a while.'

'That's so cool,' he said. 'Thank you.' He then pushed a present at Madison.

She tore it open. It was a bottle of her favourite perfume. She tried to hide her disappointment. Yes, it was generous – this stuff was expensive – but she wasn't even halfway through the previous bottle, and she'd been craving something a bit more . . . thoughtful.

'I've been meaning to sort something else, too,' said Rich, quickly. 'So consider the other part of your present an IOU for a weekend away.'

'Sounds good,' said Madison, deflated.

He nodded, pleased with himself.

'Did you have anywhere in mind?' she asked.

'Uh, maybe Paris again?' he said.

Madison knew that a trip to Paris was an amazing gift, but he'd just come up with it off the top of his head, and it clearly hadn't been planned much beyond that. She would have preferred something smaller, but a bit more personal. Something that showed he'd been thinking of her.

'Right, guys, can you gather up the wrapping paper and put away the gifts you're not playing with?' Rich instructed. 'Then you can choose a film to watch, play games, help Mummy in the kitchen, whatever you want.'

Madison gave him a death stare. As the kids tidied up and put their presents to one side, she zoned out as Chloë and Jordan fought over what to watch. In the end, Rich flipped a coin, and Chloë won.

'Yes! *Aladdin*. Let's watch *Aladdin*.'

Jordan grumbled, but soon got into it, as always. They'd both seen it so many times and Chloë, as usual, was in her element singing. Madison beamed with pride at her mini-me.

Rich and Jordan clapped, and the doorbell sounded. Madison went to answer it, to find her dad waiting on the doorstep. He looked dapper and unique in his brown trilby hat, with a long Puffa jacket with smart boots. 'Merry Christmas, darling,' he said, as he enveloped her in a hug. She smiled as she breathed in his familiar smell of mild leather and spice with citrus under-tones. 'Now, where are those little monsters?'

The kids came shrieking into the hall, shouting, 'Happy Christmas!' and flinging their arms around him.

'What if I told you I'd forgotten your presents?' he said, with a wink at Madison.

The kids stood back and looked at each other.

'I don't care,' announced Jordan. 'I'm just happy you're here.'

Madison's dad nodded slowly. 'You're raising these kids right,' he said. 'But I'm glad to say that . . . presents are here!' He reached to the side of the door where he'd stashed a bag out of view.

'Come in, come in,' said Madison.

Her dad and Rich shook hands, and Rich offered to get him a drink, which he declined as it was a little too early.

They all piled into the living room, where the kids tore open their gifts like hungry hyenas. 'Slow down, guys,' murmured Madison, as they excitedly held up their gifts from Granddad D, then crashed into him with kisses. A silver charm bracelet for Chloë, adorned with a musical note, heart and angel Gabriel to match Madison's necklace. Jordan received a pair of Michael Jordan trainers that he'd been banging on about for ages. 'And your mum's gift was too big for me to bring over,' her dad said.

She rolled her eyes. 'If you forgot to get me something, just say. Selfridges sale is on soon.' She smiled, her full set of pearly whites on show.

'What is it?' clamoured Chloë. 'Is it an elephant?'

She's definitely had too much sugar, thought Madison.

'Why, yes, it is!' said her dad, causing Chloë's mouth to drop open, before she realized he was teasing her and collapsed into giggles. Madison smiled. She loved to see the relationship the kids had with their granddad.

'Here you go,' said her dad, and he handed her a slim, A4-sized package. 'I even wrapped it myself.'

She squeezed his hand. It had been Madison's mum who did the wrapping in their household – Madison could still remember being taught how to fold the corners of the paper perfectly and tuck them in, before taping them.

Carefully, she opened the package. 'It's sheet music?' she said, confused, flipping through the book, which was a collection of favourite gospel tunes.

'It is,' said her dad, enjoying drawing out the mystery.

'I don't get it . . .' Madison began.

Her father took a deep breath, gathering himself. 'Well, I have decided that you should have your mother's piano.'

'Dad,' gasped Madison, tears swelling. 'Why? You've got so many fond memories. It belongs with you.'

'We all have fond memories.' He reached out to hold her hand. 'She played with such ease and filled the house with music, through the piano and her voice. It pains me seeing it there, silent, only touched when I dust or polish it. It deserves to be played and I'm too old to learn new tricks, but you're not.'

Madison had no words. She leaned forwards and embraced her dad tightly.

'Thank you,' she said softly. He patted her on the back.

'Oh, I've also arranged for some lessons so it's not too torturous for everyone while you're learning to play.' Chloë and Jordan chuckled loudly.

Madison laughed, too, while swiping away the tears that streaked down her face. 'I'll be no match for Mum, but maybe I'll give Finn a run for his money.'

'Why are you crying, Mum? Don't you like it?' said Chloë, concerned.

'She's happy-sad,' said Jordan, sounding very wise.

'And I have no idea why you two are laughing,' said Granddad D. 'Chloë, that musical note means you'll also be having lessons and so will you, Jordan. Look in your trainer.' Jordan did as he was told and pulled out the music for 'Jingle Bells'.

'We'll have to think where to put the piano,' said Rich. 'I might just have an idea about that, though.'

Madison looked up at him, wondering what he meant, but then the doorbell went – it would be Tina – and they rushed to answer it. Madison looked at her dad and took his hands. 'It's the best present I've ever had,' she said simply.

'Get away with you,' her dad said, flapping a hand at her, but she could see his eyes were shining with tears.

Then Tina was bustling round the door and greeted everyone with warm hugs.

'Keep her out of the kitchen,' muttered Madison to Rich – but too late, Tina was already in there, lifting lids from the saucepans, stirring the sauce and telling Madison she needed to have the oven up higher or more seasoning needed to be added.

Time passed in a blur – music was on, a Christmas film playing in the living room, which no one was watching, the kids hyped up on chocolate and the excitement of new presents.

Madison told Chloë and Jordan repeatedly to set the table, then gave up and did it herself. She scattered some snowflake sequins over it as a final touch, stood back and exhaled.

Tina came to peer at her handiwork and Madison was relieved when her mother-in-law nodded in approval. 'I think you need a drink, my dear,' Tina said, and Madison smiled. She loved Tina, deep down, and knew she only wanted the very best for her family.

Soon, they were all gathered around the table, heads bowed as Granddad D blessed the food they were about to receive, ending in the chorus of 'Amen'. Rich carved the turkey, and served it with dollops of cranberry sauce, gravy and crunchy roast potatoes.

'Not bad at all,' said Tina, looking at the full spread on the table, which was way too much food for the number of people seated.

'This is all so good,' said her dad. 'I'm so happy to be here.'

Chloë turned to her granddad and insisted on pulling a cracker, which he allowed her to win, and she insisted he wear as many paper hats as possible. Madison took a few photos with her phone, capturing the joy. She reminded herself that, whatever the turbulence of the last few weeks, *this* was what mattered. Her dad, his head bowed as Chloë tried to *manoeuvre* yet another hat on to him without ripping it. Rich, leaning in to talk to Jordan, promising to test his new drone. Tina, watching the scene unfold, her eyes soft with pride. This was family.

'Anyone for seconds?' Madison asked, and was met with a chorus of 'Yes, please!' from around the table.

'Oh!' said Tina. 'A message from your brother. Look, it's a picture of them!' She held up her phone and aimed it close to everyone's faces, so they could all see. Lloyd had indeed sent a picture of himself, his glamorous wife and their kids on an impossibly white beach in the Maldives, the sea a stunning turquoise. They were grinning over a Christmas lunch of grilled seafood.

'Doesn't it look marvellous!' said Tina.

'That'll be us next year, babe,' said Rich.

Madison winced. Was he joking? She liked Christmas at *home*. But he had that edge in his voice he always got around his brother – defensive, keen to show that he was just as good. 'I'll get dessert sorted,' she said, heading into the kitchen and preparing the Christmas pudding, dousing it with brandy and lighting it, then whizzing through to the table while the blue flames leaped around it.

Once the flames had gone out, she served it with ice cream.

Tina peered at it and frowned. 'How long have you had this steaming?' she asked.

It had been in the microwave for about eight minutes, but Madison wasn't about to tell her that.

'Oh, long enough, Tina,' she said sweetly.

Tina was prodding at the pudding with her spoon. 'And what recipe did you follow?'

It was a supermarket's finest brand – she'd had neither the time nor the inclination to make Christmas puddings this year, or any other year. 'Bit of improvisation,' Madison lied. 'Do tuck in.'

'It's delicious,' said her dad. 'So much better than the shop-bought ones.'

After they'd finished eating, the adults topped up their drinks, sparkling elderflower for some, wine for others. Madison didn't dare make Sorrel. Although she had mastered her mum's recipe she was not willing to let Tina scrutinize it. Everyone went into the living room to watch *Elf*, the grandparents snoozing before too long, to the delight of the kids, who mimicked their snores.

'I'll make a start on the kitchen,' said Madison. She liked a moment or two to herself in the chaos of Christmas. To some peaceful gospel tunes, she began rinsing plates and stacking them in the dishwasher. Today was going well. Rich seemed relaxed and happy to be back. She couldn't expect miracles. There were bound to be bumps in the road as they reconnected and worked out what the future looked like.

She heard a buzz and looked round. It was Rich's phone, plugged in to charge.

She stared at it, intrigued. She didn't know the password, and even if she had, snooping in your husband's messages was a no-no.

The phone buzzed again. Quietly, she picked it up and looked. It was a text message from an unknown number, but the phone showed a preview of it.

COME BACK TO TINDER! Reactivate your account with 50 per cent off premium membership for the whole of Jan.

Madison put the phone down, the blood pounding in her ears. Why the hell was Rich getting messages from Tinder? He clearly had an account. He'd clearly *been* on it, if the message was to reactivate an account. She felt sick. She'd taken the decision to trust him again. Was he playing her for a fool?

Footsteps down the hallway. She didn't want to see anyone. Especially not Rich.

'Want a hand with the clearing up?' he said, before clocking her face. 'You OK?'

'Shut the door,' Madison said. Something inside her snapped. She was sick of being careful. She was going to get to the bottom of this.

21

'What's up?' Rich pushed the door shut.

Madison took a deep breath. 'Why are you getting notifications from Tinder on your phone?'

He frowned. 'Why are you checking it?'

'Don't deflect. I picked it up to wipe the kitchen surface. And then I saw this message pop up about reactivating your Tinder account.'

He gave a snort of disbelief that incensed Madison. 'It's spam,' he said. 'Those kind of messages get sent out all the time.' He picked up his phone and shoved it into his pocket. 'I don't appreciate the accusation. Not when I'm here, really trying.'

'Are you actually kidding me?' Madison said, furiously. It was all she could do to keep her voice down. 'What the hell am I *meant* to think? You walk out, saying you need space. You're heading off to mysterious art-gallery events, making appointments – even talking about a hair transplant, which is a pretty significant financial outlay that you might actually want to discuss with your wife—'

'How the fuck do you know this stuff?' said Rich, his eyes wide, then narrowing. 'Have you been . . . *following* me? What the hell, Madison? I don't even know . . .'

There was an awful silence between them. Madison had never really understood what it meant to feel that trust was completely broken. Now she did. 'You left me no choice,' she said. 'So yeah. I did some of my own investigations.'

'I cannot believe this,' said Rich. 'I trusted you.'

'Don't act like you're the victim here!' said Madison, her voice breaking. 'I trusted you too. I trusted you not to break our family. I trusted you to talk to me. *All* I wanted was to discuss this with you. You know, when I discovered the hair thing, I wondered what I'd done wrong that you were feeling so insecure you were thinking of that! That you doubted I was still attracted to you.' Tears were flowing down her cheeks, and she swiped them away.

'This is fucked up,' muttered Rich.

'Be honest,' Madison said. 'Be honest. Why are you getting these notifications from Tinder?'

Rich cupped his face in his hands, and rubbed his beard in a gesture of frustration. 'I told you. It's probably a scam to get my card details.'

And again, Madison felt that plunging doubt. Was it as simple as that? *Was* she the bad guy?

'But just what have you been doing in this time?' Madison said. 'I still don't get it. You were gone, and now you're back, and what's changed? What did you need to leave us for? Do you realize the hell you've put me through these last few weeks?'

'You think I don't feel shit enough about that? I've been working on our future. Thinking of what that looks like.' He gave a deflated laugh.

'But why wouldn't you include me in it?' she said. 'That's the bit I don't get.'

The kitchen door was shoved open and they jumped.

'Granny T's snoring loads!' said Chloë, delightedly. 'Come and listen!'

'In a minute, hun,' said Madison, swiping at the kitchen surface. When Chloë was gone, she turned back to Rich. 'I have no idea what to think. But I want you to stay at your mum's tonight. Maybe *I'm* the one who needs some space now.'

He looked stung, then folded his arms defensively. 'Yep. At least Mum won't be looking through my phone.'

'That is a *low* blow,' hissed Madison.

The door opened again and Jordan ran in, begging them to come and watch TV. Madison couldn't bear faking it any more. She pleaded a headache and went to lie down upstairs for an hour. *Just get through today*, she told herself. *Please, Mum. Help me make it through today.*

She looked at her phone, at the photos taken only a couple of hours before. It seemed like a joke now. She scrolled through her WhatsApps. Messages from the girls and Finn, sharing pics of their own Christmas Day. A message from Nathan too, wishing her a very happy Christmas. She couldn't bear to reply to any. Her whole life felt like a lie right now. She scrolled down to Savine's number, hesitating before typing a message.

How's your Christmas?

It's not my favourite, Savine typed back. *I'll be honest about that. My son is with his dad this year. And you can't help but feel that everyone else is with their happy families.*

Madison paused to take in her words.

Sorry, Savine went on. *That's a bit too much honesty after some day-drinking. And believe me, if you're with your happy family, then I am glad glad glad.*

That's how the day started, messaged Madison. *But I found something on his phone.*

Swiftly she explained what had happened.

You've done the right thing asking for your space. He's not helping matters by going on the defensive, Savine typed back. *If – and that's a big if – there is an innocent explanation, he should know he needs to work for your trust.*

I feel like I've exploded things already, Madison replied.

That's not on you. Do NOT blame yourself. You aren't the one who set this all in motion.

Thanks, Savine. Your words mean a lot. I'm sorry it's not been a great day for you.

I'll get through it. I've had worse, believe me.

Do you want to come over later? After the kids are in bed? I'd like the company, if I'm honest.

Well, if you're sure? You can spare me from watching The Holiday *and falling into a spiral of depression.*

Madison snorted. *I'll message you later, if that's OK? I might just pass out.*

Sure. I'm here if you need me. And you AREN'T going mad.

She must have fallen asleep at some point because she woke up, mouth dry, completely disoriented. What time even *was* it? She reached over and looked at her phone. It was 6.30 p.m. She forced herself to go downstairs and peered round the living-room door. Everyone was there apart from Rich.

'How can you fall asleep at Christmas, Mum?' said Jordan, indignantly.

She gave a comic yawn. 'Maybe I was helping Santa last night.'

She heard the front door go. Rich walked in, barely glancing at her. 'Where have you been?' she asked.

'Literally for a walk, for twenty minutes,' he said, and there was no disguising the tension between them.

'Let's watch an old classic before we go home,' said Tina.

Madison could hardly refuse. At least if they were watching a film, she wouldn't have to talk to Rich.

'I'm going to get a glass of water. Anyone want anything from the kitchen?' Madison said. Everyone either took her up on the offer, or declined, but Rich was quiet.

'Do you want anything or shall I leave you to get it yourself?' Madison said, and she couldn't take the sting out of her tone.

'No, thank you,' said Rich, stiffly.

She took orders for drinks and snacks, and padded through, breathing deeply. She could cope with watching a film. Then the kids would be in bed. And she could think what to do with this latest crisis.

As she sipped a glass of water, she heard her dad shuffling down the hallway.

He peered around the door, then came in and patted her shoulder. 'Are you all right, my girl?'

'Fine, Dad.' Madison smiled. 'Just a headache.'

He looked at her closely and laid a hand on her cheek. 'You know I'm always here for you, don't you?'

Madison placed her hand over his. 'I do, Dad. I really do.'

He nodded slowly. 'Anything you need, I'm there.'

Any more of this and she'd crack. Part of her desperately wanted to tell him what was going on, but where would she even begin? She had a tragicomic vision of her dad's confusion over Tinder, and let out a snort that was half tears, half laughter.

'What am I like? I'm emotional today,' she said, pulling a piece of kitchen towel and blowing her nose. 'Always this time of year. Gets to me.'

'I know,' he said. 'Let's watch the film. Then it'll be my bedtime.'

'You know you can stay here?'

He chuckled. 'No offence, but the thought of getting back to the peace and quiet of my own little home is quite appealing. I'll have a chat with your mother before bed.'

Madison was startled.

'Don't look at me like I'm losing my marbles,' he said. 'You know she's always with us. Just some days she seems to fancy a chat more than others.'

Madison remembered her mother's voice coming to her so strongly: *Trust yourself.*

Easier said than done, when your instincts were pulled all over the place.

22

Finally, she was alone. She'd put her dad into an Uber, and as Rich hadn't been drinking during the afternoon, he'd been able to drive Tina home. She'd deliberately hidden from him in the kitchen as they left – she had no idea how long this goodbye was for. Mercifully, the kids seemed to have exhausted themselves and fell into bed without too much complaint, their eyes fluttering shut.

If only she was sleepy. Instead, her mind was ramping up, running over the possibilities endlessly. Maybe it was a scam text, and she'd betrayed Rich's trust by letting slip what she'd found out about him. But, if so, why wouldn't he see her point of view, that her behaviour was a desperate measure? And what if the account was genuine? Had he been meeting other women all month? Awful visions rose in her mind of Rich flirting with them in a bar, Rich taking them to a hotel room or, worse, back to theirs. She felt sick. There was no way she could deal with this alone.

She picked up her phone. *If you're still up and would like to come round, I can feed you leftovers and wine. Price of entry is working out what the hell I do next. But I get it if you've decided* The Holiday *is a better option.* She added her address, and Savine texted when she was outside, avoiding ringing the bell so as not to wake the kids. She held up a massive bar of chocolate. 'Thought you might need this.'

Madison laughed, and ushered her through to the living room, settling them with wine, the chocolate and blankets.

'Where's your head at?' said Savine. Just her friend's presence made Madison feel calmer. Savine knew exactly how this felt.

'All over the place again,' Madison said. 'Just after I'd decided to try to put all this weirdness behind me. Today, it felt like he was trying, like he wanted to be here.'

Savine nodded slowly. 'He might be confused too. Doesn't mean he's innocent.'

Madison blew out her cheeks. 'So how do I find out the truth about the Tinder message? I mean, maybe it *was* spam.'

Savine thought for a moment. 'You might not like this. But. He received a notification. That can only mean he has a profile on the app. We just have to find him.' She pulled out her phone. 'Now, I swore off the apps for a bit. But we could make a fake account. See if we find him, then if he replies.'

Madison took a long swallow of wine, her hands shaking.

This was the only way.

'I feel like I'm sending you to war,' said Savine. 'We don't have to. You can try and talk it out with him again.'

Madison shook her head. 'That's the problem. He *won't* talk to me. He won't let me in.' She took another swig of wine. 'Let's do it.'

'You sure?'

'As I'll ever be.'

'Well, this is uncomfortable . . . but you have to decide on what kind of woman would appeal to Rich.'

Madison's heart plunged, and she groaned. 'I need more wine for that.'

Savine raised an eyebrow. 'Maybe she could say she's into bald men. Appeal to his insecurities.'

Despite herself, Madison giggled. 'And she loves listening to men talk about obscure acid house jazz? For hours?'

Savine chuckled. 'Let it out, girl.'

More wine later, 'Lola' was born. She was thirty-five, single and ready to mingle. She loved socializing, travelling to luxury hotels ('He'll like that,' Madison had hiccuped) and, yes, she was a big fan of acid house jazz too. They'd searched online and found some photos of a model on Instagram who was stunning. They'd downloaded pictures of her in Dubai, on a beach sipping a cocktail from a pineapple in a trendy bar, her face illuminated by neon lights.

'I feel bad using someone else's pics,' said Madison.

'These are gonna be up for an hour or so, then we'll de-activate it,' said Savine. 'Ready to go live?'

They launched Lola's profile and set her preferences to Rich's age-range and location.

'Not bad,' said Savine, eyes gleaming as an attractive forty-two-year-old man popped up. 'Look, Madison, what do you reckon?'

'Can we stick to the mission?'

'Sure, but maybe you can enjoy a little light window-shopping along the way. Nothing wrong with that.'

Madison looked at the smiling profile of Shane, who was divorced with one kid, and looking to find someone to enjoy Friday nights and weekend lie-ins with him. He *was* quite good-looking, even she had to admit.

'And he's sent Lola a like!'

'She can't get likes!' Madison exclaimed. 'She's got one job.'

'She can enjoy herself on the way,' purred Savine.

'Give me the phone,' said Madison, and soon she was swiping swiftly through profiles. 'Woah, but *this* guy is hot.' She'd stopped on a man with a gorgeous smile and kind eyes.

'Does he have a good body, though?'

Madison rolled her eyes. 'I like his *face*. He looks really kind.'

'Kind face good, hot body better.'

Madison spluttered. 'You going to get that on a motivational-quote poster?'

'Yeah, maybe.' Savine grinned. 'Words to live by.' She looked back at the phone and scrunched up her face. 'Babe, swipe past. Any man who thinks posing with a drugged tiger is cool is far from it. Next!'

How was it possible she was having a good time? Madison thought. It felt fun gossiping about men with her new friend. It had been a while but it was like being single again. Every time Lola got a like – and they were coming in thick and fast – they checked out the profiles and either murmured in approval or gasped in shock at some of the more out-there messages. As time went by, Madison felt herself relax even more and they flicked through more profiles, on a mission and at a faster rate, swiping left like a soothing but addictive game. Maybe Rich *wasn't* on there. Maybe what he'd said was true. Lost in the rhythm of swiping left and talking to Savine, she double-guessed herself on a few pictures and pressed the undo button to make sure it wasn't him before continuing. And then.

She gasped.

There he was.

She froze. The air in the room felt heavy. Savine looked at Madison, then her phone.

'Ah, babe.' Savine let out a slow breath. 'I'm so sorry.'

Madison felt like she was having an out-of-body experience. The profile was brief. In fact, he was barely recognizable – only one photo was a close-up, and he had a cap pulled down low, showing only his jawline and the corner of one eye. There was another, a bathroom selfie, of just his bare torso.

'I recognize the tiles,' Madison said, and let out a weary laugh. 'I fucking picked those.' *How could he?* she thought. How could he take topless selfies in their bathroom mirror, the place where the kids did their teeth? Where she took a shower most mornings? In their family home? Without any respect or boundaries. He was only called 'R' on his profile. There were no other details, other than that he was London-based.

Madison stared at the photos for a long time.

So he'd lied to her about having a profile.

And just how much had he been using it?

Slowly, she dragged her finger right across the screen. There was no match.

That was some relief, in a bizarre way.

She put the phone down, trembling. The two women sat in silence.

'It gets better,' Savine said softly. 'That's the only thing I can say for sure.'

'Does it?' said Madison. 'Because right now . . .'

There was a ping. Rich had matched with Lola.

'It only seems to be getting worse.'

Savine picked up the phone. 'Do you want me to message him?'

'I don't know. Just let me think for a moment.'

But as Madison was processing this latest development, Savine gasped.

'His profile's gone.'

'What does that mean?'

Savine shrugged. 'He's either unmatched her or he's deleted it.' She glanced at Madison. 'Either way, we don't have proof. We didn't screenshot the pictures.'

'And I'm left with more questions *again*,' said Madison, her voice croaking.

'What are they? If you want to share them?'

'I just cannot get a read on what he's been doing,' said Madison. 'This man, who's meant to be my husband. Has he been meeting women constantly? Or is he just on there as . . .'

'Some kind of ego boost?'

Madison nodded.

'It happens,' Savine said. 'The number of guys who match you and then disappear.'

'I mean, none of it is good,' said Madison. 'Not the fact he's on there. Not the fact that his half-naked pic was a conscious decision. Not the fact he's lying.'

'But you just want to find out how far he's gone?'

Madison nodded slowly. 'Yeah.'

Savine glanced at the clock. 'Look, I've got to make a move as the Uber price shoots up when it's late. But I can stay if you want me to. You'll just have to explain to the kids who this new crazy lady is.'

Madison managed a short-lived smile. 'It's OK. Thank you – again – for coming round.'

Savine put on her coat. 'You don't have to thank me. Do you want me to deactivate Lola?'

Madison nodded. 'She's served her purpose.'

The two women embraced, and Madison went to bed, where she fell into an uneasy sleep, full of disturbed dreams.

23

Rich must have come back early to the house: when Madison woke, she could hear him moving around downstairs. She couldn't bear to look at him. Not when she knew he'd been lying to her face. Her heart had hardened. She would do whatever she needed to do to get to the bottom of what had been going on – or what might still be going on.

'Hey,' she said, walking into the kitchen.

At least he looked terrible too, as if he hadn't slept much either. 'I want to sort this out,' he muttered.

'I do too, but I'm doing it in my own time now,' she said.

The plan had always been that Rich would take the kids to see his relatives on Boxing Day. Normally, out of a sense of duty, Madison went too, but today she was having the space for herself. She made herself a coffee and went back upstairs, listening to Rich getting the kids up, ready and then out of the house. He must have told them she was asleep, as they didn't open the front door with their usual gusto.

Although the house was peaceful, the questions in her mind caused her head to pulsate. She needed some fresh air and a change of scenery. Madison took a long, luxurious shower. She daubed herself in her favourite moisturizer and spritzed on perfume – the most expensive one she owned and usually saved for special evening occasions, different from the one Rich had bought her. She took time to apply her makeup. If she was going to face this, she wanted to look and feel great, as regal and strong as the women in Dreph's street portraits.

She sat down and peered at herself in the mirror. 'So what do you know, and what do you need to know?' she whispered.

She knew he was on Tinder. She knew he'd lied about it. What she didn't know was if he'd met anyone from it and physically cheated on her. And how could she find that out? She threw on her warmest tracksuit and hoodie, wrapped up and left the house. Hands tucked into her pockets, she walked along briskly, making decisions about her next direction when the option presented itself. She turned left, went through the park gates, followed the narrow, winding path until eventually she arrived on the other side, then walked on to the high street. Most of the independent shops were shut, but a few were open. She didn't mind: it was clarity she was looking for, not bargains. This time last year they'd all chilled for a large part of the day, then grabbed their bikes and gone riding around East Dulwich Park.

What was Rich doing now? Sneaking off to message someone from the app? Or maybe he'd joined more than one. She shivered. It was starting to spit with rain. She put up her hood and stepped into the nearest shop to take shelter briefly, hoping it would soon ease off. Noticing she was in a phone shop, she glanced at the brightly coloured cases.

'Need any help, love?' said the man behind the till.

'No, thanks,' she said – and then an idea struck her. 'Do you sell SIM cards? Like, unregistered ones?'

He nodded. 'Yeah.'

'So I could just put it in my phone and message off that number?'

He nodded again.

Madison's heart rate increased. 'I'll take one, please.'

Back at home, the house silent, she switched the SIM cards and watched as her phone registered the new number. Was she seriously about to do this? She pondered for a minute or two, then tapped and saved Rich's number in her new phone. She typed:

Hey. It's me. Message me back only on this number. Can we talk?

She pressed send.

Time dragged. It felt like eternity. The message had been delivered. No reply. As a distraction she tidied her wardrobe, refolding jumpers, putting shoes into their boxes and facing all items on hangers in the same direction. The trashiest reality TV show played in the background. The wait was agonizing, made harder by her pretence that she didn't care. Two hours later, there was a message.

I thought we said no contact.

She threw her phone on to the bed and clapped her hand over her mouth, feeling as if she might be sick. So there was someone else! Her head raced, making her feel dizzy. She sat on the edge of the bed and read the message again in case her eyes had deceived her. *No contact.* What had Rich and this woman started and what had changed?

Her fingers trembling, she typed back.

I know. But I really need to talk to you. In person.

She waited an agonizing ten minutes.

OK, Rich typed back. *When? Where?*

Madison scrambled to look at her calendar. *29th? Boca bar at 12 noon?*

It was a bar in the next borough from theirs.

OK, said Rich. *It has to be lunchtime.*

That's fine. See u there.

She flopped back on the bed. Tears rolled down her face. She wondered what the woman looked like. Were they similar, or completely different? Was she younger, a lot younger? Was he in a mid-life crisis stage? She sighed heavily and wiped her eyes as she stared at the ceiling in a daze. Then she jolted up. The trap was set. She had the messages from Rich – they were proof. She would turn up to this meeting, give him the shock of his life when she was there and not the other woman. She imagined the scene. He would be forced to come clean – or would he come up with an excuse? She wished she had a screenshot of his Tinder profile but she'd tell him she'd seen it. *I want answers. I deserve answers.*

She swapped the SIM cards back and texted Savine an update of what she'd done.

I cannot believe he denied it all. Spam, my arse, Madison typed furiously.

I'm afraid I can, hon, said Savine. *If he's decided that the grass isn't greener, then of course he's not going to fess up now.*

Madison put down the phone. Another thought was taking hold. If he had cheated on her, could they ever move past it? Could she ever move past it? Instinctively, she'd always thought no. That it was a red line. She was loyal to a fault, and she expected the same from other people. But then she found herself down an internet rabbit hole, reading stories and posts in forums about people who *had* moved past infidelity, some saying their relationship was better than ever, others regretting staying. She felt a headache coming on. She felt that her life, which had previously seemed so secure and stable, was dissolving.

She checked her other notifications.

One from Rich, confirming the time he'd drop the kids back, that he wouldn't stay over and hoped they could talk later.

'Oh, we'll be talking all right,' Madison muttered. Although she was tired after the rollercoaster ride of emotions, she was ready for this confrontation.

24

Madison put on her 'all is well' mask. She walked confidently into the restaurant, and over to where Jess, Abiola, Ladene and Finn were already seated with a bottle of Prosecco. Finn was expertly topping up the glasses. He waved at her. 'Come and sit down! Let me pour you some bubbles.'

The atmosphere between them all was relaxed and happy. Even though Abiola looked exhausted, she was full of tales from the ward on Christmas Day – and she also mentioned a handsome new registrar several times.

'I don't have to be a doctor to diagnose mentionitis,' said Ladene, grinning.

'He's just a colleague,' protested Abiola.

'Uh-huh,' said Finn, raising an eyebrow skywards. 'And you've just happened to notice professionally how good he looks in his scrubs?'

'I didn't *say* that!' said Abiola, but then everyone was teasing her and encouraging her to ask him out.

Madison followed the conversations, and made herself laugh at the jokes, and sympathized with everyone's Christmas moans, but she felt one step removed from them. She was there but not fully present. She took another swig of her bubbles, unsure they were helping. They felt acidic in her mouth. She drank some tap water and picked at her food when it came.

'How was your Christmas, babe?' said Jess.

Finn peered at her plate. 'If you're not eating that, I will.'

'Finn!' scolded Jess, but Madison slid her plate across to him. She had no appetite.

'It was OK.' They raised their eyebrows. 'We're having our annual celebratory lunch. I didn't want to bring this to the table,' Madison said, speaking slowly while trying to remain somewhat upbeat. She didn't want the focus to be on her stuff, but pretence would have been short-lived and they would have got it out of her anyway. She sat up tall. 'As you know, Rich and I have been having some troubles. But at Christmas I found out he was cheating on me.'

Gasps went round the table. Finn reached over and squeezed her hand silently.

'How do you know?' said Jess, taking a sip of water.

'I saw a text message from Tinder appear, inviting him to reactivate his account. He said it was spam, but he was so defensive – I just didn't know what to believe. We had a bust-up . . . Look, I've been so paranoid these last few weeks that I've done things I never thought I would. I did things like follow him, desperate to know what he was up to.' She hung her head.

'None of us knows how we'd react in that situation,' murmured Finn, 'so no judgement here.'

'To be honest, I'd have done way worse, way sooner,' said Ladene, and Madison managed to smile at her.

'So, yeah. My mind was spinning. So I created a fake profile on Tinder. And I found him.'

More gasps of shock.

'OK, so . . . you don't know if he was on it just looking?' said Abiola. 'Like, you'd be surprised at how many men are on it as a weird ego boost.'

Madison nodded. 'Yeah, that's what I thought too. And then his profile disappeared. So . . .' She took another gulp of bubbles. 'I sent him a message from a SIM card I bought. My thinking was, if he replied saying, "Who is this?" or "You've got the wrong number," or something, it'd look innocent. But he said, "I thought we said no contact."'

Finn dramatically clapped his hand over his mouth.

Madison felt anger surge through her again. Why was her festive lunch taken up with this? She wanted to be telling her friends about the other stuff she had going on: about Mellow, about the kids, about Nath— *not* Nathan: there was nothing to tell.'I am *so* sick of being lied to,' she said. 'I'm sick of him taking advantage of my trust.' She leaned forwards, tapping her finger on the table for emphasis. 'I'm not going to be made a fool of any more. I told him on the burner phone to meet me at Boca bar, two days from now, at twelve noon. And that's where I'm going to confront him.'

She looked around the shocked faces of her friends. 'And you guys need to be there to support me,' she said, the words flying. 'I want people to *see* how he tries to wriggle out of it. I want him to feel ashamed of what he's done. I am *sick* of covering for him!'

Finn laid a hand on her wrist. Madison realized she'd raised her voice and people were staring.

'Sorry,' she muttered.

'Babe,' said Ladene. 'I am so on your side. I cannot believe he's treated you like this. But a public showdown? It's giving an *EastEnders* vibe. Are you sure that's the best way to handle it?'

Madison snorted. 'He's rebuffed *any* opportunity to speak honestly to me. He's literally avoided being in the same room as me for weeks, so, frankly, a public showdown where he's forced to hear me out is sounding pretty good right now.' She glanced around the other faces at the table. 'You're with me, right?'

Jess picked at her nails. Abiola's gaze was darting to and fro.

'We're with you, Madison,' murmured Finn. 'But think about this. Please. Something in me is saying confrontation isn't going to turn out well.'

'I cannot believe my own friends aren't backing me,' Madison said, tears rising hot in her eyes. 'If it was *any* of you, I'd be there, cheering you on.' She got up and pulled on her coat.

'Babe, please don't go,' said Ladene. 'Let's talk this out. We're just trying to make sure you handle it in the best possible way for you.'

'OK, like you know me best?' said Madison, sniffing back tears. 'I'll fight my own battles, then. I'm asking for support from my friends!' With that, she got up, threw some money on to the table and stormed out. She was sick of being told to be calm, to be rational, to be understanding. This was Madison on the warpath, putting her feelings first, doing what she thought was right, and it felt good.

Outside, she paused, unsure of what to do next. She wasn't ready to go home. She looked at the notification on her phone. She'd forgotten all about the meeting tomorrow with Mellow. She decided she wanted something new and expensive to wear. If Rich was contemplating spending thousands – literally *thousands* – on a hair transplant without her knowing, she was going to buy herself a designer outfit so that she, too, could feel good and more confident. She almost laughed at how sweet and understanding she'd been of his insecurities, even trying to overlook the money issue. But no more. She was going to do what *she* wanted, too.

She messaged Savine: *Shopping SOS. Want to join me? Selfridges sale?*

You're a brave woman, replied Savine. *Why not? But let's go to Harvey Nichols instead. I'll see you there in an hour.*

Deal. Text me when you are near.

At Harvey Nichols Madison moved down the rows of sale clothes, nothing catching her eye. She discarded skimpy, delicate dresses, swept aside rails of boring trousers. She wanted something that made her feel like a real warrior. Something that had the right balance of masculine and feminine energy, bold yet serene.

'Hey,' said Savine, coming up beside her and giving her a hug. 'I see you're taking out some of that anger on the rails.'

Madison looked at where she'd shoved all the clothes up together and had to laugh. 'I didn't realize,' she said.

'Retail therapy, is it?'

'Something like that,' said Madison. 'I just feel I deserve something that makes me feel amazing. I want to go into that meeting tomorrow and not think of myself as Rich's wife or anyone's mother. I just want to be *me*. Pitching my designs.'

Savine nodded. 'Let's find that outfit, then,' she said, casting an eye over the sales stuff. 'I'm not sure we'll find it here, though.'

Madison looked at her. 'You're talking full price?'

'We're worth it,' said Savine, steering Madison towards the tranquillity of the new-season clothes, the collections laid out perfectly in front of them. This is more like it, Madison thought. 'The rule is, if it catches your eye, you try it on. The goal is ten items.'

'OK.' Madison smiled nervously. Every time she saw something beautiful, or different, she ignored the voice in her head that said maybe it was too expensive, or it wouldn't suit her, or it had been made for a different kind of woman. And pretty soon, with ten items of clothing each, Madison and Savine entered the changing rooms usually reserved for those using the personal-shopping service. The assistant smiled at them as they walked into the large vacant space.

'I figured that the kind of people who use personal shoppers probably wouldn't be coming in during sale time. Seems I was right! Now,' Savine said, turning to Madison, suddenly business-like, 'as I said, just try them on. The old Madison may hate it, but we're looking for the new Madison, so keep an open mind. Don't look at the price tag, and call me when you have it on.' She closed the curtain on Madison, who took her time to change into the first item, a navy jumpsuit, and emerged.

'What do you think?' said Savine.

Madison stared at herself in the mirror. 'I can't decide whether I like this or not, and that's worrying because I'm not an indecisive person.'

'Heartbreak fogs everything,' Savine reassured her. 'Focus on how it makes you feel. How does the fabric feel against your skin? Does the colour work with your skin tone? Do you feel good in it?'

Madison watched her face shift through different expressions, before deciding on a shrug.

'OK, put it to the side and try on the next one,' Savine said. It was a red, flute-sleeved, bodycon midi dress. 'So, this is giving me bold, chic, warm, but sexy. How do you feel?' Savine asked.

'It's nice, I guess.' Madison shrugged again. 'I don't know. I don't know who I'm looking at in the mirror any more.'

'Hon, we clearly aren't seeing the same thing. Look in the mirror, and let's do an affirmation.'

'I do those with my daughter,' said Madison, 'but I'm a grown-ass adult.'

'A grown-ass adult who needs affirmations! Say it enough times and you'll soon believe it.' Savine stood next to Madison in front of the large mirror. 'I love myself. I love all of me. Come on, repeat the words after me.' Madison did as she was told. 'My situation doesn't define me. I am powerful, I am confident, I am successful. Endings are also beginnings. I am open to the bigger version of me.'

Madison finished slowly, and hugged Savine. 'Thank you for that . . . and for all of your support.'

'My pleasure,' said Savine. 'And now may I suggest you try on a few of the items I picked for you?'

Madison chuckled. 'Is my taste *that* bad?'

'Not at all,' said Savine. 'But sometimes you need someone else's perspective. And I have a feeling that this little number might just be the one to start with.' She handed her an exquisite, deep-plum leather dress.

'Oh, that's . . .' said Madison.

Savine held up a hand. 'If you're going to say way too short, or tight, I don't want to hear it.'

Madison mimed zipping her mouth shut and went back into the changing room. As soon as she stepped into the dress and zipped it up, she felt it hug her body, just the right amount. When she glanced at herself in the mirror, she could see how the plum colour set off the glow of her melanin skin to perfection.

She stepped out of the changing room.

Savine's eyes widened and she nodded slowly. 'I hate to say I was right, but . . .'

'You were right,' said Madison. 'I feel *amazing* in this dress.' She turned this way and that, looking at herself in the mirror, smoothing down the leather, feeling how butter soft it was under her hands.

'Want to try another one?'

Madison considered the offer. 'I think when you know you know.'

'Yep, trust your instincts.' Savine grinned.

Madison reached around and looked at the price tag. 'Oh. My. God.' She was panicking now. 'OK, so reality just called.'

Savine looked at the amount too. 'Can you literally afford this?'

'Literally, yes. But I just cannot spend this amount on myself. Not when it could go on a holiday with the kids or doing up the kitchen or—'

'When was the last time you bought something just for you? That you really *wanted*? Not something practical. Or that would do.'

Madison thought back and couldn't remember.

'We're taking this one,' said Savine, handing the dress to the sales assistant.

'You'd be crazy not to,' said the assistant. 'Plus it's the only one we have in store.'

'There you go,' said Savine. 'It's meant to be.'

Despite her financial reservations and the beads of sweat pricking her scalp, Madison affirmed she could afford it and happily punched in her credit-card pin. The green tick confirmed the most beautiful dress was hers. 'Thanks so much, Savine. I really needed this.'

'Have you thought about your next moves?'

'Yeah,' said Madison. She explained the plan to Savine. 'And I've been thinking,' she added. 'Maybe I need to go further. Maybe I need to expose him to the papers or something, and then see how long his family-man image lasts!'

Suddenly she was imagining lurid headlines, Rich exposed for the cheater he was. It felt awful. It felt good.

She saw Savine flinch.

'Madison,' Savine began softly. 'I've been where you are. You know that. But just . . . don't go that far. I know what it's like to want revenge. But the best revenge of all is going on to live a life where you look back and wonder how you made him the centre of your world.'

Madison pressed her lips together in defiance . . . and then they softened. Something clicked in her that hadn't before, when her friends had told her the same. Savine had been in the same situation. She cleared her throat. 'I guess the tabloid headlines were a tad dramatic,' she admitted. 'But I do want to know who he's been cheating on me with. I want him to confess everything.' She paused, sensing the need to deflect the conversation and keep the vibes high. She could only expect people to come so far on the journey with her. Ultimately, this was between her and Rich. 'Shall we go and check out the makeup counter?'

'Absolutely,' Savine agreed. 'That dress needs a new lipstick.'

25

Madison smoothed her new dress and affirmed silently, *You've got this*, before she pressed the intercom on the solid black gateposts at Mellow's house.

'Hey?' Her voice crackled out of the speaker.

Madison smiled as she spoke, putting a positive inflection into her greeting. 'Hi, Mellow, it's Madison.'

'Amazing, come on in.'

The sound of a buzzer, and the gates swung open to reveal a gravel drive, leading up to a beautiful modern house: sleek, low level, with huge windows. Madison ran back to her car and drove in before the gates closed.

Mellow was waiting at the door. 'Come in. I'll grab your coat but best leave your shoes on. As you'll soon see, some areas are still a building site.'

Madison shook off her brown longline teddy borg coat.

'Great dress, by the way,' Mellow said immediately.

'Oh, thanks,' said Madison, trying to sound nonchalant.

As she followed Mellow through the house she didn't see any building sites. She saw only potential. The space was . . . *amazing*. The kitchen and living room were open plan, with a beautiful, spiralling wooden staircase leading to the upper floor.

'Checking out the staircase?' said Mellow.

'Yeah,' said Madison. 'It's stunning.' She crossed over to it and ran her hand over the wood.

Mellow smiled. 'Glad you like it. That's the one thing I commissioned myself before I decided I needed some help.'

'You have a great eye. That staircase is everything!' said Madison. 'Hmm, perhaps we could look at echoing this pattern, this wood, in the designs?'

'Yeah, I'd love that,' said Mellow. 'Want to see the rest?' She showed Madison where the downstairs bathroom would be – 'It's presently a room with some plumbing in it. Everything's up for grabs.' They walked back out to the open-plan living area. There was already a kitchen island, with cabinets and worktops.

'How do you feel about this?' said Madison.

Mellow wrinkled her nose. 'Don't love it.'

'How come?'

'I'm just not sure,' said Mellow, the words sure to strike fear into any designer's heart. It was way harder having a vague brief than a clear one.

Madison tried another approach. 'OK. So let's visualize this. How do you see yourself using this kitchen? Do you like cooking?'

Mellow laughed. 'I'd *like* to like cooking but, with life as it is, I just don't have the time.'

'OK, so tell me what you want this space to be for.'

'What I imagine is, when I'm back from a shoot or something, I can tell my friends to come over. There's loads of room for them to perch while I pour us a glass of wine and maybe make something quick for us . . . or order in.'

'So the kitchen is a social space for you?'

Mellow was nodding. 'Definitely. I'm not gonna shut myself away and stir pasta sauce for hours.'

Madison smiled.

'The other thing,' Mellow said, warming to the theme, 'is that I do want this to be a party house. So the space has to adapt easily. I'm not talking about massive raves but if I want everyone over, I want room for them. I want different spaces for people to congregate in.'

'Dancing?' said Madison, before they both said, 'Of course,' and laughed.

'What about upstairs?' Madison said.

Mellow beckoned, and they walked up the beautiful staircase to the landing.

'Different vibe up here already, somehow,' Madison mused. It was carpeted, which felt warmer, cosier.

'Yeah,' said Mellow. 'This is the house bathroom.' She pushed open the door to a room with a high ceiling and a beautiful skylight.

'Nice,' breathed Madison.

'Then there's two guest rooms,' said Mellow, showing her into each one. 'And here's my room.'

Madison would have expected Mellow to take the biggest and best room in the house, but hers was at the back, with a sloped ceiling and only one smallish window. There was a simple, wooden-framed double bed, made-up with soft pink linen, and a small table lamp on the floor, with several large suitcases and boxes in states of unpacking.

'As you can see, it's early days,' said Mellow, shifting awkwardly.

'Why did you choose this room?' said Madison, intrigued.

Mellow widened her eyes. 'I'm not sure. Just liked the feeling of it.'

'It's your sanctuary,' Madison said suddenly. 'I get it. You're tucked away at the back of the house. It's cosy. It's quiet.'

Mellow clapped her hands. 'Yeah! That's it.'

Madison was finally understanding her prospective client, and an idea was forming in her mind.

Mellow led them back downstairs. 'So did you have any more designs for me to look at?'

Madison shook her head. 'No. I wanted to come here first to get a sense of this space and of you.'

'And what are you thinking?'

'That this house is your castle.' She looked around again. 'I want this house to be an ode to the strong, independent woman you are. I want you to arrive back here, and feel *reflected* in this place, that it's a space for you. That, yes, it's a place for you to invite others to, but that you're in control.' She paused for a moment. 'It's a space that looks after you.'

Mellow beamed at her. 'Yes! That's exactly how I want to feel!'

Madison let out a relieved laugh. 'And now I just need to figure out how to turn that feeling into reality. But I tend to find, once I know the feeling we're going for, the rest follows.' She held her breath. She felt like she had this in the bag.

'Do you want to see outside too?' said Mellow.

'Sure.'

As they arrived at the bottom of the stairs, Mellow handed Madison her coat. She smiled and put it on. 'Just through here,' said Mellow, picking up a set of keys and unlocking a door. 'Through the garage.'

Madison stepped down into the garage – and stopped dead.

In front of her was a gleaming white SUV. With a personalized registration plate: MOM311.

'I'm hoping to get the garden done at some point,' Mellow was saying, before she registered that Madison had stopped. 'Oh, the car is cool, isn't it?'

Everything was clicking into place for Madison. *This* was the woman Rich had been having an affair with. *This* was the car that had followed him. She looked at Mellow's clear golden brown skin and exquisite features, and something inside her broke. This was the other woman. The woman whose house she was about to design.

'Are you OK?' said Mellow.

'Have you . . .' Madison was unable to utter the words. She closed her eyes and forced herself to speak. 'Have you been seeing my husband?'

Mellow looked shocked. '*What?*' she said.

Madison couldn't take this any longer. She backed away, shaking her head, then burst into sobs. She fled around the side of the house and back to her parked car. As she drove closer to the front gates she prayed there was a sensor, and the gates would automatically open. Thankfully they did and she drove out. Trembling, she parked a few roads up and buried her face in her hands.

This was the truth of it.

Rich had been having an affair with Mellow.

It was Mellow he thought he was meeting tomorrow.

Mellow. That was who had tempted Rich.

She looked at her dress, the one she'd spent a fortune on. She had never felt so stupid, undesirable and alone.

26

An eerie calm had settled over Madison. Now that she knew, she was going to confront Rich with the facts. And then she would think about what to do with her life.

Just breathe, she said to herself, as she stared out of the car window.

It was what she had told herself in the aftermath of her mum's death. The situation and the feelings that came with it were overwhelming, but she just had to breathe. Not think. Just breathe. She glanced at her watch. Her life was falling apart but she had to relieve her dad of granddad duties.

Arriving at her dad's house, she walked in and forced a happy smile on to her face.

'Have you had a good time with Granddad?' she asked.

Chloë and Jordan nodded.

'And did Granddad survive?' she asked her father.

'Oh, yes,' he said, but there was no denying he looked tired.

'Go and put your feet up, Dad,' she said. 'I'll be round tomorrow. You OK for food?'

'I'm still working my way through the Christmas leftovers.' He chuckled.

Back at home, she put the kids to bed, then sat quietly, staring at the wall. She had had a thousand conversations with Rich in her head.

But there was just one question she needed answered. *Why?* Did he love Mellow? Had it been a crazy infatuation? Why would he risk the family, the home, that they had built together? Had it been worth it?

Maybe he thought Mellow wanted to start things up again, after Madison's text. Pangs of dread washed over her. *At least you discovered it before you designed the most beautiful house for her,* she thought bitterly.

After washing off her stressful day, she got into bed and fell into a dreamless sleep, waking only when one of the kids padded through in the morning to request Coco Pops. Groggily, she reached for her phone. She'd slept through her alarm.

'Be there in a minute,' she croaked, steering herself out of bed as the events of yesterday clicked into place. In only a few hours, she'd be face to face with Rich, armed with the truth. What would happen after that, she had no idea. She checked the messages to see if any of her friends had changed their minds about coming with her for moral support. Nothing. She wasn't as angry about it as she'd been previously. At the end of the day it was her marriage and up to her to fight for it.

She dropped the kids at her dad's again, kissing them goodbye, and drove slowly in the direction of Boca bar. The radio was blaring happy tunes; she switched it off. She tried to think what she was going to say. Would she tell him it was over? Tell him never to return? Would she cry or somehow remain cold as ice? She didn't know. How would he respond? Would he beg for another chance? Two things were clear. She wanted the moment of satisfaction at having caught him out, when he couldn't wriggle away or fob her off with half-truths, presuming that she'd accept them. And she wanted him to see just how strong she was.

She managed to park nearby but not too close to the venue. She was still ten minutes early. She switched off the engine and focused on her breathing. There was no need to imagine more scenarios: she was about to see the truth.

Five minutes to noon she saw Rich walking down the other side of the road, his jaw tense, his hands in his pockets, looking around him. He'd made an effort with his clothes, Madison noticed. Clearly, the opinion of whoever he was meeting mattered to him.

She watched him pause. Her heart was drumming so loudly. She had to do this. She'd come this far. She wiped her sweaty palms on her jeans, reached for the door handle and was about to open it when—

Jess came flying round the corner. For once, she looked less than perfect, her hair dishevelled, her face bare of makeup. Madison's heart leaped. She should have trusted Jess would come through for her!

Jess came to a halt in front of Rich. Her expression was twisted – anger, pain, something else that Madison couldn't put her finger on. Her mannerisms were erratic. Without taking her eyes off them, she pressed the window button down. The cold air slapped the side of her face. Jess's words did the same.

'She's coming now,' Jess was shouting. 'Why have you done this?'

Madison was confused. Was Jess *warning* Rich? Did she think the other woman was actually going to turn up or something?

She couldn't hear what Rich was saying, but he was holding out his hands, trying to placate her.

'This was never meant to happen,' Jess shouted, before burying her face in her hands.

Rich stepped towards her. He reached out a hand to her, which Jess slapped away. Jess was sobbing, inconsolable. Rich touched her cheek with his hand, and that gesture, so intimate, made Madison's heart turn to ice.

What the hell was going on?

She got out of the car. She walked towards them.

She heard Jess say, 'She'll be here, any minute,' and then Jess saw her, and stepped back, her hand over her mouth. Rich turned too, and his expression was one of utter horror. Madison realized what the other emotion on Jess's face was. Guilt.

She stopped and looked at them, the people she'd trusted more than anyone else.

Jess took some gulping breaths. 'Please, don't—'

'So it was you,' said Madison. 'Not Mellow.'

'*Mellow?*' said Rich.

Madison felt as if she was in a dream. She knew she should be angry and upset, but somehow all she felt was a terrible calm. It all made sense now.

'It was you,' she repeated to Jess. 'Look at me.'

Jess met her eyes for a millisecond, before she looked away. But that was all Madison needed. Jess's expression had been agonized and guilty.

Then she turned to Rich. 'You cheated on me. With my best friend.' She couldn't believe she was saying those words. It was almost ridiculous. Rich stepped towards her, but she backed away. She didn't want to be near either of them.

'Madison, please, it was a mistake,' said Jess, her voice trembling. 'It was one mistake.'

'Pretty big mistake,' said Madison. 'Wouldn't you say?' She still couldn't take this in. 'How could you do this? *Why* did you do this?'

'We never slept together, I promise. It was just a kiss. Tell her,' Jess pleaded to Rich, and he nodded. 'Me and Michael, we've been having problems. For well over a year. I don't know if we can fix it.' She let out two shuddering sobs. 'And one night a few weeks ago, Rich and I bumped into each other. Back at the beginning of December. He walked me home, came in for a nightcap. We were tipsy, Madison, we were talking, and it was a relief to talk to someone who understood, and then, somehow, we kissed.' She swallowed. 'And it was such a mistake; it was a huge, huge mistake.'

Jess rounded on Rich. 'And I told you to fix it! I told you to fix it with her! I told you to make your marriage better and you did nothing!'

So that was why Jess had been so encouraging, Madison thought, telling her that she and Rich would work it out.

'You let me suffer,' Madison said slowly. 'You let me wonder what the hell was going on. For weeks. You were the first person I told. The person I trusted more than anyone else, really.'

Jess was crying again now. 'I thought I was doing the right thing,' she croaked. 'I thought you guys would rebuild it. Madison, please, I am so, so sorry.' She reached out to her.

Madison couldn't even look at her. She stared at Rich, who was completely silent. 'And you have nothing to say for yourself either?' Madison shook her head in disbelief.

Rich lifted his eyes and met hers briefly, then dropped his gaze once more.

Madison turned away from them. She walked towards the car and didn't look back.

At the house, she went into the hallway and shut the door. It was dark and cold. She was shivering now. She looked at the coat rack: garments that belonged to her, to Rich, to each of the kids. She slumped to the floor and collapsed in tears. Their family would never be the same again. Her mind raced. Had Rich always wanted to kiss Jess? Had she always fancied him? Anger pulsed through her as certain things now made sense. The massage was a guilt gift. The encouragement and support were embedded in guilt. She wiped her tears on her sleeve as more clarity came. Chloë and Sienna's friendship had suffered: the lack of sleepovers and after-school time made sense now too. And when Rich hadn't acknowledged Jess or Michael at the nativity, she had thought it was because he was late and flustered, but it had been more guilt. She didn't know how much time passed, but eventually she raised her head and looked at her phone. It was later than she'd thought.

She rang her dad. 'Hi, Madison,' came his familiar voice. 'How's my girl?'

She tried to push the tears from her voice but her throat was raspy. 'Yeah, good,' she said. 'I was wondering if – if . . .'

'Madison, what's wrong?'

She pressed her fingers against her mouth.

'Are you sick?' She heard the panic in his voice.

'No, Dad, no.' She tried to pull herself together. 'Dad, I think my marriage might be over.' She was braced, somehow, for his disappointment. She felt like she had let him down.

'I'm here, Madison,' he said. 'For whatever you need.'

'Could you . . .'

'Take the kids?'

'Yes. Just for tonight.'

'For as long as you need.'

'Dose them up on junk food.'

He chuckled. 'I love you, Madison. And remember: you're strong. Whatever is going on, you'll be OK. I promise.'

'Love you too, Dad,' she whispered.

Madison sat on the floor in the living room and rocked herself to and fro. No husband. No best friend. No dream job designing for Mellow. She shut her eyes and cringed when she thought of how she'd accused her. But that was the least of her worries now. This, she decided, had to be rock bottom.

'You still have the kids,' she said aloud. 'You still have your dad. You're still breathing.'

The hours rolled on. Then, the doorbell went. She forced herself upright and answered it.

Rich.

'Can I come in?' he said, his voice small. 'Please. We need to talk.'

27

She pushed the door open to let him in and walked into the living room. Rich closed the door behind him and followed. She could see he was shivering. He sat down and wrapped the sofa throw around his shoulders.

'I've been walking round since I saw you,' he began. 'Trying to think how to explain things.' He looked at her. 'I need to start by saying how sorry I am.'

'For which bit in particular?' said Madison. 'For cheating with my best friend? For lying to me? For leaving me guessing for weeks?' A tidal wave of anger rose inside her.

Rich put his head into his hands. 'All of it,' he muttered.

'Let me explain something to you first,' she said. 'Do you know how much you've hurt me?'

He looked at her then, as if seeing her for the first time.

'Do you know how devastating it was that you walked out? With no explanation? And to think back on all the chances I gave you!' Her voice was loud. 'You took me for a *fool*. You thought I'd believe any little scrap you gave me! How could you treat me like that? Your *wife*?'

'Please,' said Rich. 'I know what I've done is terrible, I really do. Let me explain. What Jess said is true. There was a kiss. A one-off drunken kiss. It was a mistake.' He swallowed. 'But it threw me into a total tailspin. I couldn't be around you. Not while I worked stuff out. I was so confused.'

'About what? Why you did it? How you felt about her? How you felt about me?'

'Honestly, everything. I wanted to tell you but . . .'

'Were you even at your cousin's?'

'Yeah, of course I was. And there was all the stuff going on with the TV show. And at the same time, I was thinking about our future, about the kids, almost constantly. What it would look like if we stayed together. What it would look like if we split up.' He ran a hand over his face. 'I know what you must think of me, Madison, but I was trying to work it out. I was in bits. And the Tinder thing was so dumb. Yes, I created an account. I matched with people. Wanted to know if I was still attractive, or something.' He sighed. 'It sounds pathetic, I know.' He moved to sit beside her, and tried to take her hand.

'Don't touch me,' she said. His words were swirling in her brain with confusion. He still didn't get it. He still wasn't seeing the impact he'd had on her. He was so preoccupied with justifying what he'd done.

'Madison, I realize what a complete idiot I have been. And in these few weeks, I've understood how much I want to be with you. I've been thinking of our future.' He took a deep breath. 'I've been talking to my brother about buying somewhere together. Somewhere way nicer than here, maybe out West London. Then I'll have the show. You can work on it, if you like. Or you don't have to. We'll be able to afford so much more. Send the kids to private school. Holidays. You deserve so much more than this. And I'm going to give that to you.'

Madison sat silently as his words sank in.

'I can see our future so clearly now,' said Rich. 'And maybe it took this wobble for me to really *know* that we're meant to be together.'

Something was niggling at the corner of her mind. She narrowed her eyes. 'When Jess said it was about speaking to someone who understood – understood what, exactly?'

He looked at her, clearly surprised. 'Well, not being happy. We'd not been happy for ages, Madison.'

She let out a half-sob. '*I* was happy. I *liked* our life. Don't put it on me – that I wasn't happy when I was. Own it. You weren't happy. And instead of talking to me about it, you just shut me out.'

'I guess I was frustrated. Like, what had happened to all the dreams we'd once had? All the big ambitions?'

'But we were having kids. A family. That was our big ambition within this partnership.'

'I know, babe. I know. And I love the kids more than anything. It's just, with them older now, *we* can start to do more. We can start to move on up in the world.' He took her other hand and turned to face her. 'Madison, please. I need you. I need you by my side. Just imagine the life we'll be having in a year! I'll be so much more famous. We'll have more money, a beautiful house that you can decorate however you want, holidays . . .'

There was a silence as Madison processed everything he was saying. He *needed* her? He'd decided that after weeks of pushing her away? And he wanted her to move past everything now that he'd taken the time out to have his crisis? What about what she *needed*? Or, better, what she wanted and deserved?

She thought back to him saying he hadn't been happy. *She*'d been happy – or so she'd thought. But in the past few weeks, when had she felt like herself? When she'd been out exploring. When she'd been talking to artists. When she'd been messing around with the kids, just her. When she'd been with her dad. When she'd been laughing with Nathan. When she'd been thinking of designs for Mellow.

None of that featured in Rich's vision for the future. And that was when she made a decision.

'I think this is over,' said Madison. 'You and me.'

'Don't say that,' said Rich, his voice breaking.

'Rich, I don't want the future you're painting. I don't want to move. This is my home. Our community. My dad lives around the corner. I'm *happy* here.'

'We don't have to go far,' said Rich. 'But a fresh start, after what happened.'

She shook her head slowly. 'And I don't want a bit-part on the show. I want my own thing.' She sighed. 'You know, these weeks, even though they've been awful, I realized some things. You didn't ask me once what was going on for me, or include me in the discussion. You just presumed I'd go along with it all, once you'd decided. You weren't even going to tell me the truth about what had happened with Jess. And it's more than that, isn't it?' She looked at him sadly. 'We've just grown apart. So slowly that we didn't realize it. But if you weren't happy for a long time, and I was, and it took this to show us how things really were, and that the kind of future we want is so, so different . . .' She shrugged 'Then we need to find our own paths.'

A tear ran down Rich's cheek.

'You know what I'm saying is true,' Madison said. 'That's why we're sad.'

He nodded. 'Just . . . please, don't take the kids away from me.'

'I would never, ever do that,' said Madison, shocked. 'We will still be a family. Just a co-parenting one now.'

They sat in silence for an age. Then Rich got up. 'We'll sort stuff out, yeah,' he said, his voice shaky. 'Whatever you need.'

Madison stood up. They embraced by the door, leaning their foreheads together, their eyes closed. Was she really doing this? Was she really turning her back on her marriage? A tiny voice told her, *Yes. You are doing the right thing.*

28

Early next morning, there was another ring at the doorbell. Madison hauled herself out of bed, wrapped herself in a fluffy pink dressing-gown and went downstairs, her eyes puffy from crying. She'd woken up, on her own, and for a brief moment couldn't remember what had happened the previous day. But then everything had come tumbling back and whatever strength or resolve she'd felt last night had disappeared.

There, on the doorstep, stood Mellow.

Madison was shocked. 'Oh, God,' she said, her stomach fluttering. 'Mellow – you're here – I, umm . . .'

'I got your address from Nathan, and he got it from your boss,' she said. 'Yes, I could have called but I wanted to speak to you face to face.'

Madison felt herself crumple as she remembered her accusations. She was mortified. She cleared her throat. 'I owe you an apology. Come in.'

Mellow walked into the hallway and Madison closed the door behind her. 'I can't stay long, so here's fine,' said Mellow. 'I've been trying to put two and two together, after your outburst.' She raised an eyebrow.

'I'm so sorry about that,' muttered Madison. 'The stress . . .'

Mellow waved a hand, and then – to Madison's surprise – folded her into a warm hug. 'I hate cheaters,' she said, pulling back, her voice impassioned. 'They are the worst. Believe me, I know. Look, I did meet Rich after that gallery event. I followed behind in my car and we went for dinner. We're meant to be doing a TV show together. Both signed as presenters.'

Madison nodded. That made sense.

'I googled him after the other day, and saw a picture of you with him, so that's when I twigged – you're his wife, and you thought I was having an affair with him.' She shook her head sympathetically. 'That must have sucked.'

'It did,' said Madison. 'Especially when I discovered you had nothing to do with it. And I'd completely blown my chances of ever working with you.'

'Well . . .' said Mellow, slowly. 'It led to a few things. As I said, I'm not a fan of cheaters. And I wasn't a fan of the way that show was heading. If I'm honest, and no disrespect meant, Rich's energy is fame-hungry and I'm not about that. So, I dropped out.'

'Really?'

'Yeah. Sometimes in life, what you say no to is as important as what you say yes to. And I couldn't shake what you said about how you wanted my house to be. You just *got* it. So – if you want the job, it's yours.'

Madison beamed. 'I don't know what to say – thank you so much,' she managed, her heart filling with joy. 'Is it just one room or . . .'

'The whole house,' said Mellow. 'It's a big job. Look, let's discuss rates when you've had a chance to think, but it might end up being full time. I've got to go – call me when you get the chance. I'll ping my number to you.'

Madison saw Mellow out, then opened the door again and called, 'One more thing, what does Mom Three One One mean? It's been bugging me.'

Mellow scrunched up her face. Madison pointed to her car.

'It says Model Mell,' she called, before climbing into the SUV and pulling the door shut.

Duh! Of course.

Madison nodded, waving as she closed her front door.

She made herself a cup of black tea, dumping two sugars into it. She'd barely eaten in the last twenty-four hours. She went into the living room and sat quietly, trying to process everything that had happened in the last few weeks and days. She'd been betrayed by her husband and her best friend. They were two wounds that wouldn't heal quickly. But she had also felt something she hadn't in a long while: the first glimmers of excitement. The sense of an open horizon, of possibility. Her first client. She'd be paid to design the most beautiful home for Mellow. And that wouldn't have happened if she hadn't taken the leap to put herself out there. And if she hadn't met Nathan. *He's been a real cheerleader,* she thought.

A chain of events had unfolded that had started with Rich leaving. Savine had been right. Things couldn't go back to how they had been. But maybe Madison had to trust herself, and let go.

Taking a long, slow sip of her tea, Madison opened her emails. She typed a single message: an email to Jenson, subject line: I QUIT.

29

Six months later

The evening sunlight streamed through the windows, hitting the champagne flutes that were lined up on the table, bathing everything in a gorgeous golden glow that was exactly how Madison had wanted it.

She walked around Mellow's house one last time, completely focused, tweaking the placement of a vase here and there, plumping a cushion. She stood back and looked at her work.

'Happy?' said Mellow, descending the spiral staircase, a goddess in a gold-sequined gown.

Madison surveyed the room. 'You know what? I think I am,' she said, with a smile.

'I've got the journalist from *Elle Decoration* coming round this week,' said Mellow. 'She's coming socially tonight, and then on Friday to do a shoot and an interview.' She paused. 'And I'm gonna make sure your name is mentioned.'

There was a time when Madison would have felt nervous, or insecure, or like she didn't deserve the spotlight. Not any more. She lifted a bottle of champagne out of the ice bucket. 'Shall we get this open? A toast to a team effort?'

And it *had* been a team effort between them. It had been a steep learning curve for Madison, and Mellow had been demanding – there'd been some robust discussions along the way, but Madison had learned how to stand up for her vision, too. Now it was Mellow's official housewarming party – a milestone achievement.

Madison popped the cork and poured two flutes of champagne. She clinked her glass against Mellow's.

'I never used to look forward to coming back from shoots,' said Mellow. 'But you've given me a proper home.'

Her words meant the world to Madison. She opened her mouth to reply as the buzzer went. Mellow squealed and ran to it, welcoming the first wave of her glamorous friends. Soon music and laughter filled the air.

What a difference six months made, thought Madison. She wasn't going to sugarcoat how hard it had been. Telling the kids that their parents were splitting up had been incredibly tough, although with plenty of reassurance and positivity from her and Rich, they seemed to be managing. Rich had rented a small flat nearby – she knew it was for the interim, but all grand plans of moving west seemed to be on pause, and his priority was being there for the kids.

Work on converting the attic into Jordan's new bedroom had begun and Madison had bought Chloë a puppy, a golden Cockapoo called Bobby. Her daddy had left, her big brother was soon moving into his own room and she saw Sienna only at school. Getting the puppy was the best thing Madison could have done. Her bright, chatty, playful child was back. Rich had landed the new show, but had negotiated clauses about how much time he was expected to be away, which meant they could split parenting evenly.

Madison took a sip of champagne, enjoying herself as Mellow introduced her to various friends as 'the designer'. She wouldn't get tired of hearing that.

'And Nathan you already know,' said Mellow.

There he was. It had been months since she'd seen him properly. He'd dropped in once unannounced for coffee at Mellow's, and they'd had a friendly chat about how it was all going. She'd thought of him, though. Possibly more than she cared to acknowledge.

'I hoped you'd be here,' he said. 'You look great. *This* looks great.'

'Thank you,' she said. 'I'm so proud of it. And I have you to thank, really.'

He tutted and looked down.

'I didn't do much.'

'You gave me that push.'

He raised an eyebrow. 'Are we talking about Stretch 'n' Flex now?'

Madison laughed. 'I've been back a few times with Savine. She's coming tonight too.'

'I must keep missing you,' said Nathan.

'Yeah, it's tricky getting there now, with so much going on,' Madison admitted. She hesitated. She wasn't sure how much to tell Nathan about what she'd been through.

He was looking at her nervously. 'Would you . . . want to go to a class together sometime?'

Was he asking her out? She wasn't totally sure. Or was he just being friendly? But she was done with thinking that no one would be interested in her. She'd looked into the mirror tonight, and a confident, smart, creative, *smoking-hot* woman had looked back at her. 'I would,' she replied. 'But . . . the last few months have been a lot.' She raised an eyebrow.

'I get it,' said Nathan. 'Sounds more complicated than the Double-headed Sea Monster move. But it would be nice just to chat. Find out what you've been up to, what you're planning, because this' – he gestured at the room – 'this is going to lead to things.'

A tap on her shoulder, and Madison squealed as she embraced Savine. Then Abiola, Ladene and Finn were coming up behind her. Of course, there was no Jess. At times like this, Madison still expected to see her, and her absence hurt. Jess had sent letters, tried to reach out in the past few months, desperately hoping they could find some way to repair things. Madison had asked her for space. Maybe, in some possible future, they might be able to reconnect, but she just didn't know.

'Look. At. This,' said Savine, turning around and gazing in awe at the room. 'It is absolutely magnificent.'

'Truly,' said Finn, handing each of them a glass of fizz. 'We're so proud of you, Madison.'

'You guys,' said Madison. She raised and clinked her glass with everyone else's. She noticed something and moved closer to Finn. 'I see you came out of denial,' she whispered.

'I thought you set me up when you asked me to drop the poinsettia to Ethel. She spilled the tea and, girl, that doctor's worked magic on my hairline.' He beamed.

'This is gorgeous,' breathed Ladene. 'I'm afraid I'm going to have a snoop. Give us an MTV *Cribs*-style tour?'

The others moved away to begin looking round, and Madison put a hand on Savine's arm to stop her. 'I wanted to say thanks to you especially,' Madison said. 'It's not often you meet such a special person who becomes such a good friend.'

Savine had been a rock to her over the past few months, providing emotional and practical support as Madison moved through the stages of separating.

'I really couldn't have done it without you,' Madison said. 'I don't know how to thank you.'

Savine hesitated a moment, choosing her words carefully. 'Madison. I always knew you'd be fine.'

'Did you?' Madison said, tears pricking at the corners of her eyes.

'Yeah, I did,' said Savine. 'Just as soon as you learned how to trust yourself. And I've a feeling this is only the beginning. Have you thought about what's next?'

Madison hadn't told a soul yet, but maybe now was the time to start talking about her ambitions. About what she could do. About what she had planned. 'Actually, yes,' she said. 'I'm going to set up my own design consultancy.' As she said the words, an enormous grin stretched across her face.

Savine clapped her hands in delight. 'Of course you are! Any ideas for the name?'

She'd turned over a few options, but in that moment, Madison decided. 'Yeah. It's Bombshell Designs.'

Savine raised her glass.

'We need a toast.'

'To Bombshells,' said Madison.

Acknowledgements

Firstly, thank you to God. Without you, nothing is possible.

Thank you to Lisa Bent, my co-writer. Who would have thought, from that first meeting at White City House, we would be here now. Thank you for doing all the heavy lifting and constantly waiting on my edits and rewrites. I love what we have created and I am so happy I got to work with you. Special thanks to Sophie Wilson, too.

Thank you to Transworld and Penguin Random House for being so patient with me in actually getting this book out there! We finally did it and I'm so proud of what we've achieved.

Thank you to my son, Aidan, for being just the best son anyone could ever wish for, and my gorgeous big sister, Saundra. Thank you to Daniel Hammond and Ashley Jenkins for your inspiration.

Thank you to Becca Barr Management for your constant love and guidance on this incredible journey.

Lastly, thank you to my mum, because without her I wouldn't be here. God rest her soul! I miss you, Mum.

Adored for her quick wit, big heart and infamous laugh, Alison is one of the UK's most popular TV presenters, famed for her hilarious celebrity interviews. The queen of our hearts presents ITV's *This Morning* alongside Dermot O'Leary, gearing viewers up for the weekend.

Alison also co-hosts the ultimate televised baking battle, *The Great British Bake Off*, and *The Great Stand Up To Cancer Bake Off* for C4, receiving a nomination for the 'Entertainment Performance' category in the 2024 RTS Programme Awards with Noel Fielding.

As a firm family favourite into the evening TV schedule, Alison is a team captain on Sky TV's *Rob Beckett's Smart TV* and continues the late, great Paul O'Grady's legacy, hosting *For the Love of Dogs* for Battersea Dogs Home and ITV.